CRIME CLASSICS

The Whip Hand

A REX CARVER MYSTERY

VICTOR CANNING

ABOUT THE AUTHOR

Born in Plymouth in 1911, Victor Canning was a prolific writer throughout his career, which began young: he had sold several short stories by the age of nineteen and his first novel, *Mr Finchley Discovers His England* (1934), was published when he was twenty-three.

Canning was primarily a writer of thrillers, and wrote his many books under the pseudonyms Julian Forest and Alan Gould. *The Whip Hand* (1965) was the first of his four Rex Carver books, which were written, unusually for Canning, in the first person. These were his most successful in sales terms. Interestingly, Canning's fiction is well-represented in the Oxford English Dictionary, with 37 citations from the Carver books alone.

Canning's later thrillers were darker and more complex than his earlier work. In 1973 he was awarded the CWA Silver Dagger for *The Rainbird Pattern* and in 1974 was nominated for an Edgar award. Canning also wrote for children: his *The Runaways* trilogy was adapted for a US children's television.

Canning died in Gloucestershire in 1986.

This edition published in the UK by Arcturus Publishing Limited
26/27 Bickels Yard, 151–153 Bermondsey Street, London SE1 3HA

This edition published in Australia and New Zealand by Hinkler Books Pty Ltd
45-55 Fairchild Street, Heatherton Victoria 3202 Australia

Design and layout copyright © 2011 Arcturus Publishing Limited
Text copyright © Charles Collingwood, The Estate of Victor Canning 1965

Cover artwork by Duncan Smith
Typesetting by Couper Street Type Co.

AD001953EN

Printed in the UK

MIX
Paper from
responsible sources
FSC
www.fsc.org   FSC® C018072

CONTENTS

CHAPTER ONE

NEVER REFUSE A KIPPER

I had my feet up on the desk, smoking and staring at the far wall, going over in my mind the horses for the first race at Kempton Park that day, when my secretary came in.

Hilda Wilkins, spinster, forty-three, living at 20 Circus Street, Greenwich, with her father, a retired ship's steward, was efficient, intelligent, unattractive, and always right – a splendid secretary, but a non-starter for a gay night on the town. We had a reasonable dislike of each other, and got on fine.

"Ring Duke's," I said, "and put a fiver on Moorwen. First race Kempton. What are you doing?"

"Larkspur."

I gave her a little pitying smile. Of course, Larkspur came up that afternoon.

She put a card on the desk, and said, "The bank telephoned. I said you were out."

I nodded. No matter how much money I made, and from time to time I made a lot, I never seemed to shake off an overdraft that was a constant worry to Wilkins.

I picked up the card. The edges of the pasteboard were lined with gold leaf. It said – *Hans Stebelson, Cologne*. A good, big address.

"He's waiting to see you," said Wilkins.

I could tell from the tone of her voice that she didn't like him. But that was no surprise. There were few people who came into the outer office of whom Wilkins approved.

"How do you read him?" I asked her.

She paused for a moment, silently shuffling the categories into order, and then said, "He looks prosperous. But he's not a gentleman.

There's something flashy about him. Perhaps a little common. He's not worried – like most of them. I've had him there for ten minutes and he hasn't fidgeted once. His English is better than yours – except when you want to make an impression."

She wasn't giving me everything. She always kept a little something back to toss from the door as she went out. She was a snob, of course – particularly about clothes and education. A made-up bow tie could give her a headache for a day, and the one thing she disliked most about me was that I had gone to a provincial grammar school in Devon.

"Divorce?"

"No. I asked."

She always did because she knew it was something I never touched.

"Wheel him in."

She got as far as the door, and then turned and looked at me. She had a habit, just before she tossed anything at me, of raising her right hand and tucking her hair back a bit over her right ear. Her hair was red, a kind of dirty rust, and she had the bluest, most honest eyes in the world. Although I could never imagine myself in bed with her, I knew she was a treasure.

"I have a feeling," she said primly, "that whatever it is, you ought to say no."

"You have a twenty-five per cent interest in this business, Wilkins. I own the rest and make the decisions." I'd never called her Hilda in my life, and never would.

Hans Stebelson was a big, fleshy man, with an enormously round, overgrown, unsmiling baby face. His eyes might have been made of brown plastic – and they would certainly never know tears. He sat down bulkily and made the chair creak, and he looked calm and monolithic. He wore a dark-brown suit, probably Italian, and a thin strip of knotted tie against a silk shirt, the tie held by a little gold clip shaped like a hand. He had a gold signet ring, and a fat gold watch on his wrist which was probably nuclear proof and must have set him back a couple of hundred guineas. There were two gold-topped fountain pens stuck in his outside breast pocket, which must have made Wilkins wince.

He rested a large, dough-coloured, regularly manicured hand on my desk and said, "I'm over from Cologne for a while, and I want you to find a girl for me." His brown eyes dared me to misinterpret this, and he went on, "She's a German girl who came over here on an *au pair* job. But she gave that up and went to Brighton. At least she sends cards from there to my sister in Cologne."

"No address, of course?"

"No address."

I wondered if they were the usual kind of cards people send from Brighton.

"Is she a friend of your sister?"

"Yes."

"Then why no address?"

"Because she doesn't want me to know where she is."

"Why not?"

"Her father and mother – they're both dead now – did me many kindnesses when I was young. I feel like an elder brother towards her and try to keep an eye on her. She's headstrong, irresponsible. But she resents any interference from me."

I said, "What's her name?"

"Katerina Saxmann. She's a blonde, about twenty-two years old. Very attractive. Blue eyes. She came over from Cologne last March. She speaks English, French and some Italian."

"And what does she do in Brighton?"

"I don't know. Some job – because she writes to my sister that every morning before work she takes a walk on the pier."

"In that case it wouldn't be very hard for you to find her yourself."

"Maybe, but the moment she saw me she would move on. I would prefer just to know where she is and what sort of life she's leading."

It sounded very straightforward, but then it always did when they had decided not to tell you the truth. But the trouble in this game was to spot when they had decided not to tell the truth. For the moment I was not committing myself.

I said, "Where are you staying?"

"Brown's Hotel."

"What sort of trouble do you imagine this girl could get into?"

He shrugged his big shoulders. "God knows. She's young, head-strong, adventurous, a big appetite for living. She thinks she can look after herself. We all do at that age. I just want an eye kept on her for a while. Then, when I know what kind of life she's leading, I can make a decision. She could be sent back to Germany for breaking her *au pair* contract, no?"

I shrugged my not-so-big shoulders non-committally, and then, deliberately pitching it high, said, "The preliminary work would cost you a hundred pounds, plus expenses. Money in advance. This kind of job takes up a lot of time. Half the fee returned if I'm unsuccessful, but the expenses stand."

Money talk usually sorted them out. Without hesitation, he took out a gold-tipped wallet, eight months' pregnant, and counted out twenty five-pound notes, recounted them, and passed them to me and, to show perhaps that he was reading me as I read him, he said, "This assignment is perfectly legitimate."

"Who recommended you to come to me?"

He hesitated and made no effort to cover it. Then with a slight convulsion of the gross baby face which I took for a smile, he said, "I work for a very big international organization. My chairman – who knows of my concern for this girl – suggested you. Not that he knows you. But he has a friend called Manston who told him that you were the best in London."

I didn't even let an eyelid flicker. But if this Stebelson touched even remotely the edges of Manston's world then I knew that I hadn't overcharged him.

After I had ushered him through into the outer office for Wilkins to see out, I went back to my desk.

Manston could have recommended me, maybe. But I didn't see it. I'd worked with him a few times, but not on anything which got publicity.

So, just to make sure, on what could, after all, be quite a simple job, I called a man I knew at the Yard and said Katerina Saxmann and Hans Stebelson to him. Unless it was vital I always liked to keep on the right side of the boys and, when I couldn't, I always tried to be polite about it. I called them or they called me. Friendly. But it only needed one step out of line to prove just how deep friendship with the law could be. Deep, deep and far under. And that was only the law. Beyond the law, you could go deeper still, deep and dark, down below the anemone and coral line where the big security sharks lurked. Down there they've never heard of friendship. Some of them screened their own wives before they kissed them goodnight.

This man said no to both Katerina Saxmann and Hans Stebelson. That was at five o'clock.

Five minutes later I left. I stopped in the outer office. Wilkins was sitting behind her typewriter, darning one of her father's socks.

I said, "I know it's high season, so I'll bet you five pounds that you can't get me a room at the Albion, Brighton – overlooking the entrance to the pier. For tonight and maybe a few more."

She nodded, raised the sock to her mouth and bit off the end of the wool to free her needle.

"Phone me at the flat."

She nodded again.

I went down the stairs and stood in the doorway, looking out into Northumberland Avenue. A girl went by in a summer frock, and there was a long ladder in the back of her right stocking. Two pigeons, doing a courtship display in the middle of the road, made a Ford Consul slow almost to a stop. From the angry movement of the driver's lips I could tell that he didn't think it was love that made the world go round. The dropping sun winked redly on my brass plate, which said – *Carver and Wilkins*. It had just been *Carver* until, in a bad year just after I'd begun, Wilkins had insisted on emptying the old tea-caddy on the mantelshelf in Circus Street and coming to the rescue – with a look in her eyes which had dared me to show even a two-second flash of gratitude. Without saying anything to her I had had the plate changed.

I went down to Miggs's place for a half-hour workout. Behind his garage, Miggs had a small gymnasium. It was a couple of guineas a session – dear – but a lot of people went. Miggs had been a sergeant in the Commandos. I had a pint with him afterwards and then got the tube home.

Home was a flat near the Tate Gallery: a bedroom, sitting-room, bathroom and kitchen, nicely, and expensively for the most part, furnished, but somehow always damned untidy. From the sitting-room window I could see the river.

It was a quarter past six when I opened the door.

He was sitting in my deep club armchair, wearing a raincoat, and holding a glass of my whisky and soda in his hand, but having the decency to smoke his own cigarettes. I never asked him how he got in. Doors don't present any problems to them. He was new to me.

I said, "Nice evening," and went and fixed myself a whisky and soda.

He said, "Feels like thunder to me."

I went to the window and looked out. It was a warm evening and a light breeze brought me a tangy whiff of river mud and petrol exhaust. The tide was running up and three barges went by low in the water, like sodden black sausages. So far as I could see, he hadn't got anyone parked outside. I sat on the window-seat and lit a cigarette.

Blowing smoke, like a goldfish breathing, I said, "Well?"

He said, "If Manston hadn't been on holiday, they would have sent him."

"Nice of them." But I knew they would never have sent Manston. He didn't run errands.

"He's got a high regard for you. In fact, the whole Department has – so I'm told."

"Told?"

"I don't run with them normally."

He yawned, flicked ash at a cigarette tray and missed it, and then with a coy look said, "Stebelson."

I said, "The liaison has been tightened up. I only phoned the Yard at five. I suppose that's the result of the recent stink about co-operation between police and security. I'm glad to see it."

"Stebelson," he repeated.

Now, in my business, nothing is given free. Everything has a price. If they want to put the screws on they can. But they usually wait until they get really annoyed. That's the weakness of the whole system. They wait until they see red and then it's often too late.

I said, "Property recovery. He had certain things nicked from him in a night club, and he doesn't want any publicity. Recovery is a speciality of mine."

"Oh, yes. They told me that, too."

"He's from Cologne. Staying at Brown's. Has a fancy line in cards."

I flicked Stebelson's card across to him and he caught it as it skimmed through the air.

His eyes on the card, he said, "It wouldn't be ethical to ask you what the property was?"

"No."

"What has Katerina Saxmann got to do with it?" His eyes were up and on me, going right through to the back of my head.

"She was," I lied, "a girl he met in the club. He was none too sure that he'd got her name right. Bit tight at the time. Any more? If there is, you can come and help me scramble the eggs, and we'll open a very cheap bottle of Spanish white wine."

He shook his head. "Some other time. No, there's no more, except—"

I waited and then gave him his cue. "Except what?"

"Except that you won't mind if I call and have the occasional chat? Just to keep in touch. Nothing official. Just informal."

"Do. I'm a great one for informality."

"Fine."

He stood up and moved to the door. When he put his fingers on the handle and half turned to me I knew he was going to do a Wilkins.

"They tell me," he said, "that they gave you a chance to come in once. Why'd you refuse?"

"I like being alone and making my own working hours. You know, take the odd day off to go fishing."

He nodded. "I should watch the fishing. You could end up in the river." He winked and then was gone.

I opened the door after him and heard him go down the stairs. From the window I checked him across the street. He turned the corner without looking back and that was fair enough because if they were going to watch me somebody else would take over from there.

Five minutes later Wilkins called.

She said, "You owe me five pounds."

"Take it out of the petty cash and charge it to Stebelson. Expenses."

I cleared the line and then called Miggs.

I said, "I want something posh. Tonight at seven. Sloane Square."

He grumbled, which with Miggs is a lot of bad language, but promised. After that I scrambled some eggs and drank a glass of milk with them. Then I pulled my sitting-room curtains almost over and switched on the light. I packed a case and went into the bathroom, leaving the sitting-room light on. I dropped the case through the window and followed it. It wasn't the garden of my house. It was the garden next door and their front door opened round the corner of the street. I walked in through the kitchen, where Mrs Meld was cooking kippers for her husband's supper. He was hunched in a stupor on a hard chair watching television, completely transfixed.

Mrs Meld said, "Evening, Mr Carver. Off somewhere?"

"A whiff of sea air, Mrs Meld," I said. "The fancy just took me."

"And why not, seeing as you're single and fancy free? Have a kipper first?"

"Not tonight."

She took the pound note I handed to her, winked at me and, as I passed through, called, "It's always nice to see you, Mr Carver, even when we ain't supposed to." She said it every time and her laugh followed me out of the front door.

A taxi dropped me in Sloane Square. A few minutes later I was crossing the river on my way to Brighton. Miggs had got me a cream-coloured Jaguar. Very posh. Brighton lay ahead. If only I'd known then that I would have been a happier man if I'd stayed and shared Mr Meld's kippers. . . .

CHAPTER TWO

GIRL ON THE PIER

I was up at six o'clock the next morning, sitting at my window in the Albion, watching the entrance to the pier. There were few people about. By nine o'clock I hadn't seen any girl go on to the pier by herself, or a girl who might fit the description I had of Katerina Saxmann.

During the morning I telephoned Wilkins.

I said, "Anything interesting turned up yet?"

"They," she said, "phoned and asked for you. Wanted to know where you are."

"And you said?"

"That you'd probably gone racing for the day."

"Good."

"Is it?"

"I've a feeling – yes. Why should a man hand over a hundred pounds for a simple job like that? Where there's a hundred, there's more. Remember the bank manager."

"You're too naïve about money and men."

I could not think of an answer to that one so I hung up and went for a walk along the front, and tried three or four coffee-bars. Then I spent half an hour in the Aquarium before lunch and had a few minutes' staring match with a gigantic conger eel. I slept after lunch and frittered the rest of the day away. I can sleep and fritter the best of days away. It's one of the qualifications for my profession and it saves the feet.

She was there at half-past eight the following morning. She came along the promenade from the direction of Hove. It was a fresh morning, the wind coming up Channel, the tide well in, and the waves gargling along the long line of pebble beach. She was bare-headed, her long blonde hair falling loose about her neck. She had her hands in the pockets of an open coat. I kept my glasses on her until she went through the pier turnstile, and then I went out after her.

I was sharply dressed for the part, young man on holiday, well-heeled and looking for company.

I found her at the far end of the pier, behind the pavilion where the early-morning anglers had their rods propped against the rails, lines streaming away into the green and yellow curd of water, and little bells at the rod tips, waiting to ring when the cod or bream or flounders or whatever it was they hoped to catch gave the signal for hauling in. There was a mess of baskets, tins, and untidy gear along the boards, and nobody spoke to anybody else.

She was leaning over the rail, staring out at the smoke trail of some ship on the horizon. I leaned over the rail a couple of yards from her and stared at the smoke trail too. Then I lit a cigarette and half turned, watching a man beyond preparing to make a cast. She paid no attention to me. She was a biggish girl but there was nothing out of proportion. Her profile was good and she had a long, generous mouth and her skin was sun-brown, the kind that made me want to put out a finger-tip and touch it. I put her through all the tests: bikini, baggy old sweater and trousers, and lying on a bed with her violet eyes half shut. She came out with full marks. I knew I was going to be disappointed if this was not Katerina Saxmann.

The man cast and there was a sound like tearing calico. Her head turned from me to watch the fall of the line. I lost her profile but got the firm length of the side of her neck. When she came back into profile I was leaning on the rail a foot from her.

I said, nodding at the water, "Pretty neat, eh?"

She nodded, looked at me, and I saw that it was more a dark blue than violet in her eyes. She went on looking, sizing me up, and I did what any young man would have done. I adjusted the knot of my tie with just a touch of nervousness.

"My father was mad about fishing," I said. I knew the routine. I'd learned it years before at Weston-super-Mare and places like that. If it isn't kept running you are lost. Pile more words in, and then you can stand on them securely because you've got to have a base, you've got to warm up the emptiness which is always cold and cautious around strangers, even when neither wants to be a stranger. "Not this kind, of course. Fly-fishing. Trout up on Dartmoor. They don't come very big, but they give a lot of sport." The fly-fishing touch was good because it gave a little class. Wilkins, for instance, really believed that coarse fishing was coarse.

"Dartmoor?"

She was hooked, but then maybe she had made up her mind before she ever got on to the pier that she wanted to be. In the one word the foreign accent was clear, giving a moment's magic to the word.

"Yes. Devon. Heather, wild ponies, some deer, too. And all these streams, where he used to fish. Used to have holidays there when I was a kid. Now – Brighton's more my line. You on holiday?"

"No, I work here." She smiled, and the mouth was warm, generous, a squarish kind of mouth which could have been too much for some faces.

"Pity," I said, the lines coming pat from some old routine. "Beautiful girl like you shouldn't have to work. Take a week off, and I'll guarantee you'll forget there ever was such a thing. Take the old car and have ourselves a good time." Half my mind was groaning with the thought that there were people who did this kind of thing in earnest, even me not so long ago.

"Old car?"

"Well, not so old really. It's a Jag. Cream. Just the right colour to go with that dress."

She was wearing a green dress and I nodded at it, keeping my eyes at breast level. I was aware of the skin behind my ears pricking, and I'd known that before, and knew also that it was out of place here, because this was a job.

She laughed then, just a little edge of sound, maybe because she didn't want to disturb the anglers, and she said pleasantly, "You are trying to pick me up?"

Instinct took over. It was a line not to be wasted, and I said, "That's it. If you stay dumb, you stay alone." I took out my cigarette case, black leather from Dunhill's, and an Oriflamme lighter. I deliberately muffed the lighter at her cigarette so that I could keep her head bent over my hands for a few seconds longer. A seagull went over, and gave me a laughing scream. I had her perfume in my face, and the momentary touch of her hand on mine as she steadied the lighter to her cigarette. She withdrew in a cloud of smoke that the wind whipped away instantly, leaving the dark blue eyes on me.

She said, "You are funny." There was a lot of accent in the last word. It sounded like phoney.

"We'll have dinner somewhere," I said. "Run out into the country. Somewhere nice. Dance maybe. Carver's the name. Rex."

She said, "It's late. I must go to work."

I said, "Tonight? I'll pick you up. Just say where."

She gathered herself together in a going-away movement and I thought for a moment that she was going to brush me off with a generous smile and a misty look, but she said, "Half-past six."

"Where?"

"Outside the Ship."

"I'll be there." Before she could move, I went on, "I don't know your name."

"Katerina," she said.

"It's a lovely name. Katerina what?"

She smiled. "Katerina. Isn't that enough – for now?"

"You bet it is. May I walk to work with you?"

"No."

She was away from me and moving round the side of the pavilion and the *no* had been very definite. I leaned back against the rail and watched her go, half of me professional and half of me a cocky, bright young man on holiday with a cream Jaguar and a pocket full of money.

Two yards from me an angler took a cheese sandwich from a plastic container and bit into it hard, looking at me.

He said, "Some people begin early in the morning."

I said, "It's the early worm that catches the bird."

I walked away, round the pavilion, and down the length of the pier. I passed up the temptation of *Your Photograph While You Wait*. I knew exactly what I looked like and what I felt like. And I went firmly by the café, and the post-card stall with its beery-faced men and balloon-buttocked women, and all the way, casually, he kept about fifty yards behind me – the young man who, from the far side of the anglers, had watched every movement of my meeting with Katerina Saxmann.

He had light-coloured brown hair, duck-tailed over his ears, long and pad-like right down the back of his neck, a black leather jacket, worn open, hands stuck into the pockets with just the thumbs showing over the edges, tight black jeans, and very pointed shoes. His mouth moved most of the time, as though he were silently saying unpleasant things to himself, and his eyes were very close above the bridge of his nose, spoiling an otherwise quite pleasant face.

At the Albion I stood in the main entrance and waited. He went by the hotel still saying unpleasant things silently to himself.

She turned up at a quarter to seven.

I took the Lewes road and we sat, not saying much. The silence did not bother me. Some people would say "hello, beautiful" and keep on talking, never letting it flag until every piece of ice was broken. But it never did any good. Sometime or other, after the opening gambit, the silence has to come so that each of you can take a good, quiet look and decide for or against. I didn't know what her decision was, but mine was for. I liked everything about her, starting at the top and going right down. I took the Jaguar along without any panache, forty-five at the most, and half of me was really on its best behaviour.

As Lewes Gaol came into sight on the skyline, a grey hulk stranded on a high reef, she said, "Where are you taking me?"

"I thought we'd have a couple of drinks at the White Hart and then some dinner."

"That sounds very nice."

I parked outside the Assize Courts. I'd given evidence there once, in a watch-smuggling case, for the Customs and Excise. The gentleman involved was still down the road a few hundred yards, getting regular exercise in the sweet downland air.

She drank two large martinis, and then we had smoked salmon and *sole Normande*; then she had a large Neapolitan ice, while I waited for coffee and drank the last of the bottle of Le Montrachet 1958, which was one of the dearest Burgundies they had on their list. It was Stebelson's money, anyway.

We eased up over the meal, became natural, and she laughed when I told a couple of mild jokes. She told me that she worked in a dress shop – La Boutique Barbara – and I told her that I worked in a bank – British Linen.

After her ice she decided to go off and powder her nose. I stood up, and handed her her bag from the table. It was heavier than any evening bag ought to be and, as she walked away and I stood watching her, I could sense the bulk of it still in my fingers.

She came back, smiling, and watching her come I was reminded of a picture I'd seen once in the Tate when I went in there to shelter from the rain, a picture of Diana the Huntress or something. She was absolutely splendid. There are not many girls to say that about. Pretty, tarty, attractive, intelligent, compelling, fatal and nice . . . there was an adjective for them all. But this one was splendid.

When we got into the car she leaned back against the seat, spread her arms, and said, "Now take me where there is lots of air. And where you can see for miles . . . the whole world."

It was just what I had in mind. We went down through Lewes and then swung right-handed out along the Polegate road. A few miles along, I took a track up to the downs. Five hundred and fifty feet up and the night breeze from the Channel was in our faces and we had the whole of the South Coast at our feet . . . Brighton, Newhaven, Seaford and Eastbourne, spilling an overflow of tumbling jewelled lights into the sea. There was a smell of marjoram and warm grass, and a few sheep moved like lumpy ghosts in the navel-high ground mist. We got out, walked a few yards and leaned against a track gate and looked up at the stars. They were putting on a show that took the breath away. I heard her sigh and breathe deeply and her shoulder was against mine, just touching me lightly. I gave the stars a few more seconds, heard a sheep cough like an old man in the mist, and a June bug go smacking by overhead.

I turned to her and put my hands on her shoulders, looking into her eyes.

I thought I was going to have to speak first, but she beat me to it.

She said, "You like me?"

I said, "Yes."

She said, "I like you. I like you very much."

I put my lips on hers, and as my arms went round her, she put her arms around my neck. We stood there like that for a long time, and then slowly she eased away from me but held one of my hands, and we began to walk back to the car.

I opened the rear door of the car and she slid in and dropped back in the far corner and her hands came out and took both of mine. I moved to her and took her in my arms and she came alive then, not like when we had first kissed, gentle, warm, and quietly generous, but alive . . . hungry, breathless.

So it was no wonder I didn't hear him come. He must have eased up on a low throttle and dropped the machine some yards away. She was in my arms, looking up at me with her lips a little open and I was touching the side of her face, whispering her name, content with the first blaze of feeling.

The door of the car opened behind me, and he said, "Get out of there."

I had seen him mouthing silent, bitter, angry things to himself that morning. Now I heard him. It was a low voice with a thin, blade-like edge to it. I didn't move fast enough for him so he reached in, caught me by the neck of the jacket, and jerked me out. I went rolling on to the dew-wet grass and felt his boot go into my right side.

He stepped back and watched me noisily coax some breath into my body. What he did not know was that it was not only breath I was accumulating. I just wanted to take a good look at him and work out exactly what I was going to do. In one hand he was swinging a crash helmet by the strap. His leather jacket was open, and his jeans were tucked into black riding boots so highly polished that they took and held the starlight. The night wind just moved the duck-tailing of hair over his ears.

He stood there, and he said, "You tuppenny jerk with a fancy car."

Katerina was out of the car now, leaning against it, and her eyes, as they went from him to me, were bright, bright and intense, and her face was the same, bright and intense, the look of a woman who knows she is going to enjoy herself.

I stood up, taking my time, and I slipped off my blazer and tossed it to Katerina without looking at her, my eyes on him. He was smiling now and it made his eyes seem even closer together, but I could just see the tip of his tongue touching the inner part of his upper lip. I read it for just a little edge of doubt. He hadn't liked the way I'd come quietly up from the ground and taken off my blazer.

I let him come to me. He slung the crash helmet at my face and followed it, going with one hand for my throat and swinging the other. I took his wrist and helped him with the swing, dropping as I did so. He went over me and I jerked his arm so that he would remember it for some time in his shoulder joint. As he hit the ground behind me, I swung round and – Miggs's style – put my foot in exactly where he had used his on me. He didn't like it but he came up at me fast, got hold of my shirt and then slid his arms round me, trying to lift and throw me. He was strong but he had no technique. I jerked the top of my head into his face and took him at the water-line with my knee. As he broke away and stumbled, I let him have it twice, on the chin and just above the heart.

It finished him. He just lay there wondering what had happened. I stood over him and waited while his breathing evened out.

Then I said, "You chose the wrong kind of jerk. You've got two minutes to find your kiddy car and ride off."

I went over to the car and took my blazer from Katerina. I lit a cigarette and he was still sitting there, sounding like one of the sheep in the mist.

I said, "Your time's going."

He got up and went off with the mist rolling around his knees, and he didn't say a word. He kept his eyes on me for a moment as he passed, and then let them slide to Katerina, but she wasn't looking at him, she was looking at me.

A few moments later I heard the motor-cycle start; the headlight snapped on, wavering in an unsteady arc, and then he was away down the track.

She came up close to me and the bright, intense look was still in her eyes.

I said, "You enjoyed that?"

She said, "*Wunderbar.*"

I tossed my cigarette away. She came hard and close to me, and I could feel her hands holding my shoulders through the silk shirt, and her mouth was like a velvet whirlpool. But for me the magic that had been in the back of the car, waiting to sweep me away, was missing. If was not far away but it was not right there, ready to hand and undeniable at that moment. If it had been I shouldn't have heard the sheep coughing or a curlew crying through the darkness or, when we were both shaking from a kind of shivering that didn't come from the night mist, would I have opened the front door of the car and helped her into the seat alongside the wheel?

I lit another cigarette, and one for her, and my hands weren't shaking any longer.

She said, "*Wo gehen Sie hin?*"

I said, "To a pub for a pint of beer. And speak English."

She laughed and opened her handbag for her compact, spilling the contents into her lap. She made no attempt to hide it, and I guessed that I had been made a member of the lodge. I picked it up and said, "Where did you get this?" It was an Italian Beretta automatic with a full magazine. The light from the dashboard was not good enough for me to tell whether it was a ·22 or a ·32.

She said, "I buy it from a man in Brighton."

"Why?"

She stopped powdering her nose for a moment and made a little mouth at me. I wanted to kiss her, but I waited for her answer.

"Because I am in a foreign country, no? For protection."

"If he's a sample of your friends, you might need it."

"Him." She laughed and began to tidy her bag away, taking the automatic from me.

"You've got a licence?"

"You need one?"

"You know damned well you do. Who was he?"

"Dino. A boy I know. He was outside the hotel after dinner."

"And you said nothing?"

"This is a fast car. I think we lose him. He is very jealous."

"With reason?"

She looked hard at me then, and I had the feeling that she was deliberately considering whether to be angry or not. Then she smiled.

"No," she said. I could have kissed her then and I knew she was waiting for it. But I started up the car and we went down the hill and found a pub in a village called West Firle, and it wasn't any surprise to me to find that she could drink beer with the best of them.

I dropped her at her lodgings around midnight. It was a small street up near the station and I could hear a radio going in the house as we stood in the doorway and said goodnight.

Lying in bed, I opened up my emergency bottle and had a stiff drink, thinking it over, and wondering which kind of a fool I had been, or was going to be. Dino could have been working off his own bat. But she'd known he was there and had given me no warning. The fact that I might be pulled out of the back of the car when I was hadn't inhibited a single one of her responses. Either way suited her, either way it was excitement. I was going to meet her in the Ship the next evening.

CHAPTER THREE

ADIEU TO DINO

I drove up to London early the next morning. I parked in Berkeley Square and walked round to Brown's Hotel and found Hans Stebelson in. There was a big bowl of blue and yellow irises on the table in his sitting-room and a photograph of a small boy in *Lederhosen* in a pigskin frame on the mantelpiece. He was still in his dressing-gown and there was a strong smell of eau-de-cologne. He ordered coffee, gave me a cigarette, and seemed very pleased to see me.

I said, "Katerina Saxmann lives at 20 Cadman Avenue, Brighton. That's near the station. She works at a dress shop. La Boutique Barbara in North Street. I had a few expenses. My secretary will list them and send a statement to you."

He nodded, and made me repeat the details while he wrote them down in a little black leather-bound notebook.

He said, "You saw her?"

I said, "I did. She's a splendid girl."

He smiled, but he did it without using his brown plastic eyes so that for a moment I thought he was wincing.

"You spoke to her?"

I nodded. "I took her out to dinner. I didn't mention your name, of course."

"And your impression?"

"I've told you. She's a splendid girl. She also carries an Italian Beretta automatic for which she has no licence."

He nodded and said, "She is an unusual girl. In many ways she does not belong to this era. I am worried for her."

I didn't ask why. Either he would tell me or he wouldn't. I said, "I think she can look after herself."

He shook his head. "No. Against some things, no. That is why, Mr Carver, I would like you to keep an eye on her. Already you have made her acquaintance. If, say, once a week or a fortnight, maybe, you could see her and let me have a report of what she does, where she goes, or if she moves away. On a business footing, of course."

"If you wish."

"Yes, I do. Very much I do. I shall be here, maybe, another month. At the end of that time we could review the situation."

I stood up, strolled to the little table that held the telephone and stubbed out my cigarette in a tray.

"I'll keep in touch with you," I said.

"Thank you," he said and, as I went to the door, he added, "and if you can persuade her to throw that stupid gun into the sea, please do so."

I went round the corner and found a call box and fished out a mess of change to make a call. As I had stubbed out my cigarette by the telephone I had seen a Brighton number scribbled on Stebelson's pad.

I rang it and a woman's voice at the other end said with so much refinement that it was like a grove of bamboos whining in the wind, "La Boutique Barbara. Can I help you?"

I put the receiver down and stared at a crude drawing of a horse that someone had pencilled on the wall. I decided to make the fee for my extra duties high.

I had a glass of beer and a sandwich in a pub on the road, and I was back in Brighton by four. La Boutique Barbara shut at five o'clock. I stood on the other side of the road and watched the assistants coming out. There were two young girls, and a tall, bony-shouldered older woman. Katerina was not amongst them.

And she was not outside the Ship at half-past six. I waited an hour, and then I went round to 20 Cadman Avenue. The door was opened by a tall young man with wavy fair hair. He was in his shirt-sleeves and held a paperback in one hand.

When I asked him for Katerina, he shook his head.

"She's gone."

"Where?"

"Dunno. Ma says she came home lunch-time, packed her bag, and went."

A woman's voice shouted from the interior of the house.

He went on, "Ma says she paid up. Extra week for not giving notice."

"Did she leave a forwarding address?"

Before he could reply, his mother's face appeared over his shoulder, a worn, plump, pleasant face. Looking me up and down, she said, "No, she didn't, just went off in a big car, chauffeur-driven."

"She didn't leave any message for me, did she? Carver's the name."

She shook her head. "No message for anyone. Just paid up and went. I shall miss her. She was good company around the house—"

"When she was in, that is," said the son.

His mother winked at me. "Harold didn't take to her – because she didn't take to him."

I walked back along the road to where I had parked cay car. Dino was standing alongside his motor-cycle which was cocked against the kerb at the back of the car.

I stuck one of my cards out to him and he took it and read it.

I said, "Where's the nearest pub?"

"Around the corner."

We went into the saloon bar and sat at a corner table with two large whiskies. My card had done something to him. Probably decided him to hold off from having another go at me.

I said, "My interest is purely professional."

He said, "It looked like it."

"Nevertheless it is. Tell me about her."

He was silent for a minute, taking a sip at his whisky and deciding something. Then he said, "She had all the others licked, see? Met her at the rink a month ago. Used to come on the back of the old bike. No funny business, though. Just speed. She went crazy about it."

He finished his whisky and I bought him another.

"What about her other friends?" I asked.

"She didn't have any."

"Did you know she was going?"

"Sort of. She said she was waiting to hear about a job."

"What job?"

"She never said. Just a job. But she didn't say she was going today."

"You saw her today?"

"This morning. I gave her a lift to work. Did most mornings – except when I'm on early turn." He hesitated for a moment, and then said, "Ever dance with her?"

He had his nose in his whisky glass, not looking at me, and there was something rather sad and beaten down about him. It was easy to see what had happened to him. He was hopelessly in love with her.

"No."

"She was a dish. She could do anything. Dance, swim, skate. . . . And the old bike. Didn't have a licence, but I used to let her have a go sometimes. Mister . . . she made my hair stand on end. Like she'd got to have it, see. The big kick. She had a gun, too. Used to go up to the Dyke weekends and knock off milk bottles. Used to scare me just to watch."

"Brighton's going to miss her."

"It has – it's already dead. All the others are just cardboard cut-outs."

"And that's all you know about her?"

"Do you know any more?"

"No. She ever give you a hint about this job?"

"No. Except that I think it must have been something to do with the woman."

"What woman?"

"About a week ago. Some woman staying at the Metropole. She went there to tea. I went to meet her afterwards, but I was there early and I saw them. They took a little stroll along the front. And there was this woman, an oldish kind of doll, and she had red hair. But Katy wouldn't tell me anything about her. But it was after that she mentioned the job. She was a foreign bird."

"You mean the red-haired woman?"

"Yes. I know one of the waiters there. He checked for me. . . ." He fiddled inside his leather jacket and brought out a piece of paper. But he kept it away from me, and just gave me a look. He might have been heart-broken, but he wasn't giving anything away.

I put a couple of pound notes on the table. He took them and handed me the paper. Written on it in grubby pencil was – *Mrs R. Vadarci. Swiss passport. Comes from London. Dorch. Hotel.*

I stood up and said, "If you remember anything else, just ring me. I'll buy."

He nodded into his glass and, without looking up, said, "Sorry about the other night. It gets into you."

"Forget it."

I left him, broken-hearted, but two pounds better off, and no future except to hitch up with one of the cardboard cut-outs that were left to him. To some extent I could almost share his feeling about Katerina. She was under my skin, too. Not as deep as she was with him, but then he'd been exposed to the fall-out longer than I had.

I gave up my room at the Albion and went back to London. I

rang the Dorchester and there was no Mrs Vadarci staying there. There had been, but not now. I put off ringing Hans Stebelson, and I had a chat about the whole thing with Wilkins the next morning.

She said, "Why should this man pay you so much money for such a simple commission? You've done nothing he couldn't easily have done himself."

"He's a busy man."

"Is he? He spent yesterday morning shopping, then the National Gallery. Lunch at Boulestin's by himself. In the afternoon he took a river trip down to Greenwich."

I pulled a face. "Good work." I had one or two outside men who did such small jobs for me. I didn't bother to ask her which one she had used.

She said, "He's not the kind who deliberately wastes money."

"But now the trail has gone cold. I've lost this girl."

"Do you want to bet on that?"

I looked at her, standing in front of me, a file clasped to her bosom as though it were an ailing child, a frosty look in her eyes, and I knew I would lose my money.

"No."

"You want some good advice?"

"I'll listen."

"Telephone him. Say you've lost her and that the pressure of other work makes it impossible for you to continue with this."

"That's good advice?"

"So good that I know you aren't going to take it."

I said, "I don't know."

Wilkins said nothing. She went to the door and then paused with her fingers on the handle. I prepared to duck.

She said, "Oh, I forgot to tell you. Somebody broke in here last night. They must have used a piece of perspex on the outer Yale lock."

"After the petty cash? Wasted effort."

"No – they went through the files. The cabinet lock was forced. No attempt to hide what had happened."

"Anything missing?"

"No. But they were interested in the Stebelson file."

"How do you know?"

"They put it back the wrong way round. Maybe they were cross because there was nothing in it except his address and a copy of our bill to him for expenses."

She went out.

Half an hour later the desk phone rang.

Wilkins said, "There's a woman on the phone for you. Won't give her name."

I said, "Put her through."

There was a click, and a voice said, "Rex?"

I said, "Yes?"

She said, "This is Katerina."

I heard the click of Wilkins's phone being replaced. She only eavesdropped when she had instructions.

I said, "What do you want?"

She said, "To see you, of course. . . ." And then she laughed. I waited until she had finished, wondering whether I was going to take Wilkins's advice and stay out of this. As her laughter died, I said, "Where and when?"

She came round to my flat the following evening.

I decanted a bottle of Château Latour and smacked out a steak wafer-thin for the *Diane*. There were a dozen roses in a brass bowl on the table and my best wine glasses. While I worked away like a little beaver, squaring the cushions and clearing the junk into a cupboard, a tug going up-river hooted at me for being such a fool, and a motor-cycle roaring underneath my window reminded me of Dino. (Some weeks later Wilkins, who always has an eye for such miscellanea, handed me a cutting from the *Evening Standard* which had given four lines to the death, in a motor-cycle pile-up, of one Eduardino Mantinelli on the A23 at Patcham just outside Brighton. I guessed that he had been trying out how fast you have to go to forget.)

I had it all planned: a few drinks, a few easy records, and summer evening talk while I did the steak *Diane*, and then, after we'd eaten, some honest talking. I was as happy as a sandboy at the prospect of seeing her again. Wilkins should have seen me. I liked cooking, too – when I could keep it simple and well out of the Robert Carrier class.

The taxi drew up outside and I had the door open for her to come up the stairs and into my arms like a homing pigeon. I kissed her, swung her inside, and went on kissing her while I slammed the door with my foot. When I let her go she collapsed into the armchair, legs thrust out, arms hanging limply over the sides, handbag swinging from one hand, and smiling up at me.

"It's hot," she said. She was wearing a nice dress, white silk, with a deep square neck that showed her brown throat and just the promise of her breasts, and she was wearing her hair loose and – maybe it was the shaded light in the room – her eyes had taken on that deep violet mist. It was then that my heart made a record for bumping, and I knew that I didn't care a damn if I were being hooked. I was prepared for a while to swim on the end of the line.

"You look as cool as a Nereid," I said.

"Is that something nice?"

"Kind of mermaid, I think."

She nodded, approving, looked at the bottles on my sideboard, and said, "I want plenty of gin in a big glass, half a slice of lemon. Then fill up with soda and ice."

Fixing it for her, and a whisky on the rocks for myself, I said, "How did you know my address in London?"

She fished in her handbag and flicked one of my business cards on to the table.

"You told me a lie about what you did, Rex." She scolded me with her lips.

"And you pinched that from my jacket while I dealt with Dino?"

"Yes."

I handed her the drink and she raised it, said, "*Prosit*," and really began to punish it.

I said, "Cheers," and just sipped mine. The record player made pleasant, subdued noises in the corner and I watched one of her feet moving with the rhythm.

She had three drinks before dinner and, as far as I could see, they did not begin to touch her. With the second one she got up and wandered about the place, looking at my bits and pieces, and then going into my bedroom, calling things to me in the kitchen. Who looked after me? Mrs Meld from next door. Why did I have such a big double bed? Because it was here when I came. Why did I put sixpenny pieces in a whisky bottle? Saving up for my holiday. Who was Elizabeth Trant? Put the telephone pad down and don't be nosey.

She came and leaned against the kitchen doorway and watched me taking the skins off some tomatoes.

She said, "How you have this kind of business, Rex? I don't imagine it for you." I loved the way she said it.

"It must have been the cheap kind of literature I went in for as a boy. Sexton Blake, Nelson Lee."

"I never heard of such books."

"Never mind. Then one day I had fifty pounds to spare and I was feeling rash so I plunked it all on a horse."

"And it won?"

"Yes. Then I put all I'd won on another, and so on. I did it several times."

"And each time it wins?"

"Yes."

After dinner and coffee, she sat in the big armchair and I squatted on the carpet at her feet. We had both done ourselves pretty well. I like a girl who doesn't play with her food or drink – especially when I've prepared it. She had her hand on the back of my neck, her fingers making little pulling movements at my hair, and I was running my hand along her leg from the knee down to her toes. She had kicked off her shoes.

After a while, I said, "We'd be more comfortable in the big bed."

She leaned forward, pulled my face around to her, and kissed me. When she had finished she slid her lips from my mouth and ran them over my face, just touching the tip of my nose and my eyebrows, and finally came to rest with them warm and soft against my right ear. She whispered something and then let her lips slide back on to mine again. It was consolation and it went on for a long time, her lips and my lips, and her hands and my hands, touching, caressing, until in the end I got up and went to the window for fresh air. There was a moon coming up over the river. I telepathed a message for it to stick to regulating the tides in future and, out of the corner of my eye, I saw a man leaning against the far street corner, reading an evening newspaper under a street light.

I came back, made her a long soft drink and then squatted on a footstool and faced her.

I said, "What do you know about Hans Stebelson?"

She was rubbing the cool glass against her chin and she went on rubbing it, saying nothing.

"He hired me to trace you. Paid a lot of money. Too much. But I'm pretty sure he knew where you were all the time." I watched her all the time I spoke, but there was nothing for me to read.

"He's from Cologne," she said. "He is mad with love for me and, because he is rich, does not understand why I do not want to marry him. When I marry, it will be someone like you with the right kind of body."

"I might apply. But for the moment let's stick to Stebelson."

"His family is from Cologne. Like mine. I know his sister well. She is much younger than Hans. Her, I like. I come to England because Hans never leaves me alone. He's in England now?"

"You know he is."

"No, that is not so." She said it without emphasis and I wouldn't have liked to testify either way about it being a lie.

"Then why did he telephone you at the Boutique Barbara the morning of the day you left Brighton? How did he know you were there?"

"Nobody telephoned me at the shop that morning. At least, not up until eleven o'clock. That is when I left. So, it is Hans who employs you? He is rich, you know. Very rich. You should charge him much."

"How could he know about the Boutique Barbara?"

"I think I know. When I do it, I said to myself after it was a mistake. But I write sometimes to Greta, his sister in Cologne. But I never give her my address – this because Hans pesters her too for news of me so he can come after me. But I let her know two weeks ago that I was in Brighton and work at a dress shop. And I sent her a little cardigan. English wool. Afterwards I remember that the shop name tab is in it. You know what trouble it is to send a cardigan to Germany? All the customs forms!"

"And you think he got the shop address from her?"

"For sure. If he thought she had it, he would twist her arm until she talks."

I lit a cigarette. It held water if you didn't have far to carry it.

Stebelson was on the list with Dino and myself. And Stebelson was rich. He would pay well just to know where she was. Straightforward. And no suggestion in Katerina's manner that it was any other than that. I could have believed it all – except that there was a man on the corner right now watching my flat, and that my raincoated friend had been sitting in the same armchair that she was in now only a few days ago. I couldn't sweep that under the edge of the carpet.

I put out a finger and ran it gently down the front of her tibia. She wrinkled her nose at me.

"Next question, please," she said.

"Mrs Vadarci," I said. "What about her?"

"She is my new job. She is Swiss. Some time ago she was staying in Brighton at the Metropole. She came into the shop to buy things, but her English is not very good. I talk to her in German and she takes a fancy to me. So – she offers me a job as her secretary-companion and now I am in London."

"With her?"

"Yes, of course. We stay at Claridge's."

"Claridge's!"

"Why not? She is very wealthy. She is going to pay me well. We shall travel. She only speaks German. But I speak French, Swedish and Italian." She stood up and looked at the clock on my mantelshelf. "I must go back to her now. I said I was going to the cinema."

I helped her on with her light coat. "I'll walk down with you and find a taxi," I said.

At the door Katerina turned to me.

"Kiss me here," she said.

We kissed and everything went from my mind.

Then, as she moved gently away from me, she said, "Something worries you still, eh? Surely not this stupid business of Hans. He is mad. Perhaps you are jealous? You think I really love him, perhaps. Oh, Rex, darling, I tell you something, I love you. Yes, I think I do. I will telephone you tomorrow and let you know for sure."

She went laughing down the stairs, holding my hand, and we walked together through the warm summer evening as far as the front of the Tate Gallery before I flagged a taxi for her. She blew me a kiss with the tips of her fingers as she got in. I said "Claridge's" to the cabby. She drove off, waving back through the rear window. Over the river the moon was cutting little sharp-edged black shadows along the ridges of the up-coming tide. On the Vauxhall side I could see the buses going along like moving shop-front windows and I heard Katerina saying, "Something worries you still, eh?"

And something did. When I had checked Mrs Vadarci at the Dorchester and they said she wasn't there, although she had been recently, I had called the Savoy, the Mayfair, and Claridge's, on the off-chance of finding her. None of them had a Mrs Vadarci staying. At this very moment Katerina was probably pulling back the glass slide and giving the cabby another destination.

I turned to walk back to my flat and, as I did so, a black saloon pulled into the kerb and a hand beckoned to me out of the rear window. It was raincoat.

I went over. He gave me a tired smile.

"It's late," he said, "but he wants to talk to you."

I said, "I don't do business at this time of night. Besides I've left a saucepan of milk on for my bedtime cocoa."

"I'll send a man up to turn it off."

"Nice of you. He can do the washing up as well."

We drove off towards Westminster and, as we took the roundabout at the foot of Lambeth Bridge, he said, "You've got lipstick on your chin."

CHAPTER FOUR

HE SHALL HAVE A NEW MASTER

I'd been there before once – with Manston. They don't ask you to call at their office. Sometimes I think they are not quite sure where their offices are. It was a flat in Covent Garden, and I even knew his name, or at least the one that was listed with his telephone number. Raincoat did not come up with me. He stayed outside, yawning in the back of the car, and I was let in by his manservant. I did not know his name, but he was a snob like Wilkins. He had no time for me because he knew at once that I was not "regular" like old raincoat.

He, Sutcliffe, was lying back in an armchair, a floppy old corduroy dressing-gown wrapped loosely around him, and his feet were up on a small stool. He was a fat little number, a humpty-dumpty man, except that one look at his face and eyes told you he was never going to fall. He lay back smoking a cigar. From his dress trousers and white waistcoat it was not hard to guess that he'd just come back from some intimate dinner in the Whitehall area where they had settled the fate of nations over the port, not wasting too much time on it, so that they could get quickly on to the real business of discussing England's chances in the next Test series. But that did not mean that I underestimated his kind. For real ruthlessness the true blood line runs through Eton, Balliol and Whitehall on one side, and Wellington, Sandhurst, and the Brigade on the other.

He gave me a warm smile and waved at the sideboard and I went and fixed myself a drink.

"Cigar?"

I shook my head and lit a cigarette. I had a kind of "mute from malice" feeling that I knew would take a little time to go.

He said, less warmly, "Sit down and don't fidget, Carver."

I said, "I'm allergic to red tape. There must be a piece in this room somewhere."

He smiled and said, "Is your passport up to date?"

I said, "It always is."

He said, "Got a current visa for Yugoslavia?"

I said, "No."

He said, "Apply for one tomorrow. Cost you fifteen bob, I think. Or maybe it's seven-and-sixpence."

"If you say so."

"I do. But it's not an order."

"When do I get those?"

"You don't. You're a private citizen, running a private business. This is a free country."

I looked at him over the rim of my glass. He looked absolutely sincere, and I said, "That's what we fought the Hundred Years War for, and a few others. But when I apply for the renewal of my licence or what-have-you things could be awkward. The police will develop a habit of picking me up week after week for doing twenty-eight in a thirty-mile limit. It could be hard for an honest man to make a living. I might have to give it all up and get a job."

He chuckled. Then he said, "You should have taken Manston's advice and come in with us."

"No thank you."

"Then you can't blame us for using you now and then. A man of your talents. We'll raise your fee this time."

"I'd rather go home."

"No," he said, shaking his head sadly. "You stay."

There was no arguing against that. I had tried it on my first visit here and it had not worked. I did not try this time.

"Just brief me."

He stood, and went and helped himself to a glass of water, but in passing he took my glass and helped me to whisky.

"Hans Stebelson and Katerina Saxmann. We have a quite passionate interest in them."

I liked that. I wondered whether he knew that I had a quite passionate interest in one of them. I decided that he did.

"Where do I come in?"

"Very soon Hans Stebelson is going to extend his commission to you. I don't think you know it, but he has picked you for a special assignment. That shows good sense on his part. He couldn't have found a better man."

"Compliment?"

"No, fact. You're intelligent and not easily fooled. Also, the less sterling side of your character has been nicely assessed by him. You've got an itch for money—"

"Who hasn't?"

"And you can't resist a pretty face and a pair of well-turned buttocks."

"Thank the Lord."

"And you're as stubborn as a mule when you're crossed."

"It's a great character reference. I'll have it typed and you can sign it."

He rearranged his feet on the stool and stared up at one of the modern paintings. Without looking at me, he said, "You'll accept his assignment, give him good service, and you'll keep in touch with us and pass everything back to us."

"Two masters?"

"And two lots of fees, and two lots of expenses. You should do well out of it. Just so long, Carver, as you don't get any ideas of your own for further financial advancement. Plenty of men have had their arms broken while trying to put too much in their wallets."

"Don't I get anything, not even part of a fairy story to cut my teeth on? At least you could hint that it was in the higher interests of State, maybe World, Security?"

"I thought you knew that," he said, smiling. "Anyway, while we are on characters, don't underestimate Stebelson. And don't pay too much attention to any mistakes he makes. He knows he's making them, for your benefit, just to keep you primed with the idea that you've got him cold."

"And how do I pass this information – if I'm going to be travelling?"

He stood up, and I knew that the interview was coming to an end. He stretched his arms a little and put two fat fingers to his mouth, delicately laying the ghost of a yawn.

"There will always be someone around."

"And if I doubt their credentials?"

"Ask for the word."

"And what is the word?"

"You tell me. That way you'll be certain that so far it hasn't been compromised."

"All right. Mother Jambo."

"Nice. Mother Jambo. It came first in the three o'clock at Brighton today."

"That's right. I've a weakness for horses and Brighton. Particularly Brighton." I was drifting towards the door with him and when we got there, I pulled from my pocket the Italian Beretta which I had, without her knowledge, taken from Katerina's handbag after dinner, stroking her knee with one hand and lifting the gun with the other. "And this?" I held it up. "How much cover do I get? I'm thinking of the moment when I'm bending over my wallet stuffing too much money into it and someone comes up behind me."

"You've a right to protect yourself and your property to the limit," he said. "But not with that." He took it from me. "We'll see you get another before you move. We'd like to check this one just to see if we can discover where it came from before she acquired it."

Going back in the car, old raincoat was silent until we were going past the Houses of Parliament. Then he said, "Got yourself a job?"

I said, "Yes."

He grunted, and it said clearly that he didn't have much time for anyone who wasn't a regular. At heart he was a union man.

I went up to an empty flat, and a sink full of washing up. I ran the hot water, and wondered why they hadn't put a regular on Katerina's tail. Maybe it was their busy season and they were shorthanded. Casual labour, that was me.

A special messenger delivered it at nine-thirty the next morning. I signed for it and left it still wrapped on my sideboard. *Automatic pistol, one, Rex Carver for the use of.* I then called Stebelson and made an appointment with him. Going to Brown's I kept remembering something that Sutcliffe had said to me on the moment of my leaving him. "You serve two masters, but at the ultimate moment you obey our orders." The ultimate moment. It gave nothing away. I wondered if Stebelson would feed my curiosity a little more, not with the truth necessarily, but at least with something to stop me worrying too much before I went to sleep at night.

When I got up to his room there was a bottle of champagne waiting on a tray. He opened it while I talked. Before coming there I'd done a little quick telephoning.

I said, "Katerina came to London. She told me she was staying at Claridge's – but that was a lie. She's a great one for making life difficult. Actually she was at the Cumberland Palace – with her new employer."

"Employer?" He held his glass still, brown eyes on me, as though he were contemplating some toast. The big hand shook a little and I suddenly realized that he was nervous or, at least, apprehensive.

"A Mrs Vadarci," I said, and I watched him. But he gave no sign that the name meant anything to him. I went on, "She's got a job as a companion to Mrs Vadarci. She's a wealthy old trout with red hair. They both left for Paris this morning."

He took a sip of the champagne and turned a little away from me, and said, "How did she meet this woman?"

"In the dress shop. She took a fancy to Katerina. So there it is – they're both out of the country. That lets me out."

He picked up the bottle of champagne and came over to me. He refilled my glass and then stood looking at me, pursing his big lips, and I could guess what he was going to say. It had to be because otherwise Sutcliffe would never have sent for me.

He didn't disappoint me. He said, "It only lets you out if you object to foreign travel and a substantial fee."

I said, "I've no objection, so long as I know what is expected of me – and a reasonable idea of what it's all about."

He took his time sorting that one out. I had the feeling that he was walking a thin diplomatic edge, wanting to be sure that he kept me and yet not wanting to reveal too much.

He said, "I think I can say that you would be expected to follow Katerina. You see I am not the principal in this affair."

"You mean your little story about a big brotherly interest in Katerina wasn't true?"

"Not entirely." He was quite blunt about it, almost relieved.

"And what about the reasonable idea – the truth this time – of what it's all about?"

"It would be up to my employer. I think I could persuade him to enlighten you. Enough, anyway, to ease your mind about the legality of the commission."

"You went a hell of a way around the houses about this, didn't you? Or were you just putting me through my paces first, checking my wind and trotting action?"

He smiled, the big face contorting momentarily, then he picked up a writing-pad and began to scribble on it. "This is the address. Be there at six o'clock tomorrow evening and ask for me." He tore the sheet away and handed it to me.

Slipping it into my pocket, I said, "Katerina knows who I am. She lifted a business card from my pocket. She says you want to marry her. To be frank, that you pester her."

He shook his head. "It's not true. I have a great affection for her. Her family, long ago, were very kind to me. Katerina, as you probably know, will say anything that happens to suit her. I shall see you tomorrow?"

He sounded a little anxious.

"Yes."

As I reached for the door handle, he said, "One word of advice, Mr Carver. Please don't fall in love with Katerina. Excuse me if I sound impertinent. But, for your own good, it is a temptation which should be sternly resisted."

I gave him a reassuring little shrug, but as I went down to the lobby I had a feeling that the advice was already a little tardy. But, like a good boy, I made a mental note – temptation, resist. I gave a debby-looking number in the reception desk one of my great big diamond-drilling smiles just to check that everything was in working order and she looked right through me.

At the office, Wilkins was out to lunch, but there was a telephone memo on my desk. It read:

> Miss Katerina Saxmann called. 10.00 hrs.
> Message: Still not certain answer to question.
> If anxious for answer, try Paris, Balzac 35.30.
> Flying this morning.

At the bottom of the slip Wilkins had pencilled in *Balzac 35·30 is George V.* For the moment I was not certain what she meant about the answer to a question. Then I remembered that she had promised to let me know if she loved me.

At that moment the telephone went.

A voice said, "Mother Jambo."

I said, "I'm going to Paris tomorrow to have a chat with somebody who lives at. . . ." I fished in my pocket and brought out the slip. Slowly I read the address. It was repeated to me, and then the telephone clicked off.

They did it very neatly, in about thirty seconds flat. I had walked down to the corner just after ten to post my three-monthly letter to my sister in Honiton, telling her that I might be away for some time. I was coming back, smoking, relaxed, wondering what bundle of nonsense would be tossed to me in Paris the next day, when it happened.

Two of them reached out from the side entrance to Mrs Meld's house and jerked me into the darkness. Some sack-like affair went over my head, the loose end jerked tight around my neck. I was suddenly on my back with the cigarette which had been knocked out of my mouth burning the side of my neck. I roared once and kicked out. I caught someone on the shin as a hand clamped over the sack and my mouth. Then I lay there, held, and a pair of hands went over me, and from the way they did it I knew it was a professional . . . just the patter of tiny fingers that missed nothing.

Thirty seconds flat. I heard them run and I was free to sit up and struggle with the draw-loop of the sack mouth, and that took me a few seconds to release. When I stood up there was a cab turning out of the far end of the street, and a courting couple went by me, holding arms as though they were skating side-by-side. Mr Meld turned into the side entrance and smiled at me with a great gust of closing-time beer fogging the air.

"Nice night," he said.

"Lovely."

"Yes, very nice." He looked up at the purple sky and smiled. "Yes, a very nice night for London." Then, looking at me, he went on, "You do know you've got a lighted cigarette burning your collar, don't you?"

I brushed it off, refused an offer to come in and have a bit of late supper and watch the television, and went up to my flat, carrying my own shoe-bag in one hand. Because of the bag, I knew before I got there that they would have been through the place. But I would never have known it, except for the shoe-bag in my hand. My sister had made it for me as a Christmas present one year. There were little blue flowers embroidered to form the word SHOES.

I got myself a drink and sat down and then went slowly through my pockets. They had taken the Paris address and the message memo from Wilkins which I had slipped into the same pocket. I sat there, wondering about it all, wondering if a fifteen per cent increase from Sutcliffe was really enough – in view of the fact that the word which one of the men had used when I had caught him on the shin with my foot had been one of about the only four I knew in that language.

CHAPTER FIVE

A PILLOW FROM HONEY CHILD

Wilkins disapproved of the whole affair. There were times when I wondered why she had bothered to put money into a business which clearly offended her moral and commercial instincts. I could not believe that it was just for the pleasure of being near me. Wilkins's whole romantic life was bound up with a Suez canal pilot – a Finn – who had stayed on to work under Nasser after the Suez blow-up. She saw him about once a year. Maybe that was as much romance as she wanted.

She said, "Your trouble is that you keep expecting life to be larger, brighter, more exciting, and more rewarding than any decent person could tolerate."

"Tuppence coloured?"

"More than that. Don't you know that half the time it isn't even penny plain? You're an incurable romantic."

"I deny it," I said.

She ignored me and went on, "I've checked through your suit-case. You didn't put any spare pants in. You'll have to get some in Paris."

Raincoat was at London Airport, and I was given a discreet VIP treatment. There was no trouble about the automatic. I didn't care for it much. I would have preferred something like a Webley, say, a police model with a stubby four-inch barrel, a ·32 or a ·38 that would stop an elephant from getting too close. This was a Winfield Arms Corporation job, made under licence in France by "MAB" and with the fancy name – *Le Chasseur* – stamped on the barrel; a ·22 calibre with a nine-shot magazine, plus one round in the chamber, and an automatic safety device so that when the magazine was removed you couldn't accidentally kill yourself or somebody else by forgetting the one round left in the chamber. It was not new and I guessed that Sutcliffe's armourer had just grabbed the nearest of his turned-in stock to issue. I was not a regular so I just got what was handy.

Raincoat said, "You'll be met the other end and they've fixed a room for you. Hotels are out."

I did not like the sound of that. I said, "I was jumped by a couple of five-star bastards last night."

"I know," he said calmly. "We watched."

"Thanks."

"What did they get?"

"The Paris address."

"That's what we thought."

"You going to kick up a fuss when I claim for a cigarette burn in the collar of my suit?"

He yawned a little, but said nothing.

The plane was half-empty. The air hostess was pretty, but had no conversation, so I had a large dry martini and went to sleep.

At Le Bourget I was picked up by a man called Robert Casalis. He was a youthful looking forty, but a shade overblown with muscular fat, the way some ex-rowing men get, and fair-haired, with honest brown eyes which I knew nothing in the world could possibly shock. I'd met him once before, briefly, with Manston. He was no raincoat number. He was out of a much higher security bracket.

He drove me to a flat near the Palais Royal and tossed the key to me when we were in the sitting-room.

"I don't imagine you'll be here long. But it's all yours while you are. Grub in the kitchen. Everything works. We've booked a room in your name at the Hotel Florida, a two-star place on the Boulevard Malesherbes – in case anyone asks you for an address. Any messages left for you there I'll pass when I ring you at eight each morning. I got some whisky in for you." As he moved to the door, he added, "There's no law against it, but I wouldn't bring any visitors up here unless it's an emergency. And if you get unwelcome ones, the place is entirely soundproof."

I nodded, and said without hope of an honest reply, "Where's Manston these days?"

"God knows, and there's nothing more top secret than that rating. But I've no doubt he's enjoying himself in that quiet country gentleman way of his. Cheerio."

He was gone.

I took a shower. It was June and hot and sticky. I put on a nice, sober suit and went out. I bought six pairs of pants at a Monoprix and then went and sat in a quiet corner of the lounge of the Hotel George V, nursing my parcel and watching the world go by. I had three hours before my appointment.

They came in after about half an hour, and from the look of them I knew that they had been shopping, probably in the Rue de Rivoli. They were discreetly festooned with those slim, flat carriers and tiny square parcels that you could crook easily on a little finger. Katerina was wearing an inconspicuous suit that obviously had cost the earth, and a hat that held every eye in the lounge. She had suddenly jumped right out of the Brighton ton-up mob into another world . . . the glossy, cosmopolitan crowd which was always wondering where it could go and play next. The elderly woman with her looked as though she dressed herself from a junk shop – except that a closer look showed that it was all good.

Mrs Vadarci had a black felt hat, rather like the jobs Roman Catholic priests wear, perched right on top of a mass of closely-curled red hair. She had a square, almost mannish face, all dewlaps and wrinkles, and under a pair of shabby brows were set a pair of bright blue eyes. She wore some kind of green, slightly old-fashioned summer dress that drooped around her like a theatre curtain, all fringes and loops with a suggestion of dust in the creases. A plump strip of pearls cascaded over an enormous bosom, and she held in her right hand a long ivory-topped black ebony cane. She looked a comfortable old biddy, but there was a feeling about her that announced quite clearly that, when she wanted, she could be as tough as old boots. I got every word of her instructions to the hotel clerk to get someone out quickly to pay off her cabby. She beat time to her instructions with the tip of her cane on the floor. As she made for the lifts with Katerina she looked like some formidable old duenna trailing the Infanta of Spain behind her. If I had known how near I was to the truth then, I might have considered taking the next plane back to London.

As they went into the lift Katerina turned and saw me. She looked straight at me and just for a moment there was the faintest smile of recognition on her lips.

I gave her half an hour after that while I tried out my French on a copy of *Paris-Soir*. She came down just as I was deciding to give it up.

She came straight over and sat down beside me, and with a warm, little gesture, which hauled me right back into the magic circle again, she took one of my hands and fondled it.

"Darling," she said, "how *wunderbar*. But I can only stay for a few seconds. Mrs Vadarci would be furious."

"What is she? A jailer?"

"No. But one of the conditions of my engagement is that I don't have . . . how do you say it?"

"Followers? That's me, all right."

"So when I am with her, you must not expect me to recognize you."

"All right, but there's a hell of a lot I want to talk to you about."

"You want my answer, no. But you could have telephoned me."

"Your answer? Oh, yes. Sure I want that. But there's much more than that. Look, I've got to talk to you."

She smiled, leaned forward and kissed me lightly on the cheek. "Where you stay?"

"Hotel Florida."

"I will work something out and let you know. Right now I have to go back. She waits for me to rub her shoulder blades."

"Do what?"

"She has fibrositis. I rub her, each morning, afternoon and evening. You know I am a trained Swedish masseuse?"

I said, "I can't wait to stand in a good draught and get fibrositis. Do people only get it in the shoulder blades?"

"Rex, darling . . . naughty." She stood up and was away.

There was nothing I could do. I just sat, enchanted, watching her beautiful back and legs, and the sharp flick of ankles moving away from me. I did not believe for a moment that she was a trained masseuse. I had met quite a few congenital liars, men and women, but I'd never fallen in love with one before.

I went back to the flat, changed, and had a large whisky. Then I went down and got a taxi. We fought and hooted our way through the evening traffic up towards the Arc de Triomphe with the *Le Chasseur* rubbing gently against my lower left ribs, and myself wondering why the hell I was wearing it.

It was a small grocer's shop right at the far end of the Avenue de la Grande Armée, on the Porte Maillot, with the green trees and worn grass of the Bois de Boulogne just around the corner. I walked the last hundred yards to it, and if the place were being watched or I were being followed, I couldn't tell.

The place was badly lit and there was a pleasant smell of coffee grinding. There was a big advertisement runner for Suchard chocolates on one wall, a box of artichokes propped against the counter, and no room to swing a cat. An elderly, apple-cheeked woman, her black hair done in a bun on top of her head, was listening to a radio transmission of hot music. She turned it down a few decibels as I faced her. It still meant I had to shout.

"Monsieur Stebelson?"

She nodded, smiled, turned the volume up and flicked a finger to a glass-panelled door beyond the counter.

I went through into a sitting-room as crowded and as badly lit as the shop. Stebelson had his back to a window that looked out on to a small courtyard. He wore a black homburg and a light grey summer coat and smoked a cigar.

The plastic eyes went over me in the briefest of kit inspections and then he held out his hand. It felt like limp, synthetic rubber.

"Good," he said. "Come with me."

He turned and went out through a door into the courtyard. I followed. He took me on a quick tour of courtyards, alleyways and back passages. Then we were out in a small street and he was opening the door of a car for me. I tried to follow the route for a time. In London I could have held my own with the best taxi-driver, but Paris beat me. We ran south along the edge of the Bois for some time, then took a left-hand turn back into the maze of streets behind the Avenue Victor Hugo and after that I was lost.

"Neat," I said. "If anyone was following you must have shaken them."

He nodded but said nothing.

We finished up eventually in a narrow back street whose name I couldn't get as we swung into it. There was a blue door with the number eight on it. We went through, across a small garden, and into a dark little hall. There was a service lift. Stebelson swung the grille back and waved me inside.

"You go up by yourself," he said. "The fourth floor. You will be met."

I went up alone. When I stepped out on the fourth floor a girl was waiting for me.

She said, "Monsieur Carver?"

I nodded, and she turned and began to lead me down a carpeted corridor. She was a tall, thin girl, the kind that can make a cheap dress look like a Jacques Fath number. Her hair was smooth ebony, and there was a sort of *noli me tangere* air about her.

She knocked on a door, pushed it open, and beckoned me in with a nice movement of hand and arm. I went in and she followed me. It was an office with a big, antique desk affair, all gold leather and ormolu legs and bits of carving, and a shaded green light above it. Behind it sat what must have been one of the tiniest men in the world. He had a powder-white face, a hooked nose, a thin mouth like a turned down bracket, sad grey eyes, and two irregular patches of grey fuzz flanking the lower slopes of a sharply pointed bald head. He wore a dinner jacket, and to get his elbows on the desk he must have been sitting on a couple of cushions. He had a huge cigar in one corner of his mouth and I began to worry that the weight of it would snap his thin neck in half.

He pointed a brittle finger at a chair and I sat down, wondering how he had managed to survive from Sax Rohmer days. Somewhere there had to be an octopus tank. The girl sat down somewhere behind me and ruffled the pages of a notebook. The sound was reassuring.

In a lightweight voice that went with his size, he said, "It is nice of you to come, Mr Carver, and I shall try to be as direct with you as I possibly can. My name is Avraam Malacod, I understand from Stebelson that you have certain reservations about accepting this commission?"

"I'd just like to have some working idea of what I'm getting into. Stebelson, I take it, is your agent?"

"Yes."

He looked hard at me then, and he went on looking, and it was hard to say whether he was waiting for me to speak or whether he was making up his mind about something. I decided for the latter, and waited. After a moment or two he took the cigar from his mouth and laid it gently on a silver tray. Then he smiled and a tiny miracle happened. He was no longer grotesque. It was a heartening smile that I'd have taken odds could be trusted from Paris to Timbuktu. Perhaps he sensed the moment of confidence in me, perhaps he knew all about the effect of that smile on people . . . anyway, he spoke.

He said, "Before you came, Mr Carver, I had made up my mind to lie to you. Not because I wanted to use you to accomplish anything illegal for me . . . but simply because this matter is of great importance to me and many other people. Quite simply I was going to give you some story . . . fabricated of course . . . that would satisfy you and ensure that you continued in my service. However, I have now changed my mind."

"In the last three minutes?"

"Yes."

"Why?"

I got the smile again.

"When you leave here, Mr Carver, you know my name. You can make inquiries about me and you will know what kind of man I am. One of the factors which have made me what I am is an ability to judge men quickly. You have been judged."

I liked the way he said it. Somehow it made me feel good. I liked the way he spoke, too, in his soft, gently modulated English, no mother tongue obviously, but for him something not to be abused.

"And what does the judgement mean, Mr Malacod? That I get

the truth? Or that you are going to ask me to work for you in the dark and rely on your good faith?"

"The truth," he said, picking up his cigar, "cannot be told yet. But I have no wish to deal in lies. So, I am going to ask you to work for me and be content with the knowledge that, when you know the truth, as you will eventually, you will concede that I am a man of good faith."

I smiled. "It's a lot to ask. Faith in human nature wears very thin in my profession."

"In all professions. But this is the way I would prefer it to be between us. You can make your own terms about payment. After all, faith should be rewarded." He smiled, but it was a different one this time, worldly, acknowledging that people have to eat, drink and pay bills. "And in return, all I ask is that you follow Mrs Vadarci and this girl, Katerina. Just follow them, and report their movements to me?"

"Who is this Mrs Vadarci?"

"Someone who intends to use Katerina Saxmann – though the girl doesn't know this at the moment. What I want to know is how and where."

"And you just want me to follow them?"

"Yes. Eventually, they will settle down somewhere. And I can tell you that it will be somewhere remote. Not the kind of place where visitors will be welcomed."

"I'm sure you want this done discreetly – but Katerina knows me. If I follow her around she's going to say something about it to Mrs Vadarci."

His smile was the worldly one again.

"I think not – if you handle her correctly. She's an unusual girl. An expert in using people, I understand. You shouldn't find it difficult to come to some arrangement with her. A financial one if necessary. All I insist on is that Mrs Vadarci doesn't know she's being followed. Well?" He lobbed the last word at me, and I knew that I was going to get no more from him.

I heard the notebook pages flip behind me and knew that she was making a record of the conversation. What was I to do? I had trusted people before and it had usually finished by increasing my overdraft. But there was something about this tiny figure with its domed head and matchstick arms, about the smile, and the soft voice, that impressed me, rang the hidden bell inside which signals only when genuine contact is made.

Like a fool, charmed, ensnared, I said, "All right, I accept the terms."

He nodded, and said, "Good. And thank you for your confidence in me."

I said, "What about the details? Reporting to you and so on? I've a feeling I shall be travelling around."

"Quite, Mr Carver. And naturally, you don't want to be encumbered with administrative details. Madame Latour-Mesmin will accompany you and handle all your reports, and deal with all your travel and hotel arrangements. From now on you may call on her for any duties you consider necessary."

I turned then and looked at her. Latour-Mesmin. It was a hell of a name. She looked up briefly from her notebook. It was one of those long oval faces with big brown eyes that most of the time say nothing in a kind of dumb spaniel way, an attractive face, but without a great deal of life in it, though I got the feeling that at some time there had been a great deal of life there until she had decided against it.

"But I may not want her with me all the time," I said.

"Then, you tell her where to stay, what to do until you do want her. She's entirely at your disposal, and will send your reports either to me or to Herr Stebelson."

And that was that. I walked back down the corridor behind her, wondering just how far out of my depth I was. She pressed the lift push and, as we waited, I said, "I can't go around saying Latour-Mesmin. It sounds like a bottle of Burgundy. What comes in front of it?"

"Vérité," she said.

"We seem to be a little short on that around here," I said, but I got no smile from her. She handed me a sheet from her notebook on which she had written an address and telephone number.

She said, "Where can I get in touch with you?"

I hesitated for a moment and then said, "Well, I'm wandering round a bit. That's how Paris takes me. But you can always leave a message at the Hotel Florida."

The lift clanked to a stop, and she put out a hand to pull the grille back for me. I stepped in, turned and put my foot down so that the door could not close.

I said, "You approve of this arrangement, Vérité?"

"I approve of all Herr Malacod's instructions."

"You do? Even the bit about any duties I may consider necessary and being entirely at my disposal?"

All I wanted was either a smile or a flicker of anger in the deep brown eyes. All I got was a ten degree drop in temperature as the ice-age closed in.

I went down and the last thing I saw of her was a pair of neat black shoes, nylon ankles, and the toe of the right shoe tapping with either impatience or boredom.

Stebelson and the car had gone. I strolled round the corner and found myself on the Seine side, the Avenue de Tokio to be exact. I got a taxi back to the flat, had a couple of whiskies, made myself an omelette, and went to bed just as Paris began to wake up for the night. What I should have done, of course, was to have called up Vérité Latour-Mesmin and taken her to a night club. It would have been a riot.

*

I woke at three o'clock. I knew it was three because as I lay there I heard the chimes go from a couple of church clocks somewhere. And as the last *bong* went, his shadow slid smoothly between me and the window. I heard the bathroom door sigh open, the handle held first against the flick of the catch, and then gently eased back. He did it nicely, professionally, and one had to be awake to hear it.

Outside a neon light of some kind kept smearing washes of red, blue and green about the room. I don't know what he expected to find in the bathroom but he was not long deciding that it was not there. He came back and stood pensively between the bed and the window. I watched him with half my head under the sheet and through the faintest crack of an eyelid, just the way I used to do it when my old man would come padding into the room to fill my Christmas stocking. I even gave a faint snore just to reassure him. He relaxed in the way my old man used to relax. I was glad about the relaxing because the dark bulk of his right hand was club-rooted, but not with any Christmas stocking.

He half turned to the window and I came out of bed like the wrath of Christmas past, present and future, and with one hand gripping the corner of the hard bolster affair that the French call a pillow. I slung it at him and caught him on the side of the head. Quite a blow when not expected. As he reeled, I jabbed him behind the knees with my foot and he went down and cracked his head against the door of the wardrobe. I picked up his gun and sat on the edge of my bed, groping with my left hand for my slippers. Never walk about in bare feet, a mother maxim, drilled into me.

As he sat up, hunched over his knees and rubbing the back of his head, I said, "They tell me the whole place is soundproof, and I'm not responsible for the tidying-up when I leave."

With an American accent, he said, "Christ, what a welcome."

He turned and beat his fist against the wardrobe door. "Old-fashioned French colonial stuff, built to last, solid. A modern factory piece and my head would have gone right through. Howard Johnson's the name. For the time being, that is." He stood up.

I said, "Go through into the parlour. Light switch on your left."

He went through, switched on the light and I followed. I waved him to a chair and sat between him and the door and we looked at each other.

"Nice line in pyjamas," he said, smiling.

I said, "I'm particular about my bedwear. You never know who you're going to meet."

He nodded. "I must have been a disappointment. But don't judge too soon."

I said, "The floor is all yours."

He was one of those chunky, pleasant-looking chaps, very American, with close-cropped sandy hair, and a rugged face. I put him at about twenty-five, and he would not have been out of place in a line-up of Olympic athletes. But not on any American team. I don't know why. It was all perfect. Too perfect, perhaps, the way the bright boys of all the tribes east of the Rhine are always just too perfect when they tell themselves they must not make any mistake. He had a light silk jacket, smart brown trousers, and great boats of perfectly polished brogue shoes with crêpe soles, and a gold tie-clip with the initials HJ crested on it.

"Mind if I smoke?" he asked. His right hand made a move to his jacket pocket.

I waved the gun warningly and he stopped. Then I tossed him a box of matches and my own cigarettes from the table beside me.

"Careful. I like that." He lit a cigarette.

I said, "Come to the point. I don't like my sleep broken."

He was silent for a moment, but not still. There was a slight fidget of the crêpe-soled shoes.

Then he said, "All right, lover-boy – I'll give it to you straight. You're in business for money, yes?"

"Yes."

"We know you've got a watching brief for London, and you know that there's often a gap in the liaison between Washington and London. Sure, of course, you know. Political reasons, heads of staff jealousy . . . makes the whole thing a cow's ass of a nuisance at times. We'd just like to put you on the pay-roll. Whatever you pass to London, you pass to us. We're both working to the same end. Nothing wrong with double insurance. Of course, it would be confidential, strictly. And you'd make a fat bundle of dollars."

"You could have put all that in a letter instead of breaking up my sleep."

"Think so? No. First rule – try your man to check responses, reflex actions and blood pressure. You got an Alpha plus mark with me. I knew you were awake but even so you got me off balance. I should have thought of the pillow. What's the answer?"

I stood up and stepped back so that he had a free walk to the door.

"Briefly," I said, "no. Expanding it a little – not bloody likely. What is it about me that makes people think I've got a Judas complex?"

"Money," he said. "Lovely dollars, honey child."

The longer I was with him, the less I liked this American. I nodded at the door. "Goodnight, Johnson."

He did not argue. He said, "Okay. Your loss." And then at the door, he added, "You keeping my gun?"

I said, "It goes in the collection. When I retire I'm presenting it to the South Kensington Science Museum. Also, not that I'm impressed with the security of this place, I'll have the key you let yourself in with."

I held out my left hand and kept him covered with the right.

After a flicker of hesitation he fished in his trouser pocket and tossed me a key.

I kept the door open and heard him down the stairs. Then I checked him from the window, crossing the street below. Then I went back to bed. Lovely dollars. Sure, and I would have been paid in dollars, too. But somewhere, when the real book-keeping was done, I was pretty sure that it would have been in roubles. Honey child. . . .

CHAPTER SIX

"VOUS VOUS AMUSEZ, NO?"

I phoned Wilkins at Greenwich the next morning early. It was half-past seven and her father answered the phone, roaring down the instrument as though he had been roused by the officer of the watch saying that number two hold was on fire. He shouted for Wilkins and, while she was taking her hair out of curlers or whatever else it was that she felt she had to do to make herself decent to answer the phone, the old man gave me two runners at Longchamp that day and a brief run down on the weather prospects in London.

Wilkins came on, half-awake and disapproving of early calls. I said that I wanted everything she could find on Avraam Malacod phoned to me as soon as possible, and then, as an off-chance, because it had been worrying me a little ever since I had heard it, I asked for the same on Latour-Mesmin.

"Female?"

"Yes. Vérité," I said. "The old memory box keeps flashing hazy sorts of headlines. Or am I dreaming?"

"At this hour you should be sleeping."

I did not argue. I gave her the flat number to call back and then made coffee and two poached eggs. I sat over the coffee trying to put some order into things. Malacod through Stebelson wanted me to keep an eye on Katerina and finally let him know where Mrs Vadarci went to ground. Sutcliffe wanted the same. Then there were the two men who had jumped me in London, and lover-boy who had visited me last night . . . all on the same tack. And tied to Mrs Vadarci, flying like a gorgeous kite, so that you couldn't miss her, was Katerina. Stebelson had said that Mrs Vadarci was going to use Katerina. What for? Maybe I ought to pin Katerina down somewhere long enough to make her talk. It would not be easy, but it was worth trying. If everybody was using everybody else, and hoping to make a good thing out of it, I didn't see why I shouldn't come in on the game, no matter what Sutcliffe said about men overfilling their wallets.

I waited until nine-thirty and then phoned Balzac 35.30, a personal call to Katerina. She came on sounding very sleepy and cross, and sounded crosser when she heard that it was me.

"Ring later," she said, and I could hear the yawn.

"I want to see you today."

"Ring later."

I said, "Seven o'clock tonight. The north end of the Solferino bridge."

"No."

"Then I'll come round to the hotel now?"

"Then I don't see you."

"You'll have to. I'll say I'm from the Ministry of Health and want to see your certificate to practise as a masseuse. Solferino bridge. Seven o'clock."

"All right."

"Good girl."

"How can I tell the north end?"

"Look at the river. If it flows from your right to your left, you're at the wrong end. Cross over."

"*Mein Gott* – how difficult. I stand in the middle. And I wait only two minutes." She rang off, and I imagined her curling up in bed again. I lingered over the picture for a while.

Then Casalis came in on his own key and said cheerfully, "Morning, Mother Jambo. Sleep well?"

"All but an hour. I had a visitor. The key of this place is compromised. As though you care."

"Not particularly. Life is one big compromise." He poured

himself what was left of the coffee into the quarter-filled sugar basin and made a relishing noise as he swallowed half of it at one go. "Delicious. You've got a touch with coffee."

"He called himself Howard Johnson, or some such name. Made me an offer on behalf of the C.I.A. and guaranteed fat payment."

"Snappy dresser? Looks like a college half-back and has a manner so frank you can tell it's pure man-made fibre from east of the Urals?"

"That's him."

"Dear old Howard. He's what they call an early developer. Bright boy of the class, top marks in everything, and then when his voice broke and all the other signs of adolescence appeared he petered out. Still by that time they had a big investment in him so they keep hoping he'll get into gear again one day. What about Malacod?"

"I thought you might know about him. He hired me. No questions asked either way."

"Trusting of you."

"I liked his smile. It lit up the room."

"You should have worn sunglasses."

"He was generous," I said. "Put his secretary entirely at my disposal. Travelling companion, guide, counsellor and friend. The name is Vérité Latour-Mesmin."

"What vintage?"

"About 1935, and thin on the palate. But I'm hoping that decanting will improve it. Anyway, she goes with me on the Vadarci trail."

Casalis made a face and said, "I don't think we shall like that."

I knew what he meant by *we*, but I was not worried.

"You're stuck with it," I said. "And so am I. Now, what about this flat? I don't like visitors."

"You can handle them. But I'd better keep away. Be in the

George V bar each evening between six and six-thirty. Beginning tonight. If there is anything to be passed we'll do it there. Here, I could be jumped easily."

"That's right," I said, "you look after yourself."

"Always do." He gave me a wave and went.

At twelve o'clock Wilkins came through with her material. I sat in front of the window with several sheets of paper on the table before me, and a large glass of gin and campari in my right hand.

Wilkins had dictated to me a three hundred word summary – and Wilkins could summarize *Gone with the Wind* into three pages if pushed – of the trial of Vérité Latour-Mesmin for the murder of her husband in May, 1957. The account had appeared in the *News of the World*. It was that which had made my old memory box flicker because, if I could help it, I never missed my couple of glasses of Guinness and the *News of the World* every Sunday morning in Mrs Meld's kitchen. Vérité had been acquitted by a French jury at Limoges, and it had been a very juicy case indeed.

On Malacod, it was mostly international banking, shipping, two museum foundations, charity trusts, and research scholarships ... the same kind of set-up that you would find listed under names like Rothschild, Gulbenkian, Ford, Nuffield and so on. Malacod was a Jew, born in Hamburg, and he was unmarried. There was also a summary from an account in the London *Times* of 16 February, 1947, announcing a new Malacod research fund, and this included a précis of a second leader in *The Times* of the same day which, I had a feeling, was less than just to Malacod.

After reading it all through, I mixed myself a second drink, a big one, so that I could toast Wilkins and her industry first. The very little that was left in the glass I libated to Vérité Latour-Mesmin. Ice-maidens are made not born.

*

I got to the George V just after six o'clock. In the bar, a large American, with a Countess Mara tie and a matey manner, kept me company and told me a long story about a friend of his. I kept waiting for the point and it never came. I lost interest in him over the second martini. As it was served to me I saw Richard Manston come into the bar.

He was a sight for sore eyes, but I knew at once that he wanted no part of me. He came up to the bar, three yards away from me, and ordered a whisky and soda. He was in tails and wearing a set of miniature medals. He also had a monocle screwed into one eye and his hair was dyed a nice blond. He was so impeccable that I had the feeling that there were crumbs down the back of my collar. He looked right through me, the American next to me, and the wall beyond us, while the barman, serving him, said, "Nice to see you again, Sir Alfred." I turned my back on him and pretended to take an interest in the American.

Five minutes later Manston left the bar. As he passed me I waited for the touch and could not be sure that I had marked it. When he was out of the place, I dropped my hand idly to my jacket pocket. I had never met any man who could do it better, except one, and he was in Parkhurst, his talent rotting.

I endured the American for ten more minutes and then I strolled out of the bar. In the hotel main lobby I turned my back quickly and started to light a cigarette, hands well up to my face, and watching everything behind me in a wall mirror. Moving towards the main entrance were Mrs Vadarci and Katerina, togged up in full evening fig, and escorted by Sir Alfred. I watched them go out and it didn't even occur to me to get a taxi to the Solferino bridge. No girl was going to stand on a Seine bridge, even for two minutes, in blue chiffon and white fox, slightly vulgar, oversized diamonds, and a rising violet mist in her blue eyes. This last, I presumed, was for Sir Alfred. It did not even make me jealous because I knew she was wasting her time with Manston.

I went into the men's room and pulled out the envelope which Manston had slipped into my jacket pocket. There was a hotel key in it, a cigarette, and a letter which read:

Welcome back, old boy. Have a look around Suite 101. No need to be tidy. Smoke cigarette and leave butt. We may meet again but you don't know me – no matter what. And don't be tempted. There are no pickings in this one. Repeat *no.* Bon voyage. R.A.D.I.

The cigarette was tipped and just above the butt was the legend – *Beograd Filter.* I knew it was going to taste like hell. I tore up the message and flushed it away. Read and destroy immediately. A few moments later I was going up in the lift, pondering the future business. And ponder was the word. Wherever I met him in future I was not to recognize him. No pickings, either. I smiled at that. Resist temptation, here it was again. Then the smile went as I realized that Manston – plenty of others, yes, but not Manston – had never said that to me before. It meant I was in deep, very deep. Suddenly I had a moment's nostalgia for Guinness and kippers in Mrs Meld's kitchen.

Suite 101 was the usual modest lay-out you get for fifty guineas a day: a little lobby, a sitting-room, and off either side of the sitting-room a bedroom, each with its bathroom. I started with Mrs Vadarci's bedroom. She was clearly one of the untidiest women that ever lived. Her stuff was all over the place. I went through everything. She had a wardrobe that would have fitted out half the female cast of *My Fair Lady*, and enough jewellery to make a fair display in Cartier's window. I was tempted to take the lot and go into retirement there and then. There were times later when I wished I had. The only thing that made me at all curious – there were no personal papers of any kind to do it – was a long soft leather container. It was at the bottom of a white pigskin case that was half filled with a ghastly collection of archaic underwear that should have been in the V. and A. Inside this long container was a whip. It had a gold grip decorated top and bottom with three ivory bands. The stock or body of the whip was, I guessed, of nicely tempered steel and it was covered with red morocco leather with a small Greek key pattern spiralling round it in gold. There was one thong at the end about four feet long. It was no toy and it made the air wince as I took a couple of practice swings with it.

The sitting-room did not produce anything. There were a few magazines and papers. On a sideboard were drinks, an enormous box of chocolates with liqueur centres, genuine, I found, when I chose a Cointreau. I helped myself to a whisky and soda and smoked half the cigarette and then dropped the rest into a tray. It was not as bad as I had expected.

Katerina's bedroom was neat, everything in its place. She did not have a lot in the way of clothes, but what she had she treated with care . . . folded and pressed, shoes on trees. There was a short nightdress laid out on the bed. It was silk and as light and frothy as meringue, and pale green. In a travelling writing-case on a table was her passport – West German Federal Government. Her name was genuine – Katerina Helga Saxmann. Flipping through it to the visa section I found the big tablet stamp of a Yugoslav visa. It had been issued the previous day at the Paris Embassy. *Vazi tri meseca od dana izdavanja* – valid for three months from the date of issue. With it were two Air France tickets to Dubrovnik, via Zagreb, for the next day, and a printed slip from the Yugoslav Travel and Tourist Agency, Atlas, confirming reservations for two at the Hotel Argentina, Dubrovnik. I dropped the case and contents on the floor and did not bother to pick them up.

Five minutes later I turned out of the Avenue George V into the Champs-Élysées, found a café, bought a paper, and saw that one of my horses had come up at a good price at Longchamp, and then I telephoned Vérité Latour-Mesmin, and asked her if she would have dinner with me. She said she was just washing her hair, and was going to have supper in her flat and would be happy to have me join her.

As I came out of the café and started to look for a taxi Casalis came up to me and asked for a light. He was wearing blue overalls and a false moustache.

I said, "For Christ's sake – why the pantomime outfit? Even Howard Johnson could see through it."

"Another job later. Breaking it in. Like it?"

"All you need is a pair of sabots."

I held a lighter to his cigarette, and he said, after a puff, "Thank you, Mother Jambo. I've a message for you – left at the Hotel Florida. Also, I gather, you may have something for me."

He was strolling at my side and he might have been with me and he mightn't. I gave him a quick run down on the results of my visit to the suite, including the whip, and he slipped an envelope into my hand and melted faster than any genie.

In the cab I opened the envelope. It was from Katerina, and as I read it I wondered why I'd been working my fingers to the bone in the last hour.

It read—

Sorry, darling. Can't make Solferino. Big boring Embassy dinner date. Flying Dubrovnik tomorrow. Is there a bridge there? Love. K

Why was she so certain that I would follow her wherever she went? She was, and she was prepared to give leads which other people paid me to work for? Curious.

So far as I knew, it was the first time I'd had dinner with a woman who had shot her husband. It made me take a fresh look at Vérité. She still came out all right in my book. Her face was a beautiful piece of work, with a bone structure which, no matter from what angle the light came, created an arresting combination of shadows and light planes. Her deep brown eyes had long lashes, and the thin dark eyebrows were so perfect that they made you want to put out your finger and smudge them even though you knew they were real. Not once while I was there did she really smile, but I had the impression that when she did it would be something worth waiting for.

The flat was neat and impersonal, and the kitchen was like a small clinic. But she could cook. We had wafer-thin slices of veal done in Gruyère cheese with little slips of anchovy on top, and a bottle of Meursault of which she drank very little.

I said, "Mrs Vadarci and the Saxmann girl are flying to Dubrovnik tomorrow and staying at the Hotel Argentina. I think we ought to do the same, but not on the same plane. Day later, if necessary. Will you fix it?"

"Certainly." She was peeling a pear with neat movements – and no drip, no mean feat.

"Tell Herr Malacod that I went through the Vadarci suite at the George Cinq. There was nothing there of any interest – unless he's interested in Edwardian clothes – except a whip."

"Whip?" There was no surprise in her voice as she cut the pear in half.

"A fancy number, but serviceable." I described it to her.

When I had finished she said, "Please have some of this. I can't eat it all." She put half of the pear on my plate, and went on, "Was it necessary to break into the suite?"

"I wouldn't know they were taking off otherwise. And break is the wrong word. I borrowed a key."

"You are very competent."

I was not sure from her tone whether it was a question or a compliment. I took some of the pear and, as I knew it would, it dribbled down my chin. She reached for my napkin which had fallen to the floor. I suddenly realized what it was about her that kept us in different leagues. She was treating me like a small boy ... peeling fruit, keeping me tidy, pouring my wine ... drink it up like a good boy. I did not mind. Something told me that it made her feel safe with me. With me – and she had shot her husband three times at point-blank range and then calmly telephoned the police!

"I have to be," I said. She was half-way to the kitchen to do something about coffee.

"Be what?" she said over her shoulder.

"Competent."

"Oh, that, yes." She went into the kitchen and came back with a tray. There were a couple of cups on it with those tin percolator things on top that produce a lukewarm brown liquid after fifteen minutes of waiting and banging. As though there had been no break in the conversation, she said, "And thorough?"

"Thorough?"

"Yes." She held an open cigarette box towards me and when I took one, there was a lighter in her hand, flame waiting. "I presume you have made inquiries about Herr Malacod?"

"Such as I could, yes. His credit rating is very high."

There was no smile from her.

"He is a very good man. And me?"

"What about you?"

"You have made inquiries about me? It would be natural."

I said, "Of course not."

She lit herself a cigarette and said without emotion of any kind, "It is very nice of you to lie. It was unnecessary, but I appreciate it."

I could not think of anything to say to that, so I rapped the top of my percolator, and she said, "It does no good to do that." Small boy again, getting impatient.

"In the tourist season," I said, going on with my tapping, "you can hear this sound from English people all over France."

There was no smile. I think that was the moment that I made a bet with myself that if I didn't get a smile out of her in the next five days I would send a cheque for ten pounds to Doctor Barnardo's Homes.

She said, "Would you like a liqueur?"

"No, thank you."

"A whisky and soda?"

"Well . . ."

She was on her feet and going to the sideboard. With her back to me, she said, "You are armed?"

You had to jump to keep up with her. "Yes," I said.

"You had better let me have it before we get on the plane. I can get it through the customs much easier than you."

"If you insist." But I was thinking that with a girl of her build it was going to make a pretty obvious bulge inside her girdle. I even contemplated saying so but I knew there would be no smile. I was beginning to feel out of my depth. She put me far out into deep water as I left.

I put out my hand, French fashion, and thanked her for the meal and the pleasure of her company. You would have thought that I was wearing velvet pants and a lace collar, remembering to thank my hostess. She took my hand and her fingers were long and cool, and she said, "I very much enjoyed it, Mr Carver, but I think I should make one thing very clear."

"If you do," I said, "you'll be the first one in days."

"I think," she said evenly, "that you are a nice person. Naturally, we may see a great deal of one another, but I should like you to know that I have no intention of allowing you to sleep with me."

She riled me then.

"Was that necessary?" I asked.

"It has been in the past."

I walked down the stairs feeling like a dog that has been kicked from the step before he has even asked to come in.

As I stepped off the pavement to cross the road, a car coming at speed down the opposite side of the quiet street suddenly swerved at me, flashed up its headlights, and missed me by six inches as I started a backward jump to the pavement. It pulled up ten yards down and a man got out and hurried back to me. I was on my feet before he got to me, but not before his frank, jolly, phoney voice reached me.

"Sorry, lover-boy, but the steering on that old jalopy makes it as crazy as a one-winged snipe at times. No damage done, I hope? Jeez, I might have killed you."

Good old Howard Johnson was reaching out his hands across the steps to dust me down. I took one of them gratefully and, with a wrist and upper arm hold, I threw him over my shoulder against the house wall. I went through his pockets while he snored like a drunk and found nothing of interest, except a packet of Beograd filter-tips. Then I walked down to the car. There was no one in it, so I took it. It saved a big taxi fare from the Porte de la Villette, where Vérité lived, to my flat. I parked it a hundred yards down the road from the flat, dropped the keys down a drain, and let the air out of the four tyres. A French tart, who was slightly tight on duty, watched me and said, "*Vous vous amusez, no?*"

"Yes," I said.

As I went to move away, she said, "*Bien. Maintenant, nous allons nous amuser beaucoup plus?*"

"No," I said.

I went up to my flat, taking with me the only thing of interest which I had found in the car. It was a paper-back book written in English, published by a firm I'd never heard of in London called Unity Books, Ltd. It was a translation from the German, so the fly-leaf said, and was entitled – *Stigmata: A Study of European National Neuroses.* It sounded like light bedtime reading, but I hadn't taken it because of that, and I don't think Howard Johnson had been reading it because of that. The name of the author had caught my eye. It had been written by a Professor Carl Vadarci. I was interested, among other things, to see if Professor Vadarci took the same line on the subject as, I had gathered from Wilkins's summary, *The Times* had in their second leader on 16 February, 1947.

CHAPTER SEVEN

OYSTERS WITH OGLU

Vérité could not get seat reservations for the next day. We left the morning of the day after in a Caravelle. She turned up in a neat blue travelling suit and with one case, and she ran neck and neck with Wilkins for efficiency. She took charge and shepherded me around quietly but firmly. I began to wonder if all she had left now was a frustrated mother instinct.

We sat together and, as we took off, she handed me the daily papers and an English edition of a *Fodor's Modern Guide – Yugoslavia* (with illustrations and maps) to keep me from getting bored during the trip. I knew it would not be worth while even trying the mildest flirtation with the Air France hostess. Vérité would tell me I wasn't old enough.

I read the papers, saving the guide for later. I hoped it would not be such heavy reading as *Stigmata* by Professor Vadarci.

Part of the past day I'd spent trying to pick out some of the jigsaw pieces with straight edges so that I could get a frame for the puzzle before I began to work inwards. I hadn't found many. Beograd filter was easy. They wanted it to look as though Howard Johnson had been through the Vadarci suite. Sir Alfred and Katerina's Embassy dinner had been easier – though it had cost me a phone call to Wilkins in London. One of the Counsellors at the British Embassy in Paris was a Sir Alfred Coddon, K.B.E., C.V.O. I guessed that he had gone quietly on leave somewhere, and that when the need arose Manston was taking his place. Why? No answer, except that I would gamble that Manston was working on the jigsaw by starting with the centre pieces. Professor Vadarci was much harder. Wilkins could find nothing on him. So I just had to keep my muzzle down to the scent and jog on. The money was good, and there was always a chance that some time or other I could make it better.

I looked at Vérité. She had her eyes closed and could have been sleeping. I dipped into Fodor and started to read the serial story called "Tourist Vocabulary" at the back, which was all about an inquiring chap like myself who goes about hotels, shops, restaurants, garages and banks asking questions. I liked the episode in the restaurant best . . . "Waiter! I would like to have lunch, dinner. The menu, please. Thank you. Soup. Bread. Hors d'oeuvre. Smoked ham. Ham omelette. (God, what an appetite – right down to fruit, cheese, fish, eggs.) Serve me on the terrace. Where can I wash my hands? Beer. Bottled water. Turkish coffee." Poor bloody waiter.

Vérité woke up.

I said, "Where are we staying?"

"At the Imperial. It's quite close to the Argentina."

"Good. I hope I've got a *sola prema moru?*"

"A what?"

"If I've pronounced it right, it means a room with a view of the sea."

I didn't get a smile. I turned to a section on national dishes and soon saw that I was going to be in for a great deal of mutton stew under different names.

At Zagreb airport we changed to a DC.3 of the JAT airline, and all the way down to Cilipi airport I forced myself to sleep so that I wouldn't have to watch the limestone mountains not so far below.

I had a room with a view of the sea, though it was too dark to see much by the time we arrived. I flopped back on the bed to recover from a twenty-mile trip in from the airport over unmade roads, and I reached for the phone. It was answered by somebody who spoke English, and I ordered a large whisky up to the room and a personal call to Katerina at the Hotel Argentina. I was told that she had left the hotel that morning.

I went next door, carrying my drink, to Vérité's room, knocked and was admitted. She had a dressing-gown on, and her feet were bare. She had nice toes, but I kept my eyes off them.

I raised the glass. "Like me to order one for you?"

"No thank you."

I sat down on a chair and said, "They left this morning."

She nodded and bent over her case to get her toilet-bag. "I know. I telephoned the moment we got in."

"I could have saved a few dinars on the call then. What now?" This was me, asking her what to do. I made a note to watch that. I didn't want to become dominated.

"Most tourists in this country make all their travelling and hotel reservations through an agency . . . Atlas, or Putnik. And they keep open late. I'll go into the town and see what I can find out just as soon as I have changed."

"When you're changed," I said, "you're having dinner with me – on the terrace. La Vadarci can wait until tomorrow morning."

"But won't that—"

"It's an order," I said. I smiled and drank to her over the glass. I was back in the saddle again.

We had dinner on a high terrace overlooking the sea. Away to our right were the lights of Dubrovnik. It was warm, and there were trails of phosphorescence in the water. Most of the other guests in the hotel seemed to be Germans who all apparently knew one another and looked brown, beefy and self-assured. Professor Vadarci had had something to say about that in *Stigmata*.

I was not sure what we ate, but we drank a wine called *Grk*, and that was how it tasted. Vérité appeared, looking wonderful. I wondered how the hell her husband could ever have done it to her.

There were a few moments when she began to crowd Katerina from my mind, but I held them back firmly. Somewhere at the back of me a three-piece orchestra was playing, and the Germans, to get a tighter cargo stow for more food, now and again got up and danced.

I said, "How the hell do you travel a dress like that without getting it creased? Everything in my case comes out looking like a dog's bed."

She almost smiled, but not quite, but I could see she was relaxing.

We went through the usual plays. Yes, she'd been in Dubrovnik before. Herr Malacod travelled a lot. The island across the channel from us was called Lokrum. No, she did not speak the language. Yes, she always drank water with her wine. I tried her a little deeper when we got to the sweet – something called *struklji*, a preparation of nuts and plums stuffed into balls of cheese and then boiled, so Fodor told me later. I was not surprised that she tucked into it, because I'd met a lot of slim girls with the appetites of horses and nothing to show for it. No, she had no idea why Herr Malacod was so interested in Madame Vadarci. No, she knew nothing about Madame Vadarci. Or Professor Vadarci? No – it took a little longer coming, I thought – she knew of no Professor Vadarci.

She finished the last stuffed cheese ball and I stood up.

I said, "*Hocete li da igrate?*"

She looked at me and one eyebrow went up in a delicious curve.

"It could sound," I said, "as though I'm asking you if you've got indigestion. Actually Fodor tells me it means – Will you dance with me?"

It was then she really smiled and I thought to myself that the guy who'd made that smile a rare occurrence deserved three shots in him. I went round and took her chair and she looked up at me and said, "I shall be sorry I gave you that book."

"You're not going to be sorry about anything," I said. I wasn't quite sure what I meant by that, but it didn't matter because by then she was in my arms and we were moving away from the table. She could dance. Not what Dino would have called a "ball of fire" maybe, but she was certainly no cardboard cut-out.

The next morning we took a taxi down to Dubrovnik. By then she was back to normal, efficient and cool, and I knew that I wasn't going to get more than one or two smiles a day. She left me to make the round of the tourist agencies, promising to meet me in the main harbour café of the town in two hours.

I am not a one for sightseeing. Just give me a beach with a lot of brown legs to look at and you can keep the baroque façades. I never want to flog around city walls or crick my neck in cathedrals. There was a time when I used to think I did, but after about fifteen minutes I would find myself thinking of ice-cold beer, and bikinis. Now, I know better than to try.

Right at the top end of the town, at a cigarette-end's flick from the Onofrio Fountain (fifteenth century, designed by the Neapolitan Onofrio de la Cava: Fodor) I found an oyster bar, just a cool cave opening on to the street, bead curtains, two tables, and Adriatic oysters at four shillings a dozen. I had two dozen to begin with, and a half a bottle of a dry white wine called *Vugava* which left *Grk* standing. I sat near the door, enjoying myself and, after a while, a tubby little number came in and took the chair next to me and, with a wink, helped himself to one of my oysters. I waited for him to say it and he did.

"They're good, no, Mother Jambo?"

"If this is going to be a long session," I said, "I shall have to order more."

"Allow me." He called for another dozen, and then went on, "They grow on dead trees, waterlogged, sunk at the bottom. That's because the sea bed is no good. People don't know it, but they're better than Portuguese or Whitstables. Small but all flavour. Rotten travellers, though. Having a good time?"

I nodded. He was not English, though he spoke it well, but all in a sing-song, up and down. He was about forty, dressed in a faded blue shirt and canvas trousers, sandals, no socks, and a white cap cocked over one eye. There were streaks of paint on the shirt and the cap. He had a face like a Red Indian, the noble kind, and liked oysters as much as I did.

He said, "What the news?"

"They've gone, yesterday morning. Moved on. Any idea where?"

He shook his head and passed me a card. "You'll find me there. My studio. I'm a painter." The name was Michael Oglu and the address 21 Ulica something-or-the-other. "How's Manston?" he added.

"Fine," I said. "What can I call on you for?"

"Anything, dear boy. Come and buy a picture. Tourist scenes. Poker-work frames."

"Thanks."

"You're welcome. Two other things. One, when you move I'll know where you've gone. Two, watch out for a nice old gent, white-haired, who carries a malacca stick with a silver knob on top shaped like a half-closed water-lily."

"You're kidding." I laughed.

"Gospel. No amount of training can stop it. Personality will out. In its quiet way it's a flamboyant profession. London says he's just been assigned to this beat and he's strictly a killer. *Vide* the stick. He's not over intelligent, though. But he's a sticker when ordered." He giggled and squeezed lemon over the last oyster on the plate before I could get to it.

I met Vérité an hour later in the Gradska Kafana on the harbour and bought her coffee and a slice of cake.

"They left yesterday morning," she said, "on a coastal steamer for the island of Mljet."

"Where's that?"

"It's about four or five hours up the coast. There are two or three lakes in the centre of the island and there's an island on one of them where a thirteenth-century monastery has been turned into an hotel. They booked in there. I've done the same for us. We leave tomorrow morning, very early. Is that right?"

"Dead right."

We went back and had lunch. Afterwards she disappeared into her room and I didn't see her again until dinner. I got my evening smile for something or other and then we danced. In the main room we got blocked for a moment or two. I found myself treading water gently looking over Vérité's shoulder at a table which held a plain, dumpy woman and an oldish man with raven black, close-cropped hair and a stiff Prussian set to his thin shoulders. Resting up against the table at his side was a malacca stick with a silver knob shaped like a half-closed water-lily.

The comfortable old biddy with him laughed at something he had just said, reached across the table affectionately and patted him on the cheek. Maybe she liked him better with his hair dyed.

When we went up to our rooms I went into Vérité's with her.

I stopped the beginning of her cold frown by saying, "What do you do about your reports to Herr Malacod?"

The frown went.

"I mail them the moment I've written them."

"Copies?"

"I don't keep any."

I went across the room and opened the french windows. She had a separate little balcony. Mine was three feet away. There was nothing on the far side of hers except the corner of the hotel. Nobody could come round that, not even Sir Edmund Hillary.

I came back to her and said, "Keep your door locked and a chair up against it. Not wedged, but like this—" I demonstrated "—so that it'll go over with a crash if anyone tries to come in. If it does – scream with everything you've got. It's better than any gun and I'll be right in."

"It's very nice of you to be so concerned for me, and I shall do as you say. But—" she walked to the table and picked up her handbag "—I can also look after myself." She pulled out a small automatic. "Herr Malacod insisted on it."

"Good for Herr Malacod," I said. I began to walk to the door, intending to say goodnight from it.

She said, "In view of what you've just said, isn't there something you ought to tell me which I should report to Herr Malacod?"

She was serving her master. I had to find ways of serving both mine.

"No," I said. "It's just a hunch. When you've been on the same bus route a long time, you get to spot the man who's travelling without a ticket."

I got one of her genuine smiles, and said goodnight. I stood outside until I'd heard the key go and the sound of the chair against the door.

I went down to the bar and had a nightcap, and then I went to the reception desk and asked a few silly questions about our trip to Mljet the next day. The girl behind the desk was bored and ready for a gossip. By the time I went upstairs again, I knew that water-lily knob and his partner were listed as Herr and Frau Walter Spiegel from Berlin. I had a strong feeling that neither of them would have any trouble going from West to East through the Wall.

I lay in bed trying out a few wild ideas, but I got nowhere with them. . . . Katerina and Mrs Vadarci, and trailing behind them in an untidy wake, Malacod, the wealthy Jew philanthropist, Sutcliffe, the *éminence grise* of Whitehall, and then the hard-working beagle pack from Moscow represented by Howard Johnson and Herr Walter Spiegel. I was ready to bet that somewhere, more remote perhaps, there might be a representative of the Federal German Office for the Protection of the Constitution. . . . Bonn wouldn't let itself be left out, not if Katerina, Stebelson and Malacod were genuine West German nationals, which I felt they were. There were all the makings of a spicy pie. What I wanted to know was whether it was already in the oven, or just sitting on the marble slab waiting for the crust to be put on. Whatever state it was in, I was hoping for the chance to put in my thumb and pull out a plum.

I read a chapter of *Stigmata* and fell into a light sleep, which nothing disturbed until the porter banged on my door at five o'clock. One of the things I was soon to learn about the country was that travelling anywhere meant getting up at some ungodly hour.

A taxi took us over the hill from Dubrovnik and down to the port of Gruz, where we went aboard one of the small coastal steamers. Vérité went below and laid claim to a small corner of the saloon for us. I stayed on deck and watched the local cargo for the small islands being packed on the foredeck. There was everything from fertilizer to furniture cream, lubricating oil to lavabos, and the odd coop of chickens, eyes already jaundiced with mistrust of the sea.

There was a good stinging breeze coming in from the sea, healthy, and full of red bauxite dust from the dumps farther along the quayside, and a group of young boys and girls were singing and playing mandolins and harmonicas as though it were not six o'clock in the morning.

Michael Oglu came aboard just before the ship pulled out and handed me a note.

"Came through this morning," he said. "Couldn't catch you before you left the hotel. Read it later." He drifted off.

When the boat was well away from the quay I went below and joined Vérité. She had ordered eggs and bacon and coffee. The eggs came, swimming in lagoons of olive oil, and we shared a table with two young sailors going home on leave to one of the islands and a young girl with a month-old baby, her first – both sailors combined to tell us this – which she had produced at the maternity hospital in Dubrovnik. Her husband was a schoolmaster on the island of Sipan. The baby was quietly sick every ten minutes and I can't say that I enjoyed my eggs, but the coffee was very good. Vérité had ordered it to be laced with brandy. When I commented on it, she nodded and said, "It settles the stomach against *mal de mer.*" The French are a great race when it comes to health.

I went to sleep for an hour and when I woke she was nursing the baby while the mother went off to powder her nose. When it was sick, she handled the situation with a couple of tissues as though she were an old hand at the game, and she smiled as she looked down into its face.

I picked up my copy of *Stigmata* and, under its cover, read the note which Michael Oglu had passed to me. It ran:

Vadarci may try unexpected exit Yugoslavia. If contacted left-thumbless give all help. Mother Jambo compromised. Now Ringmaster. R.A.D.I.

I sat there, trying to think of anyone I knew who had lost a left thumb, but nothing came.

CHAPTER EIGHT

BRUNHILD IN A BIKINI

We arrived at Mljet in mid-afternoon. We had run up the coast on the inside of a long string of islands, stopping now and then to set down and pick up passengers and cargo. The young mother disembarked at Sipan and was met by her husband, a young man in a stiff navy-blue suit and open-necked shirt. Mother and child were set on the back of a donkey and led proudly off up the hill, followed by a string of aunts and uncles.

After Sipan came Lopud and Kolocep, and I sat on deck and gave up *Stigmata* in favour of Fodor. Inland, on our starboard hand, was the great grey-white run of the mountains, and seawards always the low run of green islands. According to Fodor, Mljet's chief claim to attention was that it was the only place left in Europe where the mongoose still roamed at liberty. Apparently they'd been imported long ago from the East to rid the island of snakes – and there was an argument still going on that Mljet and not Malta had been the place where St Paul had been shipwrecked and bitten by a snake. Snakes, mongooses, Katerina and St Paul. I couldn't wait to get there.

We eventually hit a small port on the north side of Mljet called Polace, humped our cases ashore, and caught a small bus that took us up over the shoulder of a mountain and down to the side of the main lake – the Veliko Jezero. Jezero meant lake (Fodor). A waiting motor-boat hauled us across to the far side of the lake where there was a small island, about the size of a football pitch, on which stood the Hotel Melita – formerly a thirteenth-century Benedictine monastery. There was a wide, gravelled run of quayside in front of the hotel set with tables and coloured sun umbrellas. The first person I saw was Katerina, wearing a yellow bikini, lying stretched out in a deckchair, eyes shut, her face turned up to the sun. Alongside her sat Mrs Vadarci, in a coffee-coloured tea dress and a big flopping brimmed hat, looking as though she had just got back from a Buckingham Palace garden party. She was knitting something on large wooden needles that looked as though it might end up as a saddle blanket.

A girl, in a working black dress that was tight about the bust and short above the knees, carried our cases up the outer stairway of the hotel, into a run of cloisters and then through a narrow doorway into a small reception hall. As I turned to enter the cloisters I looked back and saw Katerina, eyes open, watching me. We looked at one another for a moment, then she gave a little yawn – for Mrs Vadarci's benefit, I hoped – and flopped back into her chair.

We had rooms on the first floor at the front of the building, and they opened on to a long, vaulted corridor with great arched windows that looked out over the hotel quay and to the nearside of the lake which was about two hundred yards away.

There was a notice in three languages on the inside of my door stating that the hotel pumped its own water from a well on the island and supplied its own electricity from a generator. Then came a list of the times when water and electricity would not be available. There was a candle by the bedside if one wanted to wander about the place after midnight.

I began to unpack but was interrupted after a few minutes by a knock on the door. I called out and the door opened.

Katerina came in. She was wearing a loose bathing wrap over her bikini, and she came to my arms like a porpoise surfacing. I fell over backwards on to the bed, holding and kissing her, and there were no words between us for quite a while. It was some time before I realized that one of my hairbrushes was puncturing my shoulder blade through my silk shirt.

Eventually she sat up, held me at arm's length, shook her head, and said, "Only a few moments I have. She watch me like a hawk."

I rubbed the back of my hand gently across the brown skin above her navel, and said, "Why don't we just poison her?"

She giggled and ran the fingers of one hand through my hair and the whole of my scalp tingled with the electric discharge.

"Darling. . . ." She kissed me, too briefly.

"I've got to talk to you. Undisturbed. Not for five minutes but for half an hour. What about your room? Tonight?"

"No. . . ." She leant forward and rubbed her lips softly against mine. My bones felt like putty. She took her lips away and went on, "Her room opens into mine, she would hear."

"Then you come here."

She shook her head. "When the lights go out this place is like a tomb. You want I should walk around with a candle, to stumble into the wrong room, maybe?"

"I take your point. Where then?"

She thought for a moment, and the three-line frown was a thing of beauty. "She sleep after lunch for two hours. You hire a little boat and meet me round the back of the island tomorrow."

She stood up and pulled the wrap around her, smiled at me as I nodded, and went to the door. She paused there and said, "This Mademoiselle Latour-Mesmin you are with – she is very chic, no? But I am angry if you sleep with her."

"She's Madame," I corrected. "Maybe I am angry too I don't sleep with her. But how did you know her name?"

I couldn't be sure whether she hesitated. That was the trouble with her. You could never be sure. She said, "I read in the register before I come here." She put her head out of the door, and looked carefully up and down. Then she was gone.

After dinner that evening, Vérité and I sat at one of the tables on the quayside and had coffee and liqueurs. It was very peaceful.

It would have been relaxing to have just been on holiday and not to have to wonder every so often what all this was about, and who was fooling who and what for. The great lake was cradled in the bowl of the surrounding hills and with the passing of daylight they had grown a dark, velvety blue against the paler night sky. The air was warm and thick with the resiny smell of pines and arbutus. The coloured lights of the hotel were on, outlining the arches of the colonnade which fronted the dining-rooms. Fish jumped and smacked their flanks against the still water. A few mosquitoes buzzed and carried out sharp forays, and somewhere on the near lake shore an owl put in an occasional note of mournful disagreement. There were the usual crowd of Germans, two or three parties of English people and some Yugoslavs. From the far end of the gravelled strip I could now and then catch the sound of Madame Vadarci's voice, booming like a bittern . . . a dear old biddy, I thought, knitting a blanket for her favourite horse, and carrying a long thonged whip to flay its hide off when it began to act up.

I reached out and held my lighter to Vérité's cigarette. The soft light of the flame shadowed the beautiful bone structure of her face, and her eyes were bright with the reflection of the lights of the hotel. If one could start from scratch or make logic master of emotion, I thought, it would have been better to fall in love with her type rather than Katerina's. For the first time I told myself frankly that Katerina, on any score, was an odds-on favourite to turn out a tramp. She was ready to use anyone she could to get whatever it was she wanted. I knew it in my bones. But it didn't make any difference. You had to follow your instinct.

Vérité said, "I saw her go into your room just after we arrived."

"Yes. She's very anxious that I shouldn't lose touch with her. I'd give a lot to know why."

"You are in love with her?"

"I don't know. I'm having a shareholders' meeting about that tomorrow afternoon. No matter which way the voting goes – I'm a working man. What do you know about her?"

"Nothing – except one thing."

"Something profound?"

"No, something very ordinary, something women always know about women like her."

"Which is?"

"That she can only love herself. There is nothing else there."

"You want to hear something really profound? That's the kind men fall in love with. It's a challenge. They won't believe . . . I mean the particular man . . . that he hasn't got the one thing it takes, the lodestone, the magic kiss that melts the frozen heart. The literature of every nation is lousy with the theme. And don't let's get one-sided about it. It works the other way. There are men like her and some women who think that they alone have got the magic to change them—"

She got up slowly and walked away, across the gravel, not towards the hotel, but along a small path that led around the island, under cypress trees and close to the water's edge.

I got up and went after her, cursing myself because, at the time I had spoken, I had forgotten all about her story and had tossed, without malice or intent, a hard truth at her.

When I had almost caught her up, she turned and waited for me.

I said, "I'm sorry. I wasn't thinking."

She nodded her head. "I know." Then, unexpectedly, she put her hand in the bend of my elbow lightly, hardly touching me, and we walked on.

We went right around the island, which took about ten minutes, and came back on to a high loggia terrace above the main outer stairway that ran up to the hotel entrance from the quay. The hotel motor-boat was just coming back from the far lakeside where the bus dumped passengers for the hotel. It pulled into the quayside under the lights. A man jumped ashore and made it fast and then turned back and helped a man and a woman from it. I caught the flash of a silver-knobbed cane, and then the man and the woman were moving across to the stone steps, the boatman behind carrying their cases.

I said to Vérité, "That's Herr Walter Spiegel and his wife. You keep your door locked tonight and the chair in place."

I passed an undisturbed night. So did Vérité. I checked before I went down to breakfast. She had breakfast in her room. To allay her curiosity about Spiegel, I told her that he was a gent I recognized from some past work I had done on a political case in London, and that I doubted whether he would be on Mljet just for his health. She could let Malacod know this in a letter. There was no telephone at the hotel. I didn't tell her that I was sure he was no German.

I had breakfast in the sunshine on the quay. Afterwards I found a magazine in the hotel lounge and wandered up the slight slope behind the hotel into a terraced garden and sat on a seat beneath an olive and settled to idle the morning away.

I was joined after about twenty minutes by Herr Walter Spiegel. It was a stone seat, about six feet long, with a decorated, stone-carved back; no doubt the old monks, after a spell in the garden or the distillery or a long stint in the chapel, used to come up here, flop back, and wonder what it was all about. He sat at one end and I sat at the other. And some instinct warned me just how he had me figured out. Their research departments never slip up. So far as I was concerned there was a big sterling symbol over my head like a twisted halo. Sometimes I think it is the only thing that makes me useful to people like Sutcliffe and Manston. The other sides don't walk warily around me as though I were a puff adder.

He laid the silver-knobbed cane down between us, sighed a little with the heat, and then lit a long thin black cigar which smelt as though a hundred acres of good steppe were going up in flames. I lit a cigarette.

He said, "Poor Howard Johnson has a broken arm."

"Clumsy fellow."

He laughed gently. He had a very distinguished face, the skin grey and grained like pumice stone, wore a brown tussore suit, and a panama which sat on his head dead in line with the horizon. He could have been a Berlin family lawyer on holiday. Maybe he wished he were.

"May I talk frankly, Mr Carver?"

"Just as long as you keep it simple."

He nodded, and then said, "Oh, I forget. All this stupidity . . . I should say, Mother Jambo. That is the correct introduction, eh? You will forgive me. I have been in this business so long that I forget or find tiresome all the archaic paraphernalia."

"You want to watch your language. Simple, I said."

He blew a cloud of smoke at a cloud of midges and the midges moved off.

"It has been decided," he said, "between London and Moscow that this should become a combined operation. The decision was taken at high level, naturally. Where else are such decisions taken? Frankly, I'm glad. This uneasy pursuit of separate courses towards a common end only leads to confusion, double work, and – more unfortunate – distrust. It makes me very happy. Why? Frankly, because I am getting old, and it is pleasant to have a young, active man to do the . . . how shall I say?"

"Donkey work is a good phrase. Try it."

"Donkey work, yes. But no disparagement meant. Also – since it is intimated that you are specifically not on the establishment, but a private individual, co-opted because of special talents, then you are naturally concerned with the remunerative aspects."

"You mean money?" Perhaps he was too old for the job, because he was giving it far too much. Or maybe he had just gone gaga with the strain. I'd met someone who had once. Or maybe he was a furlong ahead of me and about to pretend to pull a tendon. God knows. Sometimes I got real homesick for simple insurance recovery.

"Money, ah, yes. . . . As I was saying – co-operation has been decided on, so frankness becomes possible. In retrospect you will forgive Howard Johnson for his rather clumsy stratagem."

"I'll forgive him anything, if the money is right."

"Splendid!" He brought out an envelope and delicately put it alongside the silver-knobbed cane.

I didn't rush. I could match delicacy with delicacy, too, when it came to deceit. Mother Jambo. He was going to feel foolish when his ciphers' link got around to letting him know about Ringmaster. I just let the envelope rest, and said, "And my instructions?"

"Exactly the same. We all want to know where Mrs Vadarci is going, and you have – *vive l'amour* – a special contact there. Just keep in touch, that is all we have to do. Though, naturally, when I leave this seat we will act as strangers. The only difference is that we now work together. I am at your service and you at mine. Happy would it be, if one could think that this unique example of co-operation might be the first of many, a broadening and strengthening of international feeling."

"I'll second that," I said, and I picked up the envelope and opened it. There were a hundred crisp, clean five-dollar bills in it. I counted them carefully and he watched until I looked up straight into his age-worn, cold agate eyes.

"A monthly retainer," he said.

"Very generous." I put the money in my pocket. Then, since we were now old buddies, I tried him with the oldest ploy in the business.

"If only the people at the top would trust us a little more, they'd get better results from us. I get tired of working in the dark."

He nodded. "We are too far down the pyramid for truth to be trusted to us. Of all the cases I have engaged in, I have never known the truth of more than, say, five per cent. Like cart-horses, we pull hard, but we wear blinkers so that we can only see the road ahead."

"You're damned right," I said feelingly, and I could see that it warmed him to me, a couple of outside men grumbling about the bosses.

"Matter of fact," I said casually, "if it hadn't been for a book I picked up in Howard Johnson's car, I'd be even more in the dark. *Stigmata*, by Professor Vadarci."

"Oh. . . ." He grinned. "The required reading. The master-race cracking the symbolic whip. But let us not forget that beyond the lunatic fringe there often. . . ." He tailed off, gave me a look and then smiled. He knew and I knew that he had caught himself just in time. There was no more to be had from him. But of all he had said it was the phrase "symbolic whip" which rang in my mind.

I picked up the silver-knobbed cane and gave the water-lily boss a half-turn and pulled. A thin ice-bright blade came out with a faint whisper like a finger being run down the length of a silk stocking. "Beautiful," I said.

"Toledo. I bought it in Spain in 1939. I was a tank commander. They were good days."

"Before my time," I said.

"Naturally."

I slid the blade back and the silky whisper sent a small shiver through me.

He stood up, took his stick, levelled the brim of his panama, and said, "I go now for my morning swim." He gave me an avuncular smile and went on, "Always we watch. You and I. And always we co-operate. It is a good arrangement."

"Splendid," I said.

And it was, at five hundred dollars a month.

After lunch, I hired one of the little canoes that the hotel kept for the use of guests. It was a two-seater affair with one double-sided paddle. I went around the back of the island, away from the hotel, and pulled into the bank just below an old burial tomb of the monks, a tall white vault set partly back into the slope of the ground. They'd buried them standing up, each in a narrow compartment, for the same reason that New York has sky-scrapers. The canoe let water a little because the seams wanted caulking, and I dabbled my bare feet in it and smoked a cigarette until she appeared.

She wore a green linen dress, buttoned all the way down the front, and her arms and legs were bare, and the sun set a dazzling burnish on her blonde hair. She got in and I set off, paddling westwards towards the far end of the lake where a narrow neck of water led out into a sea estuary. All the way, by hugging the shore, we were out of sight of the island. A new road had been cut, low around the shore of the island, but no one ever seemed to use it. Gorse pods cracked, the cicadas fiddled, the sun blazed down, and the air was full of scents, pine, broom, arbutus, thyme. Overhead a couple of buzzards circled lazily, and somewhere, no doubt, what mongooses there were were taking a siesta. It was a perfect afternoon for taking a girl out. It grew hot and Katerina unbuttoned her dress and slipped it off. She was wearing a green bikini underneath it.

I found a small beach, overhung with pines and tamarisks, and pulled in. We walked up the sand a way and flopped down in the shade of a rock. I lit a cigarette for her and one for myself, and told myself sternly that this must be strictly business before pleasure. She must have felt the same way for she hunched up her legs, rested her chin on top of her knees and looked solemnly at me through a loose trailer of blonde hair. Every line of her body made business seem a waste of time, but I stuck to my guns.

I said, "Have you ever heard of a man called Malacod?"

"No."

I resisted the temptation of trying to decide whether she was lying. It was too big a job. I kept at the questions and accepted the answers. I could sort them out afterwards.

"Stebelson works for him. And now I do."

"Doing what?"

"Following you. Or, more specifically, Mrs Vadarci."

"Why?"

I didn't like the way she was beginning to take over the questions, but I let it ride.

"I don't know. My brief is just to follow Mrs Vadarci and let Malacod know where she ends up. Simple. Do you know where she's going eventually?"

"No."

"A lot of other people are also interested in where she is going."

"Government peoples?"

I smiled. "That's a good way to put it. But how did you know?"

"We have our rooms searched in Paris. Nothing is stolen, so it is not ordinary thieves, no?"

"Good deduction. Now, let's come to you and Mrs Vadarci. She meets you in your shop, likes you, gives you a job as her travelling secretary – correct?"

"Correct."

"And you've never seen her before?"

"No."

"A good secretary would let her know that she was being followed. Why don't you? In fact, why do you go out of your way to make it easy for me to follow you?"

She took a deep draw on the cigarette and let the smoke trickle up the front of her face like a veil, and she dug one toe deep in the sand.

"Why? For two reasons. One, personal. I like you very much. I like the look in your eyes. I like the things you do. I like it when you touch and kiss me. I like everything about you. So, is nice to have you come everywhere with me." She put out a hand and just touched my bare foot. Business nearly broke down at that moment.

"One good personal reason," I said. "Now the other."

"Also, personal perhaps. You look at me – what you see? Beautiful body, nice to get into bed with? That's all most men want. But me, I want more. So, being a poor girl, I work for myself to get those things. Mrs Vadarci can show me how."

"Has she said so?"

"In a way. She talks a lot, and sometimes she says things."

"What sort of things?"

"Some you won't like."

"Try me."

"She is . . . how you say. . . ." She put the tips of her fingers to her brow, ". . . seeing the future . . . *das Medium*. . . . She tells me things about me."

"What things?"

"I am special . . . there is a destiny for me. Soon now my life changes. Everything which is me now, my beauty . . . this good body . . . this thing inside me which makes me feel life is good – I soon have the life outside which goes with it. Money, a great house, and everyone know me . . . like it is that everyone know of Brunhild or Helen of Troy. . . ."

"You believe that?"

"There is harm in believing it? I would like that. Also there is another thing – I get married."

"You don't need a fortune-teller to tell you that."

"But to someone special. More than special. Someone splendid like me."

"No name given?"

"No. Except that he is tall and blond and strong and like a god."

"You believe all this malarky?"

"Malarky?"

"Nonsense. You believe it?"

She smiled. "I don't know. But it is nice to think about. You are jealous about this man?"

"Naturally."

"There is no need. Always I will like you."

"Good. Now let's come down to the real business. A lot of people are interested in Mrs Vadarci and where she is going. But you and I are keeping an open mind about everything. Right?"

"Right."

"Like you, I'm a poor boy with nothing but a splendid body, a zest for life, and an eye to the main chance."

"Please?"

"If I can see a way of making something on the side out of this job, I'll take it. So will you. After all, the Helen of Troy business may not come off. But if we help one another there could be a nice profit. And, when it's all over, we could find some place where we could spend it."

"Why you think there must be a profit in it?"

"Because too many people are interested in Mrs Vadarci. Something is going on . . . somewhere along the line there must be something or some information which is worth a lot of money. Now, do we do a deal or not?"

Slowly she uncurled her arms and legs from the foetal position and lay back on the sand, staring up at the sky. Little flecks of quartz and felspar made a stippling along the smooth curve of her flanks. I sat entranced, wondering who the hell would ever bother about money at such a time and place, but then common sense whispered coldly that there is always a moment when you get out of the warm bed, shiver as your feet hit the cold linoleum, and there isn't a shilling in your trouser pocket for the gas fire.

"How we do this deal?"

"You see that I don't lose track of Mrs Vadarci. And we keep our eyes and ears open. The moment will come. Okay?"

She turned her head towards me, and her eyes had that deep, misty violet haze.

"Okay," she said. "We work something out."

She rolled on her side towards me, flipped a hand behind her back to brush sand from her shoulder-blades and then reached up for me. As her arms came up the bikini slipped free from her breasts.

Her lips were about mine, open and eager, and my hands were holding her and I didn't care if every word she'd uttered had been a lie. All I knew was that I wanted her, no matter what she was, no matter what lay ahead. I loved her, and if love wasn't the right word then there was no right word. And close to me, I could feel the same wildness leaping in her, and knew that the same fire that burned beneath my hands as I moved them over her also burned in hers as they moved over me.

Then, close by, a transistor radio began to play, loud, breaking the idyll into a thousand noisy pieces.

I'm gonna wash that man right out of my hair. . . .
And send him on his way. . . .

I rolled over and sat up. Walking down the beach a few yards away was Frau Walter Spiegel. She had on a red bathing cap, a nylon leopard-skin swimsuit, and her legs and arms and back looked like grey dough. She set the transistor down carefully on the edge of the strand and waded in. Then, when she was a few yards out, she turned towards us, half squatted, and splashed a little water over her shoulders. She then collapsed backwards in the water, and once or twice she waved a friendly hand at us. If I'd had a rifle I would willingly have shot her and left her to the buzzards.

CHAPTER NINE

SHORE EXERCISE FOR SIEGFRIED

Time ran out. Frau Spiegel splashed and wallowed in the shallows. I smoked four cigarettes and held Katerina's hand. The transistor went through all the crumby old theme songs from crumby old American musicals, and all the magic had gone from the crystal-clear air. Somewhere back in the Hotel Melita Madame Vadarci would be beginning to stir, heavy-eyed and dry-mouthed from her siesta, and Katerina had to be back.

We went down to the canoe and I resisted the temptation to kick the transistor into the water, and then again, the urge to hit Frau Spiegel over the head with a paddle as we passed her.

Out in the lake Katerina in a husky voice said, "Never mind, darling. We make it some other time."

I paddled hard in a fury of sublimation.

Then as we came into the back of the island, she turned and kissed me, so that the canoe rocked wildly. As she got out, she said, "We have a deal, no? Always to be truthful with each other, to look for this profit?"

I nodded.

"So . . . anything might be important? Small things?"

"Yes."

She put her hand into the pocket of her dress and pulled out a piece of paper and handed it to me.

"What's this?" I began to unfold it.

"I make copy of a telegram Madame Vadarci got while we were in Dubrovnik. Maybe it helps."

She turned and began to walk up the path that led back to the hotel. I watched the thrust of her long brown legs against the slope and the bright flutter of her dress until she was out of sight. The cable in my hands read:

> *Luka Pomina. Date as arranged.*
> *Komira.*

Underneath this Katerina had added a comment—

> *Sent in German from Athens.*

I put a match to the message, let it burn away, and then dropped it overboard. I paddled around to the front of the hotel and ran the canoe ashore by the generator shed. Pomina and Komira didn't mean a thing to me, but somewhere in my mind the word Luka was recently familiar.

An elderly woman was in the reception office, making out bills. I stopped and bought a couple of picture post-cards, and then asked her if she had a map of the island. She ferreted around in a cupboard for a while and finally produced a tourist map which looked as though someone had wrapped sandwiches in it. I took it up to my room and flopped out on the bed with it.

Mljet was a long, thin strip of island running roughly north-west to south-east. There were very few villages on it and most of the island was labelled – Nacionalni Park. On the southern side of the north-west end, a great arm of sea ran into the body of the land with a small entrance into the Veliko Jezero – which was the lake that had the island with the hotel on it. At the western end of this lake was a narrow entrance to another and smaller lake, the Malo Jezero. Beyond this lake a narrow strip of land separated it from the sea. There, marked in a small bay, protected by a few off-shore islands, was the word Pomina. Polace, the place where we had left the steamer, was marked on the northern side of the island, and in front of it was the word Luka. So, I guessed, Luka meant harbour or port. Fodor was silent on the subject.

At some date, already arranged, something was going to happen in – or off – the small port of Pomina. The map gave no clue to Komira.

There was a knock on the door. I slipped the map under my pillow, and called out.

Herr Walter Spiegel came in. He sat down on a chair, rested his silver-knobbed stick across his legs, gently mopped his face with a silk handkerchief, then beamed at me.

"You have a pleasant afternoon spent?"

"Not particularly."

"You learn things?"

"Self-control mostly."

He smiled, full of understanding for youth, and then because he thought he was using me, I decided to use him and get a second opinion and maybe a few crumbs of information. I said, "I don't trust this girl Katerina Saxmann. She knows I'm following Madame Vadarci, but she plays along with it, without telling the old girl. I can't figure her angle – and she gives nothing away. I thought I was good at mind reading but she has me baffled."

He nodded, pursed his lips, frowned, and thought for a while, taking his time over all of them. Then he said weightily, "I give her much thought. She is a dedicated girl. Dedicated to herself. With a face, a figure, and an intelligence like hers what else could she be? Anything else would be a waste. She accepts that she has been chosen. But that is not all. Now she looks to see, and waits to see, what most she can make of it. She keeps you coming because you may . . . sometime, somewhere . . . be useful in her plans. But, of course, a girl like that does not work alone. Somewhere behind her is a man. This is psychology. A woman, no matter how beautiful, how intelligent, how determined, must always have a man. It is a law of nature."

"Could be." He was a shrewd old number, worth his place on the pay-roll more than ever Howard Johnson would be. Old school, too, no emotions, no heroics, just a job to do and nothing he liked better than a quiet evening with a book and then to bed. I said, "You and I know little, just keep our noses to the scent and jog along. I think she knows a great deal. Everything, maybe."

"Maybe."

"Any idea who the man is?"

He smiled and it was full of friendly cunning and understanding. "I think you know that as well as I do. You do not go into some things with your eyes shut. Not these things."

"I shouldn't have thought he was her type." I was thinking of Herr Stebelson and hoped he was. Stebelson was the only candidate in my book.

"What is type? There are only men and women, and the combinations are infinite. You will not have seen his dossier since you are, let us say, a *franc-tireur*. Me, I have seen some of it, the pages below the red line, and even that is formidable." He stood up and I guessed he would have liked to have gone on, talking shop, easing a load of past experience and weariness off on to a youngster like myself, fresh to the game and not so completely involved as he. I could almost like him. There's always a lot to be learned, too, in sitting at the feet of a master for an hour or so while he rambles on. But he was well aware of the dangers of reminiscing. He said from the door, "So she tells you nothing?"

"Only that they are leaving."

He showed no surprise. "When?"

"She doesn't know."

"How?"

"By sea, she thinks."

"From where?"

"There's a village, or small town, midway down the island on the south side. It's called Babino Polje. This country's hell on names, isn't it?"

He smiled. "Not for me. There are affinities, don't forget. Why does she fancy this?"

"Because Madame V. is talking about making an overnight trip there."

He considered this, and then nodded. "Maybe I should send Frau Spiegel down there right away."

"Tell her to take her transistor set with her."

The bluff old lawyer's face crinkled with the ghost of a smile. Then, stiff-backed, one of the old kind that you don't meet often these days, he went out. I hadn't the faintest idea whether I'd sold him a pup or not. But it was worth a try.

The water and the electricity were on so I shaved and took a shower, then dressed and went down on to the terrace, to catch the last of the sun before it dropped behind the tall hills, and to have a drink with Vérité.

"Pleasant afternoon?"

"People keep asking me that," I said. "Average."

"Is there anything for me to report to Herr Stebelson?"

"Stebelson?"

"All my reports to Herr Malacod go through him, naturally."

"Naturally." But it was interesting. "No," I said. "Nothing yet."

I finished reading *Stigmata* before I went to sleep that night. It was a pretty simple overall argument, but it was put with great force and backed up with fat wads of historical evidence.

Simply, it was that conventional conceptions of national character – neuroses, as Professor Vadarci preferred to call them – were completely valid. But the validity rested not in what a nation thought of itself, but what was commonly accepted by other nations as the true national myth or neurosis. For instance, the English, broadly, were a race of stubborn hypocrites, hopeless at rational planning of their national life or national defence, but masters of improvisation in their recurring moments of crisis. Overall, they were stigmatized as being excitable, illogical, and much more concerned with saving face than the Japanese, for instance. (It was this last bit of deduction which had spurred some *Times* leader writer on 16 February, 1947, into pompous indignation – linked, of course, with the fact that Herr Malacod had appointed Professor Vadarci as director of the research foundation he was establishing for the study of national neuroses, with particular reference to their impact on international political affairs.) (Actually, a fortnight later, Professor Vadarci – for health reasons, it was said – had declined the post.)

Other nations got equally bad write-ups, so that by and large they sounded like a world community of delinquents with the odd psychopath here and there among them. Vadarci, too, was hard on communications. He argued that mass communications, like the radio, television and Press services, were inherently evil since by contracting the world and bringing it into people's front parlours they diminished its importance for people and made people indifferent to people. A breakfast paper every morning of every year full of war, disaster, murder, robbery, pillage, rape, arson, sex offences, moral looseness in persons and parties . . . all these, fed *ad nauseam* to the world, tended to decrease the natural sensibility of the individual towards the individual. Civilization was linked to communications and throughout history the highest points of civilization had always produced the most revolting examples of man's inhumanity to man. Civilized, communicable man was ruthless, vicious and contemptuous of the sanctity of human life. Behind the parties, the politics, the fancy uniforms, the urge for social reforms, and emerging nationalistic aspirations, was nothing but man the beast.

It was hard hitting stuff and guaranteed to put up blood pressures. And he finished by denouncing all forms of international co-operation – the League of Nations, the United Nations, European unity, Pan-Americanism, the World State – as useless, impractical diversions while the real business of kill and hold tight to what you had went on. In Professor Vadarci's opinion there was only one realistic solution, only one way to create a tolerable human society which would allow men to become what, spiritually, all men longed to be – real human beings – and that was by the emergence of one overriding world force. No community of nations. But one nation, overlords, ruthless at first, subjecting the other nations, and finally leading them into the promised land. In the West he put up two nominees – Italy or Germany, with a bias to Germany. And in the East he had a straight candidate in China. And he had a bundle of arguments for his choice, and I had no doubt that a lot of people would have agreed with him though they might have had their eye on different candidates.

It was good bedtime reading, and I wondered what the hell it had to do with Katerina and Madame Vadarci. Maybe Madame Vadarci saw herself as a world ruler. Well, she had the whip already to her hand. I went to sleep thinking of that whip. At the back of my mind I had an idea that I already knew something about it.

I was wakened at daybreak by a knock on my door. I called out for whoever it was to come in. But no one entered. I rolled over in bed and saw that a note had been pushed under the door.

I shuffled over and picked it up, read it, and then went out into the vaulted corridor and looked out of the tall window. Katerina, in her yellow bikini, was poised on the edge of the quay. She dived, neat and clean, came up and started away in a strong crawl. She could have given me fifty yards' start in a hundred and beaten me easily.

I went back to bed and lit a cigarette.

Her note read:

Walking Pomina late afternoon. Taking toothbrush, night-dress. Love.

I shaved and dressed and went next door to Vérité's room. She was sitting up in bed having breakfast.

I said, "I think Mrs V. and Katerina are leaving today. My guess is that some boat is picking them up here." I squatted on the end of the bed and showed her Pomina on the map.

"What are you going to do?"

I took a sugar lump from her bowl and sucked it, thoughtfully. She looked nice sitting up in bed, her dark hair tied back at the nape of her neck with a ribbon, a little bed jacket demurely buttoned close up to her neck.

"Well, I'm not swimming after them. The only thing I can do is to be out there, catch the name of the yacht – if it is a yacht – and then it can be traced. But we'll have to get back to Dubrovnik to set that going. That means a time gap. One that Katerina might not be able to bridge for me. Anyway, I think you'd better make arrangements for us to leave for Dubrovnik tonight."

"Do you want me to come with you to Pomina?"

"No. I'll take off after lunch on my own. We don't want anything conspicuous about this."

"Because of Herr Walter Spiegel?" She gave me a shrewd look and a half smile.

I nodded. She was no fool. How could she be, being Malacod's secretary? I said, "He's got an interest. He tried to sell me part of it. Not that he threw any light on the overall project. But I've managed to sell him the idea that Mrs V. will be leaving from Babino Polje, which is some way down the coast in the wrong direction. He's sending the good Frau down there. Probably on the back of a mule – there don't seem to be any roads, but she'll have her transistor to keep her company. I'd just like to know that he was taking a siesta this afternoon. Okay?"

She nodded and pushed my hand away from the sugar bowl. "That stuff is bad for the teeth."

I bared mine briefly. "They're big and strong. I've got an urge to bite something with them."

She giggled and it was like a string of soap bubbles going up into the sunlight, bursting with little iridescent pops.

"Don't get me wrong," I said. "I want to bite in anger. I'm fed up with being a follower. I'm fed up with being out in the dark. My curiosity is killing me."

She laughed and said, "I had a brother who was something like you. . . ."

I stood up and backed gently for the door. "That's a damning thing to say to a man. Puts him on the wrong side of the romantic tracks. I don't want to be a brother to anyone but my sister."

She said, "Oughtn't you – under the terms of your employment – to give me something specific to report about Herr Spiegel?"

"Why not? He's working for the Russians. Is one. An old and very tried agent. And he's paying me five hundred dollars a month for double-crossing Herr Malacod. The money's useful. And he's getting nothing from me. Not even a receipt. Okay?"

It was a pleasant walk, though maybe a bit soon after lunch. I went across the short strip of water to the near lakeside in the hotel rowing boat with a party of English schoolmistresses, who were going for a long hike collecting flower specimens. They were a jolly lot, most of them pushing forty-five, and with that hearty, semi-flirtatious manner which gets over schoolmistresses once the Channel steamer hits the Calais quay. I told them I was going wild-mongoose-watching and needed to be on my own. They padded away in their tennis shoes up the lake road, leaving a wake of sharp, bright echoes of chatter in the steel-blue, bright afternoon air. As I took a track straight up the hillside away from the road I had a moment's nostalgia for Wilkins and underground station signs, and Brighton pier seemed a long way away. Which it was, of course, but then obvious thoughts are always comforting, and I had a queer feeling in my stomach that cried out for comfort, the butterfly tickle which had nothing to do with the *dalmatinski prsut* which I had gone for in a big way at lunch. (Smoked ham: Fodor.)

I went up over the shoulder of the hill, along a very rough track and dropped down to the lake road on the far side, out of sight of the hotel. I went westwards towards the far end of the lake, and after about half an hour was on a small bridge that crossed the little water channel that connected the big Veliko Jezero with the smaller Malo Jezero. Here, I left the road and went along the north shore of the small lake for a while, and then up the hillside, through small oak and large pine, to cross the hump of land that would bring me down to Pomina.

Pomina was nothing. Just a rough road that died out among boulders and a stony beach. There were a few bamboo-thatched sheds full of lobster-pots and fishing gear, and about four fishermen's houses, stone built, and with that incomplete look of broken walls, unglazed windows, and raw wood that made you wonder whether they were just being built or slowly falling down. There was a small motor-boat moored off a wooden jetty that was only a foot above water, a yellow dog asleep at the end, and a bantam cock with six hens foraging around the water-line. A woman beat a carpet strip over a low wall and stopped to stare at me. Remembering my Fodor, I gave her a smiling, "*Dobor dan*". She hurried indoors as though I were mad.

I went back up the hill, into the trees and scrub and worked my way along the slope until I found a little open space, nicely screened from the sea. I sat down and pulled my field-glasses out of the nylon string bag I had borrowed from Vérité. In it, besides the field-glasses, I had my cigarettes, a flask of whisky, and a pullover in case the day should cloud over and make it too cold just for shirt-sleeves and light drill trousers. Inside the pullover I had wrapped the ·22 *Le Chasseur*.

I snapped off a few branches of the bush ahead of me, and had a good view of the little bay. Pomina was more or less below me and I could see my woman friend, back in her yard, hanging up strings of tomatoes against the house wall to dry. I kept the glasses on her for a moment and she jerked her head over her shoulder and looked up the hill, as though some instinct told her that the madman was still about. She had a fine, very thin line of black hair above her upper lip. I shifted the glasses away. On my left hand a longish promontory ran out protecting the south side of the bay. Away to the right, on the north of the bay, were a couple of islands, white limestone boulders thrusting up through the green shrubs on their summits. Anchored in the bay, a couple of hundred yards off Pomina, was a yacht. It was lined up dead ahead of me, so that I got the nice smooth white run of its rather bulbous stern square on in the glasses. In black letters her name and home port were painted just below the rail: KOMIRA, BRINDISI.

There was no sign of life on deck. An Italian flag flapped a few loose folds now and then over the stern, and water was being pumped out of some sluice port just above the water-line. She was a nice boat, long, low, single funnelled, radar basket above the bridge, and I didn't bother to work out how many months' work I would have had to do for Herr Spiegel to save up enough to buy her. A companion ladder ran down the starboard side and there was a small white launch moored at its foot.

I lit a cigarette and kept my eye on the rough road down to Pomina. For an hour the sun and I idled the time away.

Then there was a movement on the yacht. Two men appeared on deck and came down the companion-way to the launch. The launch moved away from the *Komira* and headed towards Pomina. It tied up at the jetty and the two men stepped ashore. I held them through the glasses. One of them was an elderly deckhand type, singlet, canvas trousers and a black thatch of hair with a bald patch dead in its centre. He was carrying, somewhat surprisingly, a couple of golf clubs and a bulging white linen bag. The other was a tall, much younger man, wearing a black silk shirt, wide open to show a façade of muscles that would have made Tarzan feel like something that had crawled out of a crack behind the bath, black trousers and black sandals. His hair was blond, close-cropped, and his face was square, regularly featured, good looking in the way that the dummies in the windows of Austin Reed's and Simpson's are, very masculine, guaranteed to crack if the smile became half an inch wider. His reflexes were perfect. As he stepped ashore the sleeping yellow dog uncoiled, resenting the intrusion, and went for his leg. He caught it with his right toe in the groin, hefted it into the water to cool off, and strode ashore without giving any impression that he had been aware of the incident.

Both of them came along the shore and then headed up the hillside towards me. I stubbed out my cigarette.

They came out on to a small grassy plateau about fifteen yards below me and halted there. Flat on my paunch, I stuck my head through a bush to get a good look at them. They were talking in German so nothing they said made any sense to me, except the occasional *ja, ja, nein, nein,* which didn't help.

The deckhand tipped up the linen bag on the grass and about three dozen golf balls tumbled out. The blond Siegfried took one of the golf clubs – it looked like a seven iron, or something in the mashie niblick range – and helped himself to a few practice swings. It whistled through the air at the lowest point of his swing with a swish like a rocket going off. Then he nodded at the deckhand, who began to set the balls up for him.

He swung at a ball and my heart bled for the polyurethane painted cover and the labyrinth of rubber guts inside it. It went off, straight and true, howling with pain and fell thirty yards short of the *Komira*, dead in line with the stern. He smacked another dozen after it and you could have covered the fall of them all with a large table cloth. I lay with my eyes popping out and wished Arnold Palmer could have been there. It would have made him take up smoking again.

Having loosened himself up with the iron, he passed to the wood, a spoon, and began to bombard the yacht and make pretty patterns of water spouts around and beyond it. One fifty yards to port. The next fifty yards to starboard. A nice bit of draw, and another curling in and beyond the bows from the right, and then a fade to match it coming in around the bows from the left. I worked it out, thirty-six new balls at five bob each. Nine quid. Well, a man has got to have his exercise and the way he did it certainly went with the yacht.

When he had finished with the golf balls, he stripped off his shirt and trousers and gave himself fifteen minutes' callisthenics, handsprings and front and back somersaults and three times round the grass plot walking on his hands. He was as brown as a mild Havana from suntan and there wasn't a hint of sweat on him.

He finished his exercises, said something to the deckhand, and then the wonder boy was off, trotting down the hillside. I watched him, catching a glimpse of his black briefs now and again as he light-heartedly leapt the odd six-foot bush that got in his way. He reached the water's edge directly below, dived in and was swimming towards the yacht in a fast crawl, a spout of foam going up behind him as though he had a ten horse-power marine engine fixed to his backside.

The deckhand was in no hurry at all. He sat down on the grass, pulled out the makings and slowly rolled himself a cigarette. It is a thing that always fascinates me to watch – done expertly, that is. And he was an expert. The fact that he had no thumb on his left hand didn't handicap him a bit.

I let him get comfortable on a couple of draws and then I flicked a little stone over the bush top. He turned his head very slowly.

I said quietly, "Ringmaster here – disguised as a bush. Or maybe Mother Jambo, if they haven't been through to you for the last few days."

He turned away and looked at the yacht. Siegfried was just going up the companion steps.

Without turning, he said, "Put a name to it."

"Carver."

"Not bad. Do a little better. Say the name of a dog. A Gordon setter, for instance."

"Joss."

"Good. The bastard ever bitten you?"

"Once. But it was a mistake." Joss was the name of Manston's Gordon setter.

"He's had me twice. With intent. I'm going to turn. Just drop your veil, but stay where you are."

His head came round slowly and I parted the branches a little. He gave me a slow look and then his head went back and he said, "Okay. You fit the frame, but we'll give it one more go. Why am I in no hurry to go back to the *Komira*?"

"Passengers to go aboard? Say a Mrs Vadarci, and a speedy blonde number."

He nodded, his eyes on the yacht, and then, the tone of his voice changing, an unexpected edge coming into it, he said, "Nice to know you. Lancing. And tell Sutcliffe I've been on this effing tub too long. They're bloody well going to rumble me sooner or later."

"You could leave now."

"They'd have a search-party after me in fifteen minutes. Besides, no orders. Stay with it Lancing they call me. Another blonde, eh? She'll have to be good to top Lottie."

"He collects them?"

"Sort of. Listen. . . . If I'd known you were going to be here, I'd have brought something ashore for you. Colour slide. I think it's the place they want. Keep your tuning dial steady because I'm not repeating anything. That redheaded pantomime dame could show any minute and I've got to be down there. Muscle boy – I spar with him – roughed me up for five rounds a couple of days back and I got riled and let him have one. So he knocked me out. He's good. I was out for quite a while. He took me into his cabin afterwards, all apologies, and a large brandy. Left me there for a few minutes. Slide projector, slide boxes locked but one slide in the slot. Pinched it. Old boy in the picture has been aboard once or twice at Venice. Sooner or later they're going to miss it and Muscles will remember me. Come under the stern first dark tonight and I'll drop it to you. Okay?"

"Yes."

"I'll jot a few notes to go with it. Not safe for me to stay up here. Somebody will have the glasses on me. You just make it tonight."

He stood up and began to collect the golf gear.

I said, "Where does the *Komira* go from here?"

"Venice if they stick to pattern. Christ, here they come. Kick Oglu's arse for me. He should have come aboard at Kotor. I could have given him everything. Just to write out a few notes for you and have 'em on me for half an hour is putting my head in a loop."

He was away down the hillside. As he reached the little jetty, I saw Katerina and Madame Vadarci come down the rough road and pick their way along the sea edge. Katerina carried a gaily coloured holiday bag that looked as though it held more than her nightdress and toothbrush. Madame Vadarci wore a woollen skirt, looping down ridiculously at one side, a man's shirt, a green straw hat, and was humping a rucksack that looked as though it were full of rock specimens. Through the glasses I saw that she was sweating so hard that it had put a fine varnish on her beetroot complexion.

They went out in the launch to the *Komira* and disappeared below deck. I sat there, knowing what Katerina's reaction would be to all that brown-tinted muscle.

To take my mind off it, I did a sweep of the near shore looking for a row-boat. A hundred yards this side of the jetty there was a battered looking number tied up alongside a bamboo-thatched storehouse. Outside the store were lobster-pots, some piles of net and a couple of oars leaning against the wall. Until it was dark there was nothing I could do.

I sat there until the sun went down, the shadows lengthening and a purple-brown smudge staining the lower edges of the sky. The mosquitoes began to use me as a free lunch counter and whined noisily about the quality of the fare. Darkness limped along but finally made it and I went down to the store shed.

There was no trouble, except that the boat had three inches of water in the bottom and I had to grope in it to find the rowlock pegs.

I went out, rowing only a few strokes to give me way and needing only an occasional dip to take me down towards the *Komira*. The whole thing was pretty neat considering my limited Serpentine training. As I got near the *Komira* I could hear music, thumping beat stuff, and there was a blaze of light forward from one of the deck saloons.

Lancing was there as I came under the stern. He took one large draw on his cigarette to show me his face and as I came under the counter he dropped a small parcel to me, and then I was away on the current and suddenly aware that whereas it had helped me out I had to row like a maniac against it to get back. I came ashore, a quarter of a mile down from the village, in a small cove and drew the boat up almost clear of the water and stuck a thousand dinar note under a stone in the bows. I faced the climb up the hill, blown and thinking of beer. I resisted my whisky flask because I knew it would be no help. Over the hill was the lake, a bit brackish, maybe, but I wasn't in any mood to be fussy.

By the time I got to the top of the bluff, a small slip of pale moon had appeared. I paused for a rest and looking back saw the lights of the *Komira* moving away. . . . Venice bound, and no need for me, I knew, to wish Katerina *bon voyage*.

I went on, down through the trees and scrub to the lake. At the water's edge, I squatted and drank, lots of water and then a swig at the whisky flask. Then I sat down and lit a cigarette. I'd had a hard day. Between my legs was the string bag. I reached in and pulled out the little parcel which Lancing had dropped to me. It was a neat job, wrapped in oilskin and, tied to it by twine, a cork float in case he should have muffed his throw.

I had the parcel in one hand, and the whisky flask in the other, when I heard a noise behind me. I jerked my head round just as Herr Spiegel stepped out into the starlight from the cover of some tamarisk bushes and said, "Just keep your hands where I can see them."

CHAPTER TEN

A CONTRACT DISHONOURED

Apart from the fact that he was breathing rather heavily and there was a gleam of sweat on his forehead, he looked as neat and trim as though he were on his way to a band concert on the sea front, panama precisely levelled on his head, not a fold in his cravat out of place. In his right hand he held his sword cane, but now it was unsheathed and the bright Toledo blade trembled a little as he held it towards me.

"Just throw me the parcel," he said. "But keep your hands well up in the open."

If the *Le Chasseur* hadn't been tucked alongside my pullover in the bag I might have disputed the order. I tossed the parcel at his feet. He half crouched and picked it up, keeping his eyes and his blade on me.

"Is this necessary?" I asked. "We've got a contract."

He put the parcel in his jacket pocket and smiled. "You climb hills much too fast for me. I just missed you as you came back from the *Komira*. You knew she was coming there. Pomina, not Babino Polje."

"It was a hunch. I followed Madame Vadarci and the girl. Look, do I have to go on sitting here like an Indian fakir asking for alms?"

"You went off before them." He came a step nearer as I let my hands waver and then brought them back.

"That's the way I follow people. I like to be ahead. Anyway, if it comes to following, what were you doing trotting after me? That's no way for a partner to act. Or did you know that the *Komira* was coming into Pomina?"

"As a matter of fact, I did."

"Well, then," I gave him a big comforting well-it-has-all-been-a-mistake smile, "that makes us quits. What I suggest is that we write a completely new contract. Complete honesty on both sides."

I glanced up at him, along the length of the blade. He shook his head.

"The contract is finished."

The blade was steady now. For an elderly man he had a hand like a rock, no nerves. I didn't wait for all the legal formalities of breaking a contract to be completed. I rolled quickly aside a second before the blade came in. The roll took me down to the water's edge, and I had my right hand groping in the net bag for my gun. As I came to my feet, Herr Spiegel swung round and I saw the starlight flash down the blade as it came at me. I jerked at the gun but it caught in the nylon mesh of the net. I threw myself sideways but he got me through the fat of my inner left arm. In and back again, and me sprawling towards the ground, and the blade whipping over my face with a fancy flourish, hissing through the air, and then the point levelled, sighted, and suddenly coming at me. His arm and blade were in perfect line. His shadowed face showed a thin line of bared teeth as he anticipated the shock of the steel driving home into me. I got my hand round the *Le Chasseur* and I fired with the gun still in the net bag.

The night exploded. Echoes rocked across the lake surface. I heard the sudden panic flap of ducks going up somewhere along in the reeds. Spiegel exploded, too, his arms flying wide, the rapier dropping away, his face briefly split with a wide gaping mouth, and the panama tilting and spinning from his head. He gave a long, rasping sigh, and then thudded to the ground, one of his loose hands smacking me across the face, hard and violent, as though it signalled finally, irrevocably, the end of a contract neither he nor I had ever meant to honour.

I got to my feet. Herr Spiegel lay on the ground, face upwards, a large dark stain spreading across the breast of his jacket.

I bent down and took Lancing's parcel from Spiegel's pocket. As I stood up I saw Vérité standing by the tamarisk bushes. She just stood there without movement or sound, a tall, slim figure in a skirt and blouse, a silk scarf loose about her throat, a thin band of ribbon across her hair. I gave another look at Herr Spiegel and then went across to her. I took her free hand and held it.

She went on staring past me at Herr Spiegel and, in a voice which seemed a hundred miles away, she said, "I followed him from the hotel. . . ." Her hands went up to her eyes, shading them, and I saw her shoulders shake.

I put out an arm to pull her to me, to put a hand round her shoulders and hold her against whatever it was of memory and horror that my gun blast and the sight of Spiegel's body had brought back, but she turned then and looked at me, and I saw her come back like someone from the dead to the present, a whole life slipping from her, her face drawn and suddenly stubborn with the effort she was forcing on herself.

She said, "You're hurt."

Her hands went to my shirt front and she began to unbutton the shirt. I was aware of the wet warmth down my left side. I slipped out of the shirt. As I raised my arm, the blood ran fresh. She picked up my shirt and now, completely herself, began to tear strips from it.

"It's only through the loose flesh. There's no real harm done."

She held my arm, twisting it slightly to get at the wound, and I stood in the darkness, letting her bandage me. When she had finished, I got the whisky flask and insisted that she should drink. She did, shuddered as the spirit hit her, and then handed it back to me. I took a greedy pull.

I made her go back along the shore a little way. When she was gone, I took Spiegel and dragged him some way up the hill and well off the track. I left him in the cover of a thick growth of bushes, but before I left I went through his pockets. There wasn't a thing on him that was worth taking. In the dell I found the rapier and the cane, slid the blade into it and tossed it far out into the lake. With any luck he would lie there for a few days before anyone found him. By then I meant to be out of Yugoslavia.

I put what was left of my damaged and stained shirt on, and then slipped my pullover over it, and we walked back to the hotel lakeside. Vérité said very little on the way back. She had made arrangements for us to have dinner, then cross the lake in the motor-boat and take the local bus the few miles down to Polace. The steamer did not go until half-past four in the morning, and for the few hours we had to wait in Polace the hotel authorities had hired rooms for us in one of the houses on the quayside. This, she said, was the usual arrangement for tourists.

We shouted across to the hotel from the lakeside and the rowing-boat came over and picked us up. Up in my room I took a shower and was finishing the last of my whisky when there was a knock on my door and Vérité came in. I was in my dressing-gown and pants, sitting on the edge of my bed.

She came over to me and said, "Slip that gown off." She had a roll of clean bandage in her hand.

I pushed the gown back off my shoulders, and said, "Where did you get that?"

"I always have some first-aid stuff in my case."

"Perhaps I should start carrying some, too." I raised my arm and she began to take the old bandage off, then swabbed the wound with some stuff from a bottle that stung like hell. When she had finished I slipped the gown up over my shoulders and stood up.

I put my right hand on her shoulder and I felt her tense under my fingers. I leant forward and kissed her gently on the cheek.

Then I stepped back and nodded at my whisky flask. "There's still a little left. Like some?"

She shook her head.

I said, "Do you want to hear why Spiegel went for me?"

I knew at once that I'd said the wrong thing. The sight of his dead body, the sound of the shot were all too fresh in her mind.

"Later." She turned away and left the room. I cursed myself but it was too late.

I went over and locked the door and then sat down on the bed and opened Lancing's little parcel.

Inside were a couple of sheets of notepaper, folded around a cellophane envelope which held a colour transparency slide, and a small studio photograph of a girl.

I took the photograph first. She was about Katerina's age and build, but a little taller, blonde and a dish. On the back of the photograph was a printed trade heading – *Spartalis Photos. Akti Possidonus, Piraeus, T.411–45.* Underneath this, written in pencil, were some notes made by Lancing, I guessed, probably just before I got out to the *Komira.* He wouldn't have put a damned thing in writing until the last moment. The notes read:

Lottie Bemans. 23. Blonde. 5' 9". München. Checked P.A.D. Chalkokondyli.A. Ident. card expired one month. Two convictions. Trivial.

The colour slide was mounted ready for use in a projector. It was an Agfa film mount. I held it up to the light, remembering Lancing saying that he thought it was the place they wanted. It showed a pair of large iron gates that formed the entrance to a driveway that ran into the background of the picture, disappearing into a thicket of pines, through which just showed the blue of a lake. In front of the gates was a man in blue working overalls, a peaked cap, and smoking a pipe. Running from the sides of the gates were small sections of very tall brick walls, cut by the limit of the film frame on either side. Close to the gate pillar on the left-hand side, there was a narrow niche in the wall which held a figure. I couldn't make out the details.

On the couple of sheets of paper Lancing had written his notes, which read:

WWK/2.
KKD boshed Kotor monthly report. Follows. Sea most of time. Kalamai – Venice, L.B. run 3 wks gone. This trip cargo lifted: 2 miles off Gulf Traste. Two hrs work, sunken buoy, radar or magnetic. Lead casket 10' × 3'. Shore leave 2 hrs but unable contact SKD.

Checked per ins. Baldy, cook. Dead right. S.W. transmitter, fitted back of store room fridge. All grins, declares C.I.A. Don't believe. Fridge fitted 4 months Brindisi.

Spotted A. Party pamphlet gash can.

Mme. V. and new blonde Pomina.

Baldy, me, both playing it too long. F. him. Give me out. Big boy misses nothing.

That was all on the first sheet. On the second, and he'd obviously had a little time in hand while he waited for me, he had written:

C. tell that bastard that like bishop said a man can only go on for so long. Big boy will miss slide and I'll be gutted.

It was meant only for me, and I knew how he felt. You can only keep a man walking the edge so long – and just at this moment Sutcliffe was probably dining rich somewhere in London and making loud ponging noises about the claret.

I wrapped everything up and put it away in my case. Then I went down on to the hotel lake terrace and sat with a drink, waiting for Vérité to come down. It was a balmy, peaceful evening. Thin scarfs of mist hung low over the lake, and the lines of mountain ridges were cut dark against the star-studded sky which cradled the idle, reclining moon. I thought of Herr Spiegel lying under his bush, cold and stiff, and Frau Spiegel away in Babino Polje. It was going to be some time before any trouble started and by then Vérité and I had to be out of Yugoslavia. I didn't see it as any great problem. Somewhere Katerina was away on the *Komira*, and we had a contract, and a contract, I hoped, that was going to be more lasting than the one recently broken with Spiegel.

Vérité did not come down to dinner. She sent a message down to me to eat alone. I had an omelette, half a lobster, and half a bottle of wine, and then the schoolmistresses at the next table insisted that I had my coffee with them and wanted to know whether my fiancée were ill. I said no, she was just tired.

The motor-boat took us across to the far side of the lake at ten, and we went down to Polace in the bus. There were half a dozen other people leaving the hotel and catching the boat. In Polace one of the hotel staff who had come down on the bus with us showed us to our temporary lodgings.

Vérité and I were led up a flight of rough stone steps to a small house on the hillside, just above the landing stage. We were introduced to the woman of the house and the hotel man left us there.

The woman took us through a spotless sitting-room, shining

with new, highly varnished furniture, into a large bedroom. There was a new suite of bedroom furniture; a large bed, a wardrobe that rose into the lofty gloom of the ceiling like a polished cliff side, and two chairs that had white cloth covers over their tapestry to preserve them. There were no curtains at the windows, but large sheets of brown paper had been drawing-pinned across them. Against the window was a wash-stand with a yellow bowl and jug.

Within a few moments it became clear that this was the only free bedroom in the house and that the hotel had made a mistake and assigned it to us on a man-and-wife basis. I tried to point this out to the woman. She thought that we had some objection to the room on the score of its furniture or cleanliness. In the end I had to let her retire hurt.

Vérité, who had been quiet ever since we had left the hotel, said, "It doesn't matter. We've only a few hours to spend, and I don't mean to undress, do you?"

"No. I'll doss down on the floor."

She shook her head. "The bed's big enough for two."

She went round the bed, slipped off her coat and shoes, and lay down.

I padded over to the oil lamp which stood on the wash-hand stand and turned it out.

I flopped back on the bed and we lay there with a good two feet of neutral ground between us.

I said, "If I snore, just kick me and say, 'Quiet.'"

She said nothing.

In five minutes I was asleep.

I don't know how much later it was that I awoke. At first I thought that I had been awakened by the brown paper at the window rattling. One of the windows behind it was slightly open and the night draught was playing a gentle drum-beat against the paper. Then I heard a noise from the other side of the bed and knew that it was Vérité who had awakened me. She made a noise, somewhere between a sob and a sigh, and I knew that she was lying there in the darkness, fighting something alone. The noise came again, and without thinking, I put out my hand and found hers.

"What's the trouble?"

She made no answer, but her hand clung to mine tightly as though human contact now was the one thing she needed desperately.

"Don't think about Spiegel," I said.

"It's not Spiegel. . . ." I heard her force her voice to be normal.

"What then? That's if you want to talk."

"I don't know. . . ."

I felt that I was holding her hand across a great pit of loneliness.

"Sometimes it's better . . . to talk, I mean. Maybe you never have."

"It was the gun. . . . The noise, and seeing him there. Everything came back. A long time ago I said I would never let it come back. . . . But out there, it did. . . ."

"You loved him?"

"Yes. . . . Oh, God, yes. But it was never any good. . . . No, no, that's wrong. Sometimes it was good. Sometimes I could tell myself, fool myself, that it would go on being good. But it never lasted. It's a most terrible thing to hate and love. Sometimes I didn't even know what I was feeling. He brought other women into the house, kept them there. . . ."

"You needn't tell me about that. I read about it."

"I knew you had. You've been nice and kind. . . . Maybe, it was just that. When people are like that, it brings it back. And then today . . . the sudden noise of the gun in my ears. . . ." She moved and her voice was suddenly higher, echoing fiercely in the dark room, "I want to forget.... I don't want the coldness, the loneliness any longer.... Oh, God, why can't it be taken from me...?"

Maybe she moved, maybe I moved, maybe the earth just gave a compassionate lurch, but she was cradled in my arms and then holding on to me. I put my lips down and kissed her gently on the brow and then she put up her lips and kissed me, and I knew that it was not me she was kissing, not anyone. Her body, pressed against mine, trembled with an eagerness for warmth and comfort. I held her tightly to me, and talked to her gently, kissed her, and cursed the past, willing it to be exorcized from her, knowing it would be easy to give false comfort, knowing that this was not the moment. That was the way I saw it, and I knew that when the morning came that would be the way she would see it. This was a night for ghosts, a night for shriving.... I held her in my arms and I talked to her and the trembling faded, the fierceness died, and I could feel her tears against my cheek. I went on holding her until she slept.

We made Dubrovnik about half-past seven that morning and took a taxi up over the hill from Gruz and down to the end of the tram-lines by the Porto Ploce where were the tourist offices of Atlas. I left Vérité to deal with the question of getting an air booking, and said that I was going into town to have a shave and, maybe, a last taste of oysters before I left. I promised to meet her for coffee in an hour at the Gradska Kafana.

I left her and went into the nearby Excelsior Hotel. On the way back in the boat I'd been thinking about the whip which I'd seen in Madame Vadarci's room. It meant something to me, something to do with politics. I was curious, too, about Lancing's reference to the "A. Party pamphlet". I got through to Wilkins and unloaded my troubles on to her, suggesting that a visit to the publishers of

Stigmata might help, and telling her to express anything she found to my Paris hotel.

After that I headed straight for Michael Oglu's place, hoping that he would have a razor I could borrow and knowing that I would have no time for oysters.

CHAPTER ELEVEN

SLIDE OUT FROM UNDER

It was a little house built close up against the city wall on the north side of the town where the ground rises. From the wide windows of Oglu's studio I could look down across the red tiled roofs and the little vine and creeper bowered balconies to the sea.

The studio was an absolute litter of junk . . . paintings, canvases, old frames, a carpenter's bench with not a clear inch on it, and a long divan on which a cat had scratched the stuffing from the upholstery to make a nest for a litter of kittens which had been born that morning. The range of colouring in the eight small kittens would have given Mendel something to think about.

Oglu fussed around with the cat and kittens while I gave him a quick run down on the events at Melita. He kept nodding and making encouraging noises at the cat to drink milk from a saucer. But the moment I had finished he stood up and said, "Let's see the stuff." He put out a hand and swept the top of a small table free of junk.

I put on the table all the stuff I had received from Lancing, except the mounted colour slide. In my report to Oglu I had made no mention of the slide or of Lancing's comment on it. So far I'd just been beagling along, following a trail made only too obvious. Nobody was trusting me with anything. Now, for the first time, I was in on my own and my pride – or a sound commercial instinct – told me I'd do well to keep a hidden bargaining counter.

Oglu went through it all, his lean Red Indian face suddenly grave and thoughtful. It was a good face and he looked like some Chief pondering the omens. As he skipped through the notes his face went graver and I expected him to say, "Much bad medicine here, brother."

Instead, he said, "Spiegel's dead. No question?"

"No question. Vérité is trying to get air tickets for us to leave today. She'll do it if anyone can."

"Paris?"

"Yes. You'll let them know?"

"Yes. You want me to send this stuff?"

"No. I can take it. Vérité knows what I've got. I'm working for Malacod. That means I must turn all this over to him."

"No problem. I'll photograph the lot."

"Not the second sheet. That was private for me."

"Okay."

"WWK/2 – that's Lancing's tab?"

"Yes."

"He's pretty far gone. What happened at Kotor?"

"I was there – but some bastard jumped me. Drove me fifty miles into the hills and dumped me."

"Spiegel?"

"Possibly. Old Baldy's clearly kept him in touch. Ma Spiegel's transistor must be a receiver."

He went to a cupboard and brought out a camera and a powerful desk lamp. "Negatives will get to Paris a day, maybe two days, after you. Pull the curtains, will you?"

I went over and pulled the heavy curtains over the wide studio windows. A butterfly flew out of one of the folds. On the way back, a thought occurred to me. I bent over, patted the cat and made noises at the kittens.

Oglu fiddled with the desk lamp and checked his camera. He worked quickly, expertly, completely at home with the white man's magic. He said, "They're not going to like the Spiegel business."

"They?"

"Spiegel's friends. They've got simple book-keeping minds.

Account will have to be balanced. So expect a visit. Or am I teaching my grandmother?"

"It had crossed my mind."

"Good. Keep your fingers off the text."

I held the notes and photo under the light, while he clicked away industriously.

I said, "What's all the Lottie Bemans angle?"

"Don't know. I'm on the fringe, like you."

"You can do better than that."

He said, "Her last known address was Munich. P.A.D. Chalkokondyli.A. That'll be the Police Aliens' Department, Chalkokondyli Street, Athens. I know it. Anyone staying for more than a month in Greece must get an identity card. Lancing checked her there and her card was overdue."

It was interesting, but not what I wanted to know. He picked up the sheet of notes and studied the script. I went over and started to pull the curtains back.

He gave me a long hard look and said, "You're sure that this is absolutely everything that you got from Lancing?"

I turned. He had the notes in his hand and he was watching me, the sunlight striking full on his face as I drew the last curtain back.

"Absolutely everything."

He said, "How did you cover this with the girl? Vérité?"

I said, "I told her I took a row-boat for a look around the *Komira* and somebody tossed it over to me."

"She that gullible?"

"I'm not worrying about her. Malacod's the snag. I'll have to expand it a little for him."

"You're in trouble."

"I'll work through it."

He shrugged his shoulders. Then suddenly he smiled, walked

to the cupboard and put his equipment away, and came back with a bottle of brandy and two glasses.

We drank to one another.

As I lowered my glass, I found myself looking into the muzzle of an automatic.

"Don't tell me," I said, "that you carry that to protect the cat."

He smiled, shook his head and said quietly, "I may be doing you an injustice. Probably. But I have a job to do. If you were regular I wouldn't be doing this."

"Just what are you doing?"

"Making sure that you didn't get anything else from Lancing."

"So?"

"Just strip off. The cat won't mind. Starkers." He fidgeted with the automatic.

I stripped. Dropping it all in a heap on the floor.

"Shoes and socks," he said. "Take 'em off standing."

I started the necessary balancing act, and said, "I'm supposed to be getting a shave."

He motioned me away from the clothes and reached out without looking to the carpenter's bench, his hand seeking for something. He tossed a small leather case to me. I caught it, and then unzipped it. There was a Philishave battery model inside.

I began to shave while he went through the pile of clothing, the automatic on the floor, too close at hand for me to have tried anything if I had wanted to make an issue of things. But I didn't. The colour slide was not on me.

I shaved and, when he had finished with the clothes, he came over to me and made me turn my back to him. I felt as though I were up for sale in a slave market. One Anglo-Saxon, fit and sound, but only reasonably honest, and not to be trusted in the harem. The cat – kittens butting at her dugs – watched me, but she didn't make any bid. Oglu's hand finished feeling around the bandage on my arm.

"Okay," he said.

I turned. "A pleasure."

He shrugged. "My apologies."

I dressed. We had another brandy and parted friends.

I went over and patted the cat and kittens good-bye, and palmed the colour slide which I had hidden under them.

At the door, as he saw me out, he said, "For God's sake don't try anything clever. The whole thing's too big for that. And don't worry about the air tickets. I'll phone and check whether she's got them. If she hasn't, just come back here in two hours and they'll be waiting."

But Vérité had got them, and we caught an afternoon flight to Zagreb, changed to Air France, and were in Paris in time for dinner. Vérité had booked a room for me at the Castiglione Hotel. After dinner, I took her with her cases to her flat and told her I'd be round in the morning. When I got back to my hotel Casalis was waiting for me, which didn't surprise me. That side of the organization was sound enough.

I said, "If you think I'm going back to that flat, you're crazy. Spiegel's stiff and Howard Johnson has a broken arm. They're the kind that like to even the score. I feel safer here."

He nodded, and said, "Up to you – until Sutcliffe arrives tomorrow."

"What time?"

"Afternoon. I'll come and fetch you after lunch." He got up from my bed where he had been sitting and cocking his head owlishly went on, "Where have you put all the stuff you brought back?"

I flicked an eye at my case on the luggage stool and knew he had been through it.

"I took a box at the American Express and left it there. For safety."

When he was gone I telephoned Vérité and told her not to let anyone in until I arrived the next morning. Myself, I slept happy in the knowledge that the colour slide was already on the way to Wilkins with very explicit instructions as to what I wanted done about it. Express delivery. Mailed at the airport.

I went round to Vérité's flat early the next morning and had breakfast with her. I don't know whether it was because she was back in Paris, close to her employer, and the old personality had claimed her again, or whether she had decided that the Melita affair and the night at Polace had lowered her defences too much and the breaches must be built up . . . anyway, she was friendly but cool and slightly standoffish. There was no question of giving her a slap on the bottom and asking her if she had slept well.

She gave me bacon and eggs with their eyes shut and some excellent coffee made from a Cona which saved my hand from all that tin-top bashing.

I said, "You've passed the stuff to Malacod?"

She nodded. "Last night."

I said, "Will you ring Malacod and tell him I want to see him this evening at six o'clock. After that I'll take you out to dinner and dancing at the Lido on the Champs Élysées – fifty-four francs all in and half a bottle of champagne. So you can see I want to be generous and nice."

She looked at me for a long time and then very quietly she said, "You've been very generous and very nice. I wouldn't want you to be anything else."

She got up and went to the telephone. It took her some time to get him and when she did she spoke in German. And that took some time too. But when it was over, she turned to me and said, "Herr Malacod agrees. He'll see you at half-past six. I am to take you."

"To the same place?"

"No."

She didn't sound very friendly.

I said, "What's eating you?"

She said, "Herr Malacod is no fool."

"I never thought so. Not with all that money."

"These notes were written by a British agent."

"So?"

"How can you explain that to Herr Malacod?"

"Carver luck. It happens."

I went across to her and she stood her ground. I put my hands on her arms, leaned forward and kissed her chastely on the cheek.

Wilkins came on the telephone half an hour after I got back to the hotel. We had five minutes' skirmishing about whether I was changing my socks regularly, not letting my hair grow too long, and why had I said I'd paid the electric light bill for the office when I hadn't – and then she got down to business. She'd had the slide on the big office projector and had spent an hour with it and various reference books. She gave me her findings under different headings, and she had made a good job of it. But then she never did any other kind of job. I finished up with a page of notes that read:

GENERAL

Picture taken some time in spring. Larch in pines background just breaking. Gentians, small crocuses, cowslips along foot of wall. Shadows, early morning or late evening.

MAN

Fiftyish. Five ten, brown eyes. Dress – French, Swiss, Austrian better working class. Smoking dropped-stem, big-bowled pipe – German, Austrian type. Sole, right boot, built up, probably walks slight limp.

WALL NICHE

Small roadside altar, or shrine. Figure, carved wood, is of Madonna and Child. No distinguishing features, but probably local workmanship (possibly Bavarian?).

OVERALL

Somewhere Germany, Switzerland, Austria or poss. Haute Savoie. Part of mountain peak background, snow showing.

Before I rang off, I said, "I'll let you know any change of address. How are things?"

"Some small jobs came up, so I called in Fisk."

"That's fine." Fisk was an ex-policeman who gave me a hand now and then. "That the lot?"

"No. Harvald is coming home at the end of the month on leave."

I smiled. Harvald was her Suez pilot boy-friend. When he turned up Wilkins took off. A royal command would not have stopped her.

"Don't worry. If I'm not back, shut up shop or leave it to Fisk. Give Harvald my love. Tell him it's time he made an honest woman of you."

There was a snort and the receiver went down at the other end.

I got up from the little table by the window at which I had been speaking and went into the bathroom. As I closed the door behind me, I saw Howard Johnson sitting on the turned down lid of the lavatory seat. He lit a cigarette and grinned at me, no malice showing at all.

I said, "How long have you been here?"

"Idle question."

I went over to the basin and turned the tap to wash my hands, watching him. "How's the arm?"

"It wasn't broken, only badly sprained. It's almost a hundred per cent now. Interesting talk on the phone with your Wilkins?"

"Yes. Her fiancé is coming back. Means I've got to close the office up for a while." I washed my hands, briefly, watching him, and stepped to the towel rail and picked up a towel. There was nothing I could do about the notes on the slide out by the telephone. And there was nothing I could do for myself, because in addition to the cigarette in his left hand, he was covering me with an automatic in his right.

He said, "All nice and clean now, lover-boy?"

"Sure." I tossed the towel at the rail and it fell to the ground in a tangle.

"Good," he said. "Not to worry, though. They haven't come to a decision on Spiegel yet. I've just got a limited set of instructions."

"We must be thankful for small mercies," I said.

"That's the attitude." He took a step towards me. "Turn round," he said.

I turned. You can't make any headway against a force ten blow when you're in a coracle. He smacked me on the back of the head and I went out like a high-voltage bulb giving up the ghost.

CHAPTER TWELVE

THE BORGIA TOUCH

Casalis took me through the back entrance of 35 Rue du Faubourg St. Honoré and left me alone in an attic room which was being repapered. There were two deal chairs in it, spotted with whitewash from the redecorating of the ceiling. My kind don't go boldly up the front steps of the Embassy. It gives the place a bad name. Still, I'd come up in the world a little. The last time, I'd been taken through the back entrance of 37 in the same street, which is the Consulate.

I sat and watched a spider wrapping gummy threads around a fly in a web as though he'd just had the idea of inventing a golf ball. I smoked one cigarette and then Manston came in. He was in a cutaway morning coat and striped trousers, soft grey cravat with a pearl-mounted pin, and he looked hot. His hair was still dyed blond, but he was good to see.

He winked at me and said, "What did you think of the Yugoslav wines?"

"Not much. Where's Sutcliffe?"

"Keeping well away from you to protect his blood pressure."

I nodded. "You might be interested to know that Howard Johnson paid me a visit at my hotel."

"What did he get?"

"Nothing." In fact he'd gone off with my notes on the slide from Wilkins. But I had a good memory.

He looked at me for a long time while he quietly tapped a cigarette on the flat of his gold case.

Then he said understandingly, "All right. What do you want?"

"I'm hired by Malacod to follow Mrs Vadarci and Katerina

Saxmann. Then I'm hired by your lot to do the same. I've got a feeling that I'm chasing shadows. It makes me uneasy, and slightly unreliable."

Manston grinned. "That's what we're all doing. Chasing shadows."

"Then I quit."

"Us and Malacod, or just us?"

"You. If you want a run-of-the-mill tail, get somebody else from the correct category. I'm a big boy with a reasonable I.Q."

"I sympathize with you. I get the same frustrations."

"But at a higher level. Either you want me in or you don't care a damn."

Manston smiled. "How wise I was to keep Sutcliffe away from you. He doesn't really understand your type. Not even after all these years."

"But you do?"

"I think so."

"So where do we go from here?" I asked.

He studied the tooling on his gold cigarette case and after a moment said, "This thing has a security rating which is used once in a blue moon. You ask the questions – and I'll decide which to answer."

I lit a cigarette and saw that the spider was still carefully wrapping up the fly. I knew exactly how the fly felt.

I decided to pitch into the middle and try working out to one end or the other.

"Old Baldy, the cook aboard the *Komira*?"

"He's an East Berliner who works for Spiegel's lot."

"Spiegel's lot, and you – you're all gunning for the same thing?"

"Yes."

"Why don't you co-operate?"

He made a wry mouth. "We would if we had any common sense. But that's a rare quality in State Departments. No trust. Professional pride. We all want to get there first – on our own. Malacod has the same idea."

"You're operating against private individuals?"

"Partly."

"They have political backing?"

"Of a kind."

"Lead packing-case. What's inside? The missing Goya?"

He gave me a fractional smile, and then he said, "I suppose you could call it a work of art."

"Period," I said. "Well, if that door's shut, try telling me something about the Siegfried type on the *Komira*. Scratch golfer, if I know one. And handy with his dukes as they used to say when I read boys' stories."

"Well, he's also first class with foils and sabre. Wimbledon standard tennis, Olympic standard swimming, and a double-first Oxford – but not under any name you could trace. Don't ever let him back you up into a corner. He'll kill you laughing and pronounce your requiem in any language you want, including Sanskrit."

"Stebelson?"

"Small beer. He could be hoping to double-cross Malacod eventually . . . if he sees a chance. You guessed this?"

"My nasty mind suggested it. Katerina?"

"She might have the same idea. But she shifts her ground rapidly. My guess is that she's waiting to decide which is really the big play. Meanwhile, she keeps you coming."

"I'll say she does. I've just followed a paper chase – big markers, half across Europe, dropped by her. I'm surprised she hasn't given me a lead to Venice – if that's where the *Komira* is going."

"She hasn't let you down. She wants you to keep coming." He fished in his pocket and handed me a cablegram slip.

It read:

Lots of bridges Venice. Love. K.

It was addressed to me at the Hotel Florida, Paris – my old address.

"Long shot," I said. "She could have missed."

"There was one waiting for you at the airport. Same message. You just didn't see your name on the board. And don't think she didn't take a chance somewhere to get them off. She's cold steel in smooth silk."

"Nice phrase. Sort of nineteen-twenty ring."

"That's when I gave up reading thrillers."

"So what do you want me to do? Keep coming on the miserable handful of information you've dished out?"

"You get two choices. You aren't going to like one of them."

He'd got his case out again and was tapping one of his thumbs with it. I knew the gesture. It was as near to showing emotion as he ever came.

"Lay them out."

He looked straight at me and I didn't like the long bracket shape of his mouth.

"You're a bloody fool," he said. "Generally – about women. Chiefly – about the main chance. This thing is big – and you're playing around with it."

"Who, me?" I gave him a big, open-eyed surprised look.

"Cut it out." The way he said it was like being hit across the face, and coming from him it hurt, hard and lasting.

"I'm going," I said angrily.

"The only way you go out of here – unless you come clean – is in a box with brass handles."

I wasn't angry then. I was scared.

I said, "You mean that?" I didn't recognize my voice.

"Unless you have something that will drop Sutcliffe's blood pressure. Get it straight, Carver. It's out of my hands, unless you come to heel – and damned fast."

I swallowed what was left of the saliva in my mouth and protested, "You can't just bloody well bump off unreliable servants. This is the twentieth century."

He smiled then. "That's just what makes it easy. Walk out and try it. You won't get down the first flight of stairs, and there will never be a coroner's inquest on you. So come clean, quickly."

"You tell me how. Hell, you can't mean this!" But I knew he did. It wasn't his line in jokes. I'd been in far before, searching for the dishonest penny, but never as far as this. My intestines were coiling about like a nest of snakes. He meant it . . . grey cravat, pearl pin, striped trousers, popping up here for a few minutes from some reception for an oil sheik. Pardon me, while I ring for someone to put the knife into you – and then back to the champagne diplomacy and the spread of democracy in underdeveloped countries – and the dirty finger sign to any crap about the liberty of the subject.

He said, "I mean every word of it. You're nothing in this. Absolutely nothing. The thing we're after is that lead case that was lifted from the Adriatic – and if we don't get it within the next three weeks all hell is going to break loose. And I mean hell – blue, bloody murdering hell! So start talking – and make it the truth!"

I'd never heard him like this before. I swallowed hard, my throat like a rusty pipe, and I croaked, "But where do I begin?"

"Try Lancing."

"What about him?"

"He went ashore when the *Komira* reached Venice to report to SKD. He never made it. He was found in the Grand Canal just below the Rialto bridge with a knife in his back."

"Poor sod."

"That isn't the point. Lancing's code name was WWK. He put it on the notes you got from him. Only it read WWK/2. Know what that means?"

"No." I'd never thought about it and it was too late now.

"It meant that there were two enclosures in his message. We got one – the photograph of Lottie Bemans. If you want to stay on your feet and go on working for us – just hand over the other, you mercenary magpie."

"But—"

"Carver, for Christ's sake! I'm not fooling. I like you, you know that. That's why I'm here instead of Sutcliffe. You're worth more than most of the types we've got. But stop playing funny Bs with us. You aren't going to get a chance to make one extra nickel out of this deal on the side. Hand it over – and go back to work for us and Malacod. Find that lead case. All arrangements as before."

"Everything forgiven – but not forgotten."

"Exactly. And you say nothing to Malacod about what you held back. What was it?"

I wanted to get out in the street again, walking, so I kissed the fast buck good-bye, and went all out for frankness.

"It was a colour slide," I said. "Slightly over-exposed. Lancing thought it might be a clue to the place where the lead case is going." I went on, describing it for him, and finished, "Wilkins has it. I'll phone her and tell her to hand it over to whoever you send." I sat down on the chair, feeling the back of my knees aching as though I'd been on parade at attention for two hours. And I hoped there was not worse to come.

Manston killed that hope at once. "What did Howard Johnson get from your room?"

"Nothing. . . ."

He looked at me, right through me. The chill from his look refrigerated the room.

"Don't play about with me."

"All right. . . ." I didn't want to play with anyone. I just wanted my feet on hard pavement, pitter-pattering towards the nearest large brandy. "He got the notes I took from Wilkins about the slide."

"Did he?" It sounded like two short sharp funeral knells going.

He walked to the window and looked out, and he said no more for a very long time. Then he came back and right up to me and he said in a frozen, gravelly kind of voice, "Get this straight – because it's something I never thought I'd do for anyone in my life. You haven't said what you've just said. Johnson got nothing. Nothing."

"That's it. Johnson got nothing."

I was cold all over and felt the size of a worm-cast.

"Good."

He moved towards the door, paused with his hand on it and said, "If you should run across me anywhere after this, you play the same rules as you did in the bar of the George Cinq."

I staggered out to the street and tottered to the nearest zinc, and called for a triple cognac. It went down like iced flame and I had another and this time there was a feeble warmth to it, and all the time I was telling myself that the bastards really would have done it, they would have written me off with no regret from anyone except Manston. . . . Don't ever let anyone tell you that the Borgia touch has been wiped out in politics.

I had thought that I was going to Herr Malacod with Vérité. But I had a phone call from Stebelson saying he would pick me up at the hotel at a quarter to six. He took me to a block of offices in a turning off the Champs Élysées.

We went up in a private lift to a flat at the top of the building. I was taken into a large sitting-room and through a long run of window I had half Paris lying at my feet. There were a couple of Picassos on the back wall behind me, a sideboard that looked like the tomb of Napoleon to my right, a gilt-legged sofa to my left on which the Empress Josephine had, maybe, curled up comfortably, and under my feet a selection of Persian rugs which most millionaires would have hung on the walls.

Stebelson went to the tomb and fetched me a large brandy while I watched the traffic rat-race up to the Arc de Triomphe. Stebelson had been very quiet and went on that way. But there was no long awkwardness between us for Herr Malacod came in almost at once.

He was dressed for some official government function, I guessed: dark blue knee breeches, white tie, and a red ribbon with some order dangling on it making a broad diagonal across his chest. He looked about knee high to a young grasshopper and I watched him with the same fascination which had taken me at our first meeting . . . the domed head, matchstick arms, powder-white face, hooked nose, and the turned down bracket of a mouth with a huge cigar stuck in it. He smiled a greeting at me, and the same tiny miracle happened again, making me ready to put all my trust and faith in him.

He went to the sideboard, stretched up to it, and filled himself a glass of Vichy water.

I sat on the edge of the sofa and he moved the window so that the evening light behind him put his face in shadow.

He said to me, "Are you a member of the British Secret Service?"

I was not altogether surprised at the question.

I said, "No. But I have worked for them on a temporary basis in the past. As a matter of fact, they have been in touch with me over this job. They seem interested in it."

"No doubt. And what have you passed to them?" The smile came again, "It's all right. I know you must have. I'm well aware of the kind of pressure they can bring."

"Are you?"

"Yes. I've known it myself in the past. If I trusted them completely I should not be employing you. Expediency is the only god they acknowledge: What did you pass to them?"

"Everything I handed to you. Mademoiselle Latour-Mesmin will have reported to you what happened in Yugoslavia."

He nodded and sipped the Vichy.

At this stage, I thought I might have trouble explaining to him my contact with Lancing. But if it did concern him he wasn't showing it. Maybe it suited him just then not to embarrass me.

He said, "You know where the *Komira* has gone?"

I nodded. "Venice. One could have presumed that from Lancing's notes. But also I've had a telegram from there sent by Katerina to my old Paris address. She knows I'm following Mrs Vadarci, and I took the liberty of hinting to her that there might be a substantial payment for her if she helped me to keep on the trail. I hope I did right?"

He nodded.

Somewhere behind me I heard Stebelson help himself to a drink.

I said, "I don't think she's likely to pass that information on to Mrs Vadarci, though. In fact I'm sure of it."

"Why?"

"Because until she knows exactly what Mrs Vadarci intends for her she is giving nothing away. She wants to see what her role is. At the moment – though perhaps she doesn't know it – I think there's another candidate in Lottie Bemans."

He nodded again then, but not the miracle smile. Just a slightly worn businessman's smile. Then, to my surprise, he said, "They are both candidates for marriage. To the young man you saw on the *Komira*. Both have been carefully chosen, but I think Katerina will be given the honours. But I am not particularly interested in that. I want to know where she is eventually taken."

"It will be the same place as the lead packing-case. I'm beginning to have dreams about this case."

"Weren't your British friends forthcoming about that?"

"No. And they said nothing of marriage candidates. But then they don't answer questions. They ask them. What is in the case? Do you know?"

He gave me a little old gnome look, and said, "Never mind what is in it. I want to know where it is going. I want it – and I've got to have it within the next three weeks."

It was the same spiel as Manston had given me.

"The fate of nations? Armageddon?"

The joke died somewhere between us, shrivelling to the ground like a dead leaf.

He said coldly, "Go to Venice. Find out where the case goes. I'm sure you will. I have complete trust in you." He moved towards the door.

"And the A. Party?"

He paused by the door. "You can drive me, Stebelson." Then to me, he said, "You were taking Miss Latour-Mesmin out to dinner tonight. I suggest you have it here. I only use this flat for changing when I have an official evening appointment. I think until you leave for Venice tomorrow, it would be better for you to avoid public places as much as possible."

"Thank you."

He opened the door and let Stebelson go through.

I caught him with his hand still on the door with the big question which had been in my mind all the time like a piece of gravel under the heel.

I said, "Why don't you co-operate with the British over this? If I read the signs, you, they and a few others are all after the same thing."

"Quite. But when we get it, then expediency will dictate what is done with it. And I am a Jew, Mr Carver. Expediency – with other races – usually works against us. Goodnight."

I got up and helped myself to another brandy and, as I did so, Vérité came in through the main door from the hall. She was wearing a black silk evening dress with gold shoes and a tiny gold flower spray brooch on the left shoulder. She looked far too good for Mimi Pinson's or the Lido. As she came up to me, there was the beginning of a smile on her lips and warmth in the deep brown eyes. Not knowing why, except that something inside me told me it was the thing to do, I put down my brandy and gathered her gently into my arms. She came like a bird tired of flying, and I kissed her on the lips and held her close to me. We stood like that for some time until, with a gentle little sigh, she freed herself from me and went towards the window. Her back to me, she said, "I'd like a Dubonnet with a lot of ice, a piece of lemon and then some soda."

I began to fix the drink.

"I've been told to keep off the streets as much as possible."

"We can eat here. A cold supper has been sent up to the dining-room."

"We shall miss our dancing." I went over to her with the drink. She was different. I could read it all over her. Maybe she really was tired of flying against the wind. But I didn't ask her.

She said, "We can dance here afterwards."

"Why is he letting me have my head? No awkward questions."

"He has many contacts. Or maybe it is instinct. And he thinks highly of you."

I looked at her over my glass. "You gave him a report on me?"

"Yes."

"Top of the class?"

"Not quite. They've found Spiegel. It's in the late editions today."

"The Melita Mystery. I'll bet the Jugs* are tipped off to let it

* Yugoslavs

die down. There's a lot of international wire-pulling going on. What time does Malacod get back here tonight?"

"He doesn't. He changes here – then goes to his house at Neuilly at the end of the evening. You sleep here and go straight to the airport tomorrow morning. I've had all your stuff sent along from the hotel."

"And you're coming to Venice?"

"Yes."

I put my arm round her and kissed her again and she held her glass away carefully so that it would not spill. After a moment, she said, "Aren't you hungry?"

I nodded.

We had avocado pears, Scotch salmon with a cucumber salad, and a bottle of Pouilly-Fuissé to go with it, then Cona coffee and a glass of Rémy Martin. She sat across the table from me and in the mirror with its ormolu frame, swagged with fruit and flowers and Napoleonic bees, I could see the reflection of the back of her head and the line of her shoulders.

We danced for a while, then watched the television, and then at eleven o'clock she looked at her little gold bracelet watch and said, "You have an early start in the morning."

"I'll see you home," I said.

"No. You keep off the streets."

I let myself be directed because I knew that I was in her hands.

She showed me my bedroom, all my stuff from the hotel was there, including an express letter which had arrived from Wilkins. I kissed her before she left the room and she ran the palm of her hand down the side of my face slowly and said, "You know the nicest thing about you?"

"My table manners. I don't gobble my food."

She gave a little chuckle, shook her head, and said, "No. You know when not to ask questions. Is that instinct or cleverness?"

I shrugged my shoulders. I knew when not to answer questions, too.

I undressed slowly, wandering around the room. It made my place by the Tate look like a dog kennel. You can say what you like about being rich, but you can't deny the fact that with everything it brings you have more chance of being in a good mood than a bad one. The sheets were silk and the lampshade was held by a jade figure a foot high, and there was a small Corot over the fireplace that would have made a handsome dowry for Wilkins. I got into bed with a hiss of protest from the silk sheets. I thumped the pillow into shape to show who was master and lay back, wondering why I felt happy – since none of this belonged to me.

For bedtime reading I opened the letter from Wilkins.

Wilkins had been to the *Stigmata* publishing offices – three rooms above a shop near the British Museum. The shop was used for display and also as their trade counter. I had wanted her to go through their pamphlets on European political parties on the odd-ball fringe to see if she could pick up anything on a party which used a whip as its sign – the memory of which had been worrying me for a long time – an organization that might be referred to shortly as the A. Party. She had found what I wanted. She enclosed a short pamphlet in German and there on the front was the sign of a whip. Since she knew I couldn't speak German she had given me a breakdown of the contents.

Behind every screwball organization in the world there is usually a purpose not written into the declaration at the head of the pamphlet. Also behind each such organization there is usually some unnamed person putting up more money than could ever be collected in subscriptions and hoping to get a fat return on it. The *Sühne Partei* smelt like that to me. Atonement – said Wilkins – was the nearest she could get to the translation of the party name.

The head offices were in Munich, on the Königinstrasse.

The Director of the Party was a Herr Friedrich Nackenheim, the Secretary was Professor Carl Vadarci, and then there was a list of names, chiefly German, of a Committee of Management, none of which said anything to me. There were branch offices in most of the big German towns.

The party declared itself as strictly non-political in the sense that it did not put up its own candidates for election to the *Bundestag*. But it claimed that members of all the parties in the *Bundestag* were also members of the Atonement Party. In the same way, I suppose, as the Quakers could claim that there were some members of all parties in the House of Commons who were also Quakers.

Its aims were simple. The German people had been guilty of starting two wars, and of pursuing a policy of racial extermination towards the Jews. The national soul was dark with guilt. The time had come for atonement, the time had come when the tremendous energy of a people impelled by a sense of great destiny – until now manipulated into the dark side channels of power – must be used to create the true German national character. Every German had a duty to make atonement to the past through his every action, every day, no matter how humble or how important his role in the national life was. The true greatness which awaited the Germans lay in adhering unswervingly to the democratic principle in political life and the Christian ethic in private and public life.

The Atonement Party, which had been in existence for three years, asked for no more from its members than that – except their yearly subscription of ten marks, nearly a pound.

It was a straightforward statement, admirably simple and commendable. If it was a bit woolly about what one had to do it was no more so than a great many other worthy causes. Most Germans, I imagined, would rightly answer – without feeling obliged to cough up ten marks – that they were already at heart members of the Atonement Party.

However, Wilkins had talked to a woman in the shop, making it seem that she was all for the party, and had been told that of the four hundred and ninety-seven members of the *Bundestag* over two hundred were members of the A. Party. There were also influential supporters of the party in other countries.

The lunatic fringe works its feelers into all sorts of places. I was convinced that Manston – in the role of Sir Alfred Coddon, K.B.E., C.V.O., was heading for the same place as myself, but by a different route.

So, there it was, a whip to drive the national guilt from the hearts of the Germans.

The real crunch, though, was that Wilkins had been told that the party was holding a grand Atonement Rally in Munich in three weeks' time. It took a little while to get to sleep after that.

I must have been asleep about half an hour when the telephone by the bed rang.

It was Stebelson.

He said, "I thought you'd like to know something that's just come over the tape."

"Go ahead. But I don't own any shares so I can't have been wiped out."

"You nearly were, my friend. Half an hour ago a bomb attached to the underside of a bed in the Hotel Castiglione exploded."

I held my breath for a moment. Then in a rather small voice I said, "What room?"

"It didn't say. But have you any doubts?"

"No. Thank you." I put the receiver back. That clever bastard Howard Johnson. He was growing up fast. The bomb had been put there before I came back from Vérité's flat. No instructions on

Spiegel yet, he'd said. That must have given him a giggle. I switched the shaded bedside lamp on, wondering if I should go and find a brandy as a tranquillizer.

The door of my room was open and Vérité was standing between it and the bed.

She said, "Who was it?"

I said, "Wrong number. What are you doing here?"

"I have the next room." She came over to me. She was wearing a long green silk dressing-gown with a froth of ruffles around the shoulders. She held it together across her breasts and I saw her two hands shake a little as though she were cold.

"Liar," she said. "I listened on the other extension. You could have been sleeping in that bed."

I reached up and took her hand and she came down on to the bed beside me. "I'm sleeping in this bed," I said.

"Don't you care?" she said. "About yourself? You might have been killed."

"Of course I care," I said. "I like being alive. For God's sake I like being alive, and so do you. I can't think of anything that's better than being alive. . . ."

I switched off the light and put my arms around her. She was naked under the gown.

CHAPTER THIRTEEN

LOVE, K. AND V.

She was gone when I woke up. The sun was coming through the partly drawn curtains, bathing the Corot with a warm golden glow, but the bed was still warm at my side and her pillow was hollowed and scented.

I went into the bathroom, shaved, and took a shower. With hot water needling my skull, I thought about the A. Party. It seemed innocuous enough – the kind of lunatic fringe party you can find in most countries. But it had to be more than that with Vadarci running it, and with Manston giving it a priority rating that had made him get more than tough with me. Now, I could paint a pretty accurate picture of things for myself. Munich, the whip sign, *Stigmata*, the blond Siegfried type on the *Komira*, and Katerina and Lottie, a couple of hand-picked Rhine-maidens – but why get so burnt up about it all? To me it didn't seem to merit any high rating – I'd have put the British Union of Fascists way above it, and they had never made Manston lose a night's sleep.

As I dried myself on the largest towel I'd ever seen and which I could just manhandle, Stebelson wandered in without knocking.

He said, "I've come to wish you *bon voyage*."

I kicked the door shut with a bare foot and nodded to the bath stool. He sat down and stared sadly at my knees.

I said, "It was my hotel room?"

"Yes." He let his eyes run up over me. "You keep pretty fit."

"I'm not bomb-proof, though." I pulled on my pants and then patted my chest with eau-de-cologne. It was something I kept secret from Wilkins. I had an idea she might not approve.

"I should take more exercise," he said.

"I'll give you some – mental. He thinks I'm working for someone else, doesn't he?"

"Yes."

"Then why did he scrub round it?"

"He trusts you. More than you imagine. He's the kind of man who knows how far to trust."

"And he trusts you?"

"In a limited way. I wouldn't be silly enough to go outside the limits, if that's what you're thinking."

"I was."

"It's a compliment, undeserved."

"How far do you trust Katerina?" I began to button up my shirt, watching him in the mirror. His face was bland.

"The question doesn't arise."

"I'm glad it doesn't. If it did I could give you some advice. Her principle is number one first, last and always. There's probably only one place she ever forgets it, and that's in bed."

That jabbed him, just the faintest quiver and a slow upturning of the eyes.

"You speak from experience?"

"No. But I took a course once in female psychology. There was a special section on her type. Does any of this interest you?"

"Not much," he said, standing up. He put his hand on the door knob. "Vérité asked whether you want one or two eggs?"

"Three and four rashers. I like to fly on a full stomach. Tell me, briefly – what are the qualifications that made Madame Vadarci pick Lottie Bemans and Katerina Saxmann as possible wives for Siegfried?"

"Siegfried?"

"You've read Vérité's reports. The blond number on the *Komira*. Katerina herself told me Madame Vadarci said she might be married, that a golden future lay ahead. You should have seen her eyes gleaming. What are the qualifications?"

"I don't know." He sounded as though someone had just fitted him with a wooden head.

He turned stiffly and went out to see about the eggs.

When I got into the dining-room he'd left the flat. Vérité was sitting beside the coffee and my eggs were waiting in a silver warmer. I went over, kissed her on the forehead and gave her good morning, and she gave me a loving smile. We might have been married for ten years and still not worked through the honeymoon haze yet. And it worried me. Not because I'm against it, but because experience had proved that I didn't have that kind of horoscope.

At the airport while Vérité fussed around with the tickets and our baggage, I went to buy some cigarettes at the kiosk. Casalis appeared from nowhere, held a lighter ready as I broke open the packet, and said, "Briton killed in hotel bomb outrage."

"Nearly, but not quite."

He grinned. "We've got a bloke in Venice. He knows where you are booked."

"That's more than I do."

"He'll find you. Severus is the name. Have a large dry martini at Harry's Bar for me."

He went, forgetting to light my cigarette.

Our hotel at Venice was a quiet, undistinguished place on the Riva degli Schiavoni, an unfashionable four hundred metres farther eastward along the waterfront from the Royal Danieli, and looking straight out across the wide reaches of the Canale San Marco to the low line of the Lido. We had two bedrooms with a small sitting-room between them. We shared a bathroom, and from the moment we entered the suite – if you can call it that – we both behaved very politely and a little embarrassed, and both knew that it would stay that way until nightfall.

I went to the window with my field-glasses and had a look at the shipping anchored off shore. The *Komira* was there.

I left Vérité to unpack for us both and strolled back up the Riva degli Schiavoni, heading for Harry's Bar, and wondering which bedroom she would choose to put pyjamas on one pillow and nightdress on the other. I also wondered whether, if I went along with the illusion, it might not turn into some kind of reality.

Harry's Bar was crowded out with the particular kind of wealthy young Italians, both sexes, that I found hard to take: the suntan and Ferrari crowd with fathers in Milan prepared to commit murder to get an extra half per cent on their business deals. A few English tourists were squashed, etiolated and subdued amongst them, and it took me five minutes to get a large martini while I cursed the obliqueness of people like Casalis. They just couldn't ever be straightforward. The Russians may run interviews in parks, paint pink circles on trees, flash an *Evening Standard* under the left arm, and so on, but get a man like Casalis, who only has to tell one to meet a certain Mr Severus (SKD) in Harry's Bar, and he'd choke rather than say it right out. *Have a large dry martini for me at Harry's Bar.* Maybe because I was feeling angry about myself over Vérité – I'd got into the "What-a-bloody-heel-you-are" epicentre – the whole thing struck me as being too flaming childish for words. I suddenly felt that I'd like to go home, have a work out with Miggs, then a pint of beer and eggs and chips at a Corner House, and finish the evening at a Continental picture house. That's what I call living.

It took another large dry martini to work me out of it, and then a greasy, suntanned number in terracotta trousers and a pale blue sweat shirt grinned at me. He pushed a lank strand – and I mean lank, it was like a wet blackbird's wing – of hair out of a red-rimmed eye and said politely—

"*Buona sera*, Signore Ringmaster."

I said, "Let's get the hell out of this."

He winked and began to burrow to the door. I followed along the same tunnel.

He walked ten yards ahead of me, giving me no time to do any window shopping for holiday trinkets, and we finished up in a little *ristorante* in the maze of alleys just north of the Piazza San Marco. There was a bar to one side of the dining-room. It was empty, except for a plump young girl who served our drinks, holding a small child in one arm that quietly grizzled until – our service completed – she went back behind the bar, pulled down the yoke of her jumper, and began to feed it. It looked old enough to me to have been knocked off the breast at least two years earlier, but maybe she had some theory about child raising.

I said, "For God's sake, why couldn't we have met here in the first place?"

Severus winked and I realized that it was not deliberate. He had some kind of tic thing that flicked on as a prelude to any speech. It made me feel uneasy.

"Orders, *signore*."

"You Italian?"

"Greek mostly, little British, too. My mother—"

"Skip the pedigree." I was still a little angry and taking it out on him. "Give – if there's anything to give. What about the Vadarci woman and Katerina Saxmann? They still aboard the *Komira*?"

"No. They went ashore when she arrived."

"Where?"

"I don't know."

"Should you?"

"No. I'm a boat movement expert. Contacts in the water guard service. They came ashore through customs at the Lido and then disappeared."

"Who let them slip?"

"Nobody. Orders to watch *Komira* reached me after they came ashore."

"Unless there's somebody else holding that end?"

"Could be."

I said, "What about cargo?"

He smiled. "They've got a fast launch. Anything they didn't want to go through customs could have been shifted at night from a few miles out – before they came in."

"True." I made a face into my glass.

He said, "Maybe you prefer whisky, not this Chianti?"

"I'm O.K. Any reason why I shouldn't go out and have a look at the *Komira* tomorrow? Sort of trip around the island."

He nodded. "I'll pick you up at the foot of the Via Garibaldi. You know where that is?"

"Yes. Since you're the maritime expert perhaps you can get me charts or maps of Venice and the coasts up and down a bit from here?"

He flicked the blackbird wing of hair back and said, "Admiralty charts: fourteen-eight-three and fourteen-four-two. Mediterranean Pilot, too, if you want it. *Volume Three – West Coast of Greece, Ionian Sea, and the Adriatic Sea.* I'll send them to your hotel tonight. I used to be a pilot in these and other waters."

I said, "I've got a friend who has a friend who is a Suez Canal pilot. And I've changed my mind about the drink. I'll have a whisky and buy you one, too."

I called to the girl who, with great good nature, interrupted feeding time and served us and also put a dish of prawns on the table. Back at the bar, I saw her feed the child one of the prawns before putting it on the nipple again. She had some theory all right.

"There is something else you should know," Severus said.

"You chaps always keep the titbit until the end."

"Frau Spiegel?"

"God – without her transistor, I hope."

"With that. She's at the Royal Danieli – calls herself Frau Merkatz."

"Alone?"

"Yes."

"She have anything to do with the Lancing job?"

"Could be. She would be in touch with the *Komira*."

"Baldy, the cook."

He nodded.

At six o'clock the next morning the *Komira* was still in the Canale San Marco. I came back from the window, tossed my field-glasses into a chair, and sat on the end of the bed. Vérité sat up and worked her way down to me, heaping the bedclothes in front of her. I lit a cigarette and she reached round me to take it. She drew on it and then handed it back to me. Just for a moment I felt her lips touch the back of my neck.

"How would you get a large lead case from here to somewhere in Europe, say – without fuss?" I asked.

She said, "Kiss me."

I said, "What for?"

"Just kiss me."

I kissed her, putting my arms around her and she collapsed gently against the bed and we lay there. Then she slid her mouth free and one of her hands began to run slowly up and down my spine under my pyjama jacket.

"Sometimes," she said, "you are too clever. Or maybe it is too careful. Why? Because you are afraid to hurt?"

"What are we talking about?"

"You – me." Her eyes were very close to mine and I could feel the beat of her heart against me. "You can't hurt me, ever," she went on. "Never. Ever. Because already you have given so much."

She put a finger up and touched my lips as I was about to say something. Then, smiling, she said, "I know how you feel. Once I felt like it, too. You remember what you said at Melita one evening? 'The magic kiss that melts the frozen heart.' Remember? Some men, some women, think they have it for that someone else . . . always the someone who really has no heart to melt. Because of you I can talk about it now. I'm free. But you're not, are you? You're still thinking about her. And that makes you feel guilty about me."

"All this is a long way from lead cases."

She shook her head and the hand on my back was suddenly hard against my shoulder blades.

"I'm here," she said firmly. "Here, for so long as you want me here. Just that and no more. There's no need to try and shield me. You owe me nothing. . . ."

Her mouth came up to mine. After a while she lay back, smiling up at me, and I genuinely wished that I had never walked on to Brighton pier and seen Katerina.

She said, almost to herself, "You know he almost dismissed you."

"Who?" I smoothed my knuckles against the lower side of her chin.

"Herr Malacod."

"Why?"

"He knows you kept something back from him. Something from Lancing's parcel."

"Did I?"

She nodded and said, "A colour slide. When you went down to dinner that last night on Melita I went into your room. The chambermaid let me in with the pass key. I went through the parcel."

"Clever girl."

"He has been good to me. More than anyone will know. I am

honest with him and also with you. It is you who should be more honest with yourself. Why do you want to keep something back?"

I lay back beside her. It was a good question.

"I don't know," I said. "I just wanted something up my sleeve. A hidden ace. Something the others hadn't got. It's always handy."

"You mean it sometimes pays?"

"Sometimes."

"Sometimes it could be dangerous. . . ." She twisted, leaned over me and held my head in her hands, shaking me. "You fool, you fool. . . ." she said, and there was the beginning of tears in her eyes.

Severus was waiting in a small launch, tied up not far from the *vaporetto* stage at the foot of the Via Garibaldi. I got the full greeting, a nod, a wink, and a flick of his black cowlick. The *Komira* was anchored some way off-shore, out of the main stream of traffic and not far from the military seaplane moorings off the Lido. We went by her on the Lido side. There she was, white and luxurious looking, and the only sign of life on her was a man at the open end of the wheelhouse bridge wearing a white shirt and shorts. We went down to the far end of the Lido and then came back on the other side of the *Komira*, keeping our distance. The man was still on the bridge, but there were now a couple of hands on deck, painting the lower works of the funnel structure.

We passed her and then headed in for the Lido shore and tied up against the stone wall of a small cut that ran up to a bungalow, where an old man was raking a gravel path as though he had the whole of a lifetime in which to finish it. Half an hour later, a launch with three people in it put in alongside the *Komira*, and picked up a couple more passengers.

Within ten minutes I was sitting by myself at a table outside Florian's in the Piazza San Marco with a jolly family party going on not five tables away from me. I'd put on my sunglasses and picked up an old copy of the Continental *Daily Mail* which some-one had left on a chair, and was pretending to read it while I iced my right hand on a tall glass of Italian beer.

There was I – cool, casual, a summer visitor enjoying a drink, while a drift of chatter went up from the surrounding tables, while occasional flocks of pigeons exploded softly from the wide reaches of the square, and the golden horses of San Marco strained at the basilica façade in their never-ending task of trying to pull it down – and there was a pit in the middle of my stomach which was full of black ice. Just seeing her again did it to me. Just watching the slide of the sunlight on her blonde hair put me right back into a feverish trance which a hundred nights of bedding down with hot whisky and aspirins would never cure. There ought to be a law against the way some women go around operating on too high a frequency for ordinary men to receive in comfort.

She was wearing a pale blue silk dress, white openwork sandals tied with little scraps of gold thread, and a choker of large white beads around her cool brown neck, and she sat turned a little away from the table, her bare legs crossed, so that I could see her knees below the dress. After I'd been there about two minutes she took off her sunglasses and stared straight across at me with those violet blue eyes and gave no sign at all that she had recognized me. But I knew that she had, some supersonic call signal whistled between us and, as she leaned forward for Siegfried to light a cigarette he had given her, a great pang of jealousy split me in two at the familiarity of his innocent movement. If I'd had a blowpipe on me I would have sent a poisoned dart between his shoulder blades. If someone had said "Vérité" to me then I should have mumbled stupidly, "Who?"

Sitting at the table with them was Madame Vadarci, bulging like a couple of sacks of potatoes around which someone had wrapped a loose length of orange cretonne and, for fun, had topped it off with a wide-brimmed gondolier's straw hat from which hung two lengths of red ribbon that matched the redness of her face. Next to her was a thin, parchment-faced man of about fifty wearing pince-nez high up on a long thin nose. He had a panama hat, a black silk stock at his neck, and he sat a little back from the table, his hands resting on the top of a very tall, black stick. Siegfried was next to him and he had taken off his pale blue woollen jacket to show a white short-sleeved shirt and bare, brown muscular arms. So far as I could hear they were all talking German and there was a great deal of laughter.

I sat there and watched them around the corner of my paper, and I remembered the beach at Melita with Frau Spiegel's transistor going, and the other beach where Siegfried had come ashore to murder golf balls. And then I thought about Lancing. It didn't do me any good.

After about fifteen minutes I saw Katerina lean over to Madame Vadarci and whisper something to her. The old woman nodded and Katerina got to her feet, waving down both the men who made motions to rise with her, and then she threaded her way through the tables and under the colonnade into the entrance of Florian's. I sat where I was. She had done exactly what any clever girl would have done, gone off to powder her nose.

She was gone for about five minutes and, in that time, I noticed that the laughter and bright chatter at the table died. The three went into a serious, dignified huddle, talking quietly, but in the concentrated way of people who were getting down to brass tacks. The moment that Katerina appeared out of the colonnade they broke it up. As she sat down at the table the bright chatter spurted once more.

Five minutes after Katerina was back I ordered another beer. A different waiter brought it to me and as he put it down he said, "*Signore, prego!*"

I looked up at him and, his back to the Vadarci table, he slipped me a folded piece of paper and winked.

I said, "*Grazie. Pago ora per le due birre,*" and fished for my wallet. When forced to it I had enough bad Italian, thanks to an earlier stint in the country, to get by with. I gave him a handsome tip and then went behind my paper to read the note. It was written in pencil on a page torn from a small diary, and said:

> Darling. My heart went bump when I saw you. Don't follow. Vadarci might remember from Melita. Tonight. Ten o'clock. Walled garden. Villa Sabbioni, Treporti. If I can make it. Love. K.

Love. K. I looked across at their table and she was at that moment laughing at something Siegfried had said and had her hand lightly on his wrist. I made a vow to myself never to go out without a blowpipe again. But the next moment I forgot all about that because, coming up to their table, was a man, bare-headed, his face full in the sunlight, a face which even if it hadn't been vaguely familiar to me would have only needed the hooked pipe in his mouth and the slight limp from his built-up right shoe, to tell me who he was. He carried a long paper-wrapped parcel under his arm. Coming to the group, he made a deferential movement of his head, stood quietly in attendance like a good servant, and waited while the oldish man with the panama paid their bill. They moved off, limp-foot leading, under the shadow of the Campanile and right-handed into the Piazzetta San Marco, and I knew they were heading for the launch which was moored at the waterfront at the foot of the *piazzetta.* Severus was there, too, in his boat. Although I did not think he would have much luck, it was over to him for the time being.

I gave them five minutes' grace and then left too. When I got back to our hotel Vérité was out. She had left a note for me:

Darling. Gone shopping, etc. Don't wait lunch for me. Love. V.

It was my day for getting *billets-doux*.

CHAPTER FOURTEEN

BE A FLYING POST

Around about two o'clock there was a telephone call from Severus. He was waiting for me at the foot of the Via Garibaldi. Vérité was not back. I slipped out and walked down the Riva degli Schiavoni and found the launch moored in the same place with Severus stretched out in the stern, smoking.

I sat down beside him. He reached over the side and pulled up a flask of wine which he had dangling on a string in the water to cool. I shook my head.

"What happened?"

He filled a glass for himself, and said, "The launch went straight back to the *Komira*. Everyone went aboard except one man. The launch took him ashore at the Lido and then it went back to the *Komira*. I reckoned there was a lunch party aboard, so I tied up at the Lido and followed the man they'd put ashore."

"Did he walk with a limp?"

"That's the one."

"What happened to him?"

"He went to the airport. He had a pass for the field, and he went over to a helicopter. It's a commercial job that I've seen there before. He took off his jacket and started to help a mechanic work on it. I waited around a bit but he showed no signs of knocking off so I went back to the launch. Just in time, too."

"For what?"

"To see the yacht party leaving in their launch. Same party, old woman, young woman, young man, old man – and they had another man with them. It's a funny thing but I got the impression that this new man was being hustled a bit between the young man and the old man, but maybe I was wrong."

"Where did they go?"

"I wish I could tell you. Their launch went off like a bat out of hell. It must have some engine. I just couldn't keep up with them. The last I saw of it it was disappearing across the lagoon."

"Ever heard of the Villa Sabbioni at Treporti? It's not marked on any of the charts or maps you gave me. I want you to find out what you can about it, and meet me here at seven o'clock this evening. I'm going to make a call up there."

He looked at me, obviously expecting more, but I let him go on expecting. He'd get it all in good time. Just at that moment I was thinking of the helicopter more than anything else.

I said, "You know about the girl with me?"

"Latour-Mesmin?" He grinned. "Yes. I checked the hotel reservations."

"I want her to handle this helicopter thing. Have you got a contact over there?"

He fished out a fat wallet and selected one of a bunch of rather dirty visiting-cards and handed it to me.

"Tell her to see him. He's an officer in the *Dogana*. He knows everything." He winked. "You can pretend to her it's a contact you've made on your own. I'll phone him and put it right."

"Did you get the registration of the helicopter?"

"Yes." He took the card back from me and wrote down the registration letters and number on the back. Handing it back, he said, "Sure you won't have some wine?"

"Not now – but bring it along with you tonight, and also something to hold in your right hand while you drink. We might need it."

He flicked his hair-lock back, winked, and then hid his face behind a tumbler of wine.

I left him and went back to the hotel. Vérité was there. Within ten minutes she was on her way across to the Lido Airport.

When she was gone I lay back on the bed and cleaned and checked the *Le Chasseur*, and I thought about the helicopter.

Vérité came in two hours later with her report. The customs officer had been very nice, given her all the information she wanted, had asked her if she would have dinner with him that evening and, when she had said she was sorry she couldn't, he had accepted the disappointment gallantly and pinched her bottom as she had left his office.

She sat on the edge of the bed and played with the lobe of my left ear as she gave me the details of her report.

The helicopter was owned by a small air transport firm which operated from Munich. It did a bi-weekly run from Venice to Munich. Apparently the company had a contract to transport glass and pottery from two Venice firms. On the trips from Munich to Venice the company brought in optical instruments, wallpaper, small machinery and other odds and ends of general cargo. The pilot of the machine was called Brandt, the man with the limp was Hesseltod, and listed as crew, and there was another crew member named Danowitz. The helicopter had been due to leave the Lido Airport the day before with a cargo, but owing to engine trouble it had been delayed, probably until around seven o'clock that evening. She gave me a copy of the cargo manifest of the load for that day which had already been cleared by customs. Then she produced a *Carte Michelin – Europe Sud – Grandes Routes*, and on it a straight pencil line which she had ruled from Venice to Munich.

The line ran just west of north from Venice, missing Treviso to the west and then, farther on, leaving Cortina d'Ampezzo to the east and then, from there on, running slap across the Tirol between Innsbruck and Kitzbühel to Munich, a fat stretch of country, without any large towns, full of mountains and lakes, where a small deviation in flight would cause no comment.

I cocked an eyebrow at her. "Is this Hesseltod a regular crew member?"

"No. He appears only on and off."

I said, "Would Malacod have anyone reliable in Munich?"

"Herr Stebelson would be able to arrange it."

"Then I'd like you to phone him or Malacod and ask them to put a man at Munich Airport right away – to catch this flight from Venice if he can – and to check on this helicopter until further notice. I want to know whether the same pilot, crew and cargo that leave Venice also turn up at Munich. Tell them I'm particularly interested in Hesseltod and would like to know whether he walks with a limp when he reaches Munich. I'd like them to phone you a report direct here."

Katerina had said ten o'clock. But as it was light very late in the evenings now and I felt that a preliminary survey of the Villa Sabbioni would do no harm, I took the usual surveying instruments with me, field-glasses, and the *Le Chasseur* rubbing a hole in my jacket pocket.

Severus was waiting with the launch. We went down the main channel to the Porto di Lido mouth that ran out to sea. We crossed it and headed up the Treporti channel, which in its deepest places was no more than four fathoms and mostly between one and two fathoms. On our port hand was the long, low line of the Isola San Erasmo, and on our starboard hand the great stretch of the Littorale di Cavallino, which hid the sea from us. Treporti was about a couple of miles up the channel at the head of a small inlet which ran deep into the Littorale di Cavallino. It was a flat, uninviting stretch of land, studded with the occasional clump of trees and the stubby silhouettes of one or two farm buildings.

Severus told me that the Villa Sabbioni was two or three hundred yards up the inlet to Treporti, well away from the village. It had been built some fifty years previously by a businessman from Rome – who had seldom used it because he had found that the place was mosquito-ridden. The kind of mistake any businessman should have been ashamed of making. He was dead now and the place was owned by his son, who never used it, but let it to anyone who was prepared to pay the modest rent and dose themselves with mepacrine morning, noon and night. It sounded to me like the kind of folly that didn't attract crowds of sightseers and casual ramblers to its gates.

Severus landed me at the mouth of the inlet and I had five yards of marshy bog-wading before I hit firm ground. I made my way across a long stretch of sandy wasteland towards a clump of three Lombardy poplars which, Severus had told me, were about four hundred yards from the villa. A hare got up and went away in front of me, ears flat, and then stopped at a safe distance and sat up on its haunches and watched me. A curlew came over, slanting down the slight breeze, and with every step I took little puffs of sandflies exploded underfoot. Now and again one bit the back of my neck and it was like a jab from a rusty hypodermic needle. The place was going to be pleasant when the mosquito squadrons took the air for their night flight. It was no place to bring a girl courting on a summer evening. Far away on my right hand, Venice was lost in the flatness of land and water and marked with a brown pall of summer evening mist.

I picked the middle one of the three poplars and I went up about twelve feet.

I settled in a leafy fork and got the field-glasses out. Villa Sabbioni was a long, two-storey building with a red-tiled roof. So far as I could see, it was surrounded on the three sides away from the inlet with a wall about eight feet high, topped with a coping of red tiles. In the angle of the wall nearest me there was a white door, its top third filled with an ornamental grille. Through it I could see part of an inner and walled garden. I went up an extra six feet and could see the inner walls of this garden plainly and, beyond them, a wide expanse of gravel running up to the house front. On this side there was a creeper-grown loggia stretching the full face of the house. If Katerina were playing fair with me, I knew that the white doorway would be unlocked.

From behind me, from the direction of Venice, I suddenly heard the sound of an aircraft engine, a heavy, laboured noise. I screwed my neck round, and there it was, coming low up the seaward side of the Littorale, an orange-painted helicopter, like some clumsy flying insect. It changed course beyond the trees and swung in towards the villa.

I kept the glasses on it, and from the moment that it sank, clanking and coughing, on the open gravel space in front of the villa things happened fast. I couldn't see everything because part of the far wall of the enclosed garden cut off some of the ground view. Two men dropped out of the machine, a stowage door was opened, and I saw them manhandling cases out. I counted three, and then, beyond the machine, I caught the movement of people coming out of the villa, partly obscured by the helicopter. I had a glimpse of Siegfried, a flick of skirt or dress which could have been either Katerina or Madame Vadarci, and then saw the two men from the helicopter lugging the cases towards the house. I couldn't see them go into the house because my angle of vision was wrong. I should have been in the tree five yards to my right. There was a lot of movement on the far side of the helicopter. Then three men came round to my side, carrying between them a long case which they loaded aboard. From the way they moved it was obviously damned heavy – and looked about ten feet long by three wide. The stowage door was closed and, with a swirl of dust from the gravel as the rotor blades cartwheeled into action, the machine was up, hovering, and then away.

The whole operation had taken about forty seconds flat, and in another twenty seconds it was away, lost behind the house and heading inland, on its proper course now, I guessed, which would just miss Treviso and take it on to Munich, except – and I'd have taken any bets on this – somewhere along the line there would be another quick deviation and temporary stop.

I lit a cigarette safely behind my leaf screen and wondered, among other things, if the pilot were a member of the Atonement Party. Maybe the proprietor of the company was, too. And all planning to go to the grand rally.

I sat it out in my tree for two hours while the daylight finally faded and a moon, which had been lurking somewhere out in the Adriatic, slowly came up like a blood orange, and the mosquito flights below me gradually gained altitude and began to dive-bomb my neck and hands. There wasn't another woman in the world but Katerina who could have kept me tree-squatting for so long, and now I wasn't even sure that she was still in the villa, waiting to come out and keep her tryst with me.

At ten minutes to ten I dropped to the ground, stumbled from cramp in the knees, and then began to move carefully towards the white door.

It was unlocked, but there was a key on the inner side. I slid through and closed the door after me. The garden was about the size of a tennis court. All around the sides were little flower beds edged with box which had grown long. The flower beds themselves were a mass of weeds. Nobody in the Vadarci party clearly cared for gardening. In the centre the ground was open and paved with great slabs of stone and there was a small pedestal with a sundial on it. On the far side of the garden was another white door, grilled at the top, which led into the big driveway at the back of the house.

To my right, shadowed in a corner of the wall, was a small summer-house with most of its window-panes broken. I moved into this, half-closed the door, and stood back so that I had a clear view of the open space with its sundial and of the short run of path up to the other white door.

I took out the *Le Chasseur* and put it on the window-ledge at my side, dismissed the idea of having a cigarette, and settled down to wait for Katerina.

It was fifteen minutes past ten when I heard a noise from the direction of the house. The far door was suddenly thrown back with a jerk and three men came through into the garden. For a moment they were in deep shadow. Then they came down the small path and into the open space which was flooded with moonlight.

There was Siegfried, walking ahead, carrying something wrapped in a cloth under one arm. Behind him came another man in shirt-sleeves, and behind him I could see the panama of the elderly number who had been in the Piazza San Marco.

Siegfried was dressed in a dark shirt and dark trousers. He walked up to the sundial and dropped his cloth bundle with a clank on to the ground. It was then that I saw clearly the man behind him and that the grey and white nightmare slowly began to take shape and gather momentum. The man was about forty, strongly built, short and bald. He wore striped canvas trousers and his hands were tied in front of him. He walked in front of panama hat docilely and stopped near the sundial. Siegfried turned and said something to him. It sounded to me as though they were talking in German. The bald man shook his head and then, almost with a resigned movement, held out his bound hands.

Siegfried stood back from him. The other man moved forward and, with a certain amount of awkwardness, undid the bonds on the bald man's hands. Then he moved back to the edge of the open space. As he did so, Siegfried bent down, whipped the cloth away from the bundle on the ground, and then straightened up. Something flew through the air, glittering briefly. The bald man caught it and the moment he had it in his hand the whole of his body tautened as though a spring had suddenly been tightened in him.

And then there they were, the two of them, a few yards apart, each crouching a little, each moving a little in a slow circular dance, each with his right hand a little advanced and held high, and in each of their hands was a sabre. It was like watching the slow crab-like stalk of a couple of murderous insects, their elongated right arms great shining spikes, ready to slash and kill.

And killing, I knew, was intended. Clear through the nightmare came the shock of understanding . . . *Baldy, cook . . . short-wave transmitter. Fitted back of store-room fridge.* The lines came back from Lancing's notes. And here I was, with a front-stall seat, at the gutting which Siegfried was staging in his own sadistic manner. I guessed now that Katerina was no longer in the villa. She'd gone off in the helicopter. This show would never have been put on with any chance of her seeing it.

There was a clash of sabres and the moonlit square was alive with the sharp movement of men and the sharper glitter of sabres. The two men drew apart, circling warily, watching each other and already I could see a dark line of blood down the right-hand side of Baldy's face. Beyond them, coolly sitting on a stone pillar at the edge of a flower bed, the dignified number in the panama lit a cigar and watched.

It wasn't, for my money, anything that was good to watch. Baldy was no fool with the sabre, that was clear, but he was way out of Siegfried's class. He must have known that it was going to be slow murder. There would be a flurry and clash of blades, the lightning leap in of Siegfried, a whirl of movement, and then the quick withdrawal with Siegfried untouched and another streak of blood on Baldy's cheek. After his face came the body's turn . . . and whenever Siegfried's face swung so I could see it he was smiling, calm, eyes bright and perfectly composed.

I don't have any strong feelings about blood sports generally, and I suppose, if I'd lived then, I'd have paid my drachmae or whatever and sat in the gallery of the Coliseum and backed net against trident with the best of them, but this was too much for me.

I reached out for the *Le Chasseur*. As I did so Siegfried came in again at Baldy. The man was forced back across the open space towards my end of the garden, and the great blade of his opponent played around him like lightning. Then Baldy staggered, dropped his sabre, and I saw his hand go down to his left side.

Siegfried paused, said something, with a gesture of his blade to the sabre on the floor, and waited. I stepped out then. I made two yards before any of them knew I was there. I raised the gun and covered Siegfried, and I said:

"Baldy – the door behind me is open. Get going!"

He began to turn and I saw Siegfried's face swing towards me and then the movement as he went for the other man. I fired. A foot ahead of him at the paving stones. He pulled up and I saw the point of his sabre dip towards the ground as he dropped his right hand slowly.

"The door. There's a motor launch at the end of the waterway."

Baldy turned fully then, both his hands pressed against his left side. His face was wet with sweat and he nodded and began to move. He went past me and I covered Siegfried, who stood watching me, his body relaxed now, no movement from him. And there was no movement from the man in the panama hat. He sat on his little pillar, the cigar stuck in his mouth, and he watched me, too.

There wasn't an idle question in either of them. They just watched me, and I stood there, heard the door go and then the dying sounds of Baldy going fast across the ground outside. I gave him a few minutes, not knowing how fast he was able to travel. Then I began to back slowly towards the door. I wasn't going to go a foot nearer Siegfried than I needed, not even with a gun in my hand. Manston had told me enough about him to make it clear that allowing him up close was asking for trouble.

I reached behind me and got the key out of the lock. As it came free Siegfried spoke. He had a good firm, pleasant voice, and there wasn't a trace of accent in his speech, or even a note of anger or any other emotion.

He said, "I look forward to the day when I find out who you are."

I said, "You don't want to bother with me. I was just passing and heard the sound of cold steel. Write me off as a nosey-parker with a love of fair play."

I went through the door quickly, jammed the key in the outside lock and turned it. Then I ran, hoping Baldy would be well on his way. I didn't let up until I reached the launch. I looked back a couple of times but no one was following. I sloshed out across the bog to Severus. Baldy was not with him.

I made him pull out into mid-stream and hang off there waiting for the man to turn up. We waited twenty minutes, listening all the time for the sound of any launch coming downstream, and watching the bank for any sign of the man. In the end we gave him up. I'd got him out of one mess and I didn't intend to get myself into trouble by searching for him. He was the kind who, given enough start, could look after himself.

Eventually we turned away, going fast down the Treporti channel for Venice, and it was a faint sort of comfort to me that all the time I had fronted Siegfried in the garden the moon had been behind me and my face well in shadow.

*

I was dreaming that I was facing Siegfried, both of us with sabres, and he was smiling all the time as he went for me. Then a telephone bell began to ring somewhere and Siegfried frowned and said, "For God's sake, why can't they leave us alone to enjoy ourselves?"

I woke then to see Vérité in a dressing-gown moving around the end of the bed to answer the phone which was ringing in the sitting-room. I sat up, rubbing my neck which was as lumpy as rhino skin with mosquito bumps. I listened to her talking in the next room. My wristwatch showed that it was six o'clock.

I reached for the water carafe and drank from it without benefit of glass. My throat was dry as though I'd had a late night and too many cigarettes.

Vérité came back into the room and sat down beside me. She put her arms around me and kissed me and then, after a few moments, she pulled away but left one hand on my neck.

"You've been bitten to death. I've got something I can rub on those."

She started to get up but I held her and said, "Who was the call from?"

"Munich. What time did you come in last night?"

"About three. You were sleeping."

Severus and I had come back to Venice and taken up station off the Lido shore watching the *Komira*. At two-thirty the *Komira*'s launch had turned up from Treporti and Siegfried and the panama-hat man had gone aboard. At three-thirty the *Komira* had pulled out. I didn't need a clairvoyant to tell me that the Villa Sabbioni would not be used again. I was due to meet Severus in an hour and go back there to have a look round, not with any great hope of finding anything. They would have cleaned up nicely. Everything destroyed or tidied away. And the tidying would have included Baldy if I hadn't butted in.

Vérité said, "So, I was sleeping. What had you been doing?"

"I'll dictate a full report later. I could never concentrate with a secretary in a short nightdress. What did Munich say?"

"It landed at Munich just after eleven last night."

Munich was about a hundred and ninety miles from Venice as the crow flew, and I suppose there have been a few crows that have done it. The helicopter could do a hundred an hour easily. Three hours to do two hours' flying. They'd made a leisurely stop somewhere.

She went on, "There was a crew of two, the pilot, Brandt, and another man, Hesseltod. Only this Hesseltod didn't limp."

"I can't say I'm surprised. What about the cargo?"

"Exactly as listed on the manifest from here."

"Neat. I saw the Venice cargo unloaded not three miles from here. They must have had a duplicate cargo waiting at their stopping point before Munich."

"What happens now?"

I looked at my watch. It was ten past six.

I said, "I'm meeting a man at seven o'clock. I'll need thirty minutes to shave, shower and dress and get to him. When I come back we'll probably have to start heading north. Meanwhile we've got twenty minutes for you to do something about these mosquito bumps."

We were at the Villa Sabbioni just after eight. We could have been there fifteen minutes earlier, only we were very circumspect about our approach. We need not have been. There wasn't a living soul there. Not a door was locked. But before we went into the house we saw where the cargo had been dumped. There was a well-head in the gravel space before the house, and they hadn't bothered to close the wooden flaps that covered it. Severus shone his torch down. Twenty feet below, we could see the edges of a couple of cases poking above the water. The other one was probably already waterlogged and had sunk.

We went right over the house and there was not a personal item of any kind to be found, except a toothbrush in one bathroom, and some ash in the hall fireplace where a few papers had been burned and crushed to fine flakes. Severus insisted on collecting them in his handkerchief. He had more faith in the marvels of scientific detection than I had. While he was doing this, I went through into the servants' quarters and the kitchen.

As I could have guessed from Lancing's remarks about him, the one thing that made Baldy a top professional was his devotion to duty in defiance of any personal discomfort. And last night he had been operating under the ultimate discomfort. But underneath the professional there must have lurked insistently, too, the instinct of, perhaps, his first and most loved *métier*, the good cook. He had homed on the kitchen like a badger to its holt, a wounded bear to its den. He was sitting at the marble-topped kitchen table and on it was an extension telephone to one I had seen in the hall. He stared straight at me, a ball-pen in one hand, and a small sheet of notepaper on the table in front of him.

He didn't smile any greeting or nod in appreciation of past services. His eyes were wide open, and he was cold and stiffening up. I had a little trouble easing the sheet of paper from between the right thumb and forefinger that held it. I took the paper and the ball-pen and slipped them into my pocket just before Severus came in.

Severus stood by me, looking at him, at the big heavy face and the sabre-ripped, blood-matted shirt.

"This the one?"

"That's him."

"If he'd come to the launch, we could have helped him. Maybe saved him. Santa Maria – look at his side!"

I didn't because I'd already seen it.

I said, "He hung around, watched them, checked them out, and then came back here to see what he could find. And he couldn't have known or believed how bad he was."

Severus moved to the table and looked at the telephone. He touched it with his finger.

"I think he did," he said. "There's blood on it. He telephoned. For help?"

"Or to pass information?" For help most likely, I thought, otherwise why start writing while he waited?

Severus said, "What do we do about him?"

"Leave him here. Tidying up isn't in our brief. Poor bastard."

Severus turned away from the table and nodded sympathetically. I saw the swift flick of his involuntary wink, and the greasy shift of his lank lock of hair – then there was a crack like lake ice splitting. He fell away from me, gave one high, animal scream, from what had a second before been his face, and thudded to the ground.

I don't suppose I remembered it then in so many words, but an old Miggs's precept worked. A standing post is easy to hit from three yards. The butt end of a post flying towards you creates problems in marksmanship. Be a flying post.

I dived for her, flat out, and she fired and took the heel off my right shoe, though I didn't know it at the time. I had her in my vision for a good half-second before I hit the ground a yard from her and belly-skidded across the stone tiles, reaching for her ankles. She wore a blue dress with white collar and cuffs like a District Nurse and a white, big-peaked cap like a jockey's, and her wide motherly face was twisted into a solid look of murder. Maybe she'd loved Spiegel truly, and this was pure vendetta, or maybe she was just as toughly professional as Baldy had been. Either way, she meant business and got in another shot, that laid a red-hot poker down the inside of my left leg, just as my hands crashed into and held her ankles. Frau Spiegel, or Frau Merkatz, came down on top of me like a house falling, a house full of a few hundred spitting, claw-ripping cats. I let her have her way while I rolled from under the weight and grabbed at her right wrist. She held it away from me, using feet, knees, and the nails of her left hand, while her teeth went through the stuff of my jacket, deep into the flesh of my right shoulder.

I got her wrist at last and gave it a twist that made her cry with pain and loosen her hold on my shoulder. The gun in her hand skidded away somewhere, useless to us both, and she pounded her fists into my face and scrambled away from me. We both came up together. It was the first time in my life with a woman that I didn't care a damn about the niceties, about gallantry, and old world courtesy. I didn't want any in-fighting with a mountain cat from the Urals weighing a hundred and ninety pounds. I slammed my right fist into her jaw. Her head snapped backwards on her shoulders and she went over, crashed to the floor, and her head jerked violently as she hit the tiles.

She lay there, breathing heavily, but out. I picked up her gun from the floor and ran to the kitchen door. There was no one outside in the hallway.

I went back. There was nothing I could do for Severus. I felt sick and I was shaking all over.

I didn't spare her. She was well out, safe from embarrassment and I was a grown man. I gave her the full search treatment. And I did the same for Baldy. For him I felt genuine sorrow and respect. I got nothing from him. And not much from her. She had a small purse in her dress pocket. Apart from some lire notes the only other thing in it was a thin flat silver pill-box affair about the size of a half-crown. The lid screwed off with a half turn and there were a dozen flat white tablets inside. I kept the box for I had an idea what they were, though I knew I wouldn't feel safe about them without a proper chemical analysis.

I pulled up my left trouser leg and wrapped an old tea towel around a messy but not serious wound, and I did what I could to my face at the kitchen sink. There was nothing I could do about the teeth marks in my shoulder except get an anti-tetanus injection and hope that Vérité would not be jealous.

From the hallway I telephoned Vérité at our hotel. I didn't go into details. I just told her to get our stuff packed and get up to the Piazzale Roma and hire a car so that we could get out of Venice fast. I wanted, I said, to see Herr Malacod as soon as possible.

It was only as I was going down to our launch that I discovered I was limping from the loss of my right shoe heel.

Her launch was tied up near ours. She had come out on her own to fetch Baldy and, seeing our launch, had been ready for company. I opened the watercock on her launch, watched the water begin to flood in, and then took off. Half a mile down the Treporti channel and I was sick, and I knew it would be a long time before I forgot that last scream from poor Severus.

CHAPTER FIFTEEN

THE TWICE-FIRED HAND

Back in Venice I left the launch at the foot of the Via Garibaldi and then went straight to the Royal Danieli.

In the lobby I found the telephones and put through a call to London. I didn't get Sutcliffe or anyone I knew. I just said, "Ringmaster. Severus is dead. I'm clearing out. I'll ring this evening for instructions."

A voice at the other end said, "Thank you," and then there was the click of the receiver going down.

After that things went on moving fast. I met Vérité in the Piazzale Roma, which is right up near the station, and close to the point where the autostrada runs out of Venice.

She had fixed us up with a chauffeur-driven car and, I discovered later, had done a lot of telephoning. She was as efficient as Wilkins and had the same gift, too, of not badgering for explanations at the wrong moment. Anyway, I didn't want to talk. I'd got too much to think about. We drove north to Treviso and then across to Trento and up to Bolzano. At Bolzano we paid off the car and spent an hour waiting in the railway-station buffet.

We were picked up there by a blue-and-cream chauffeur-driven Rolls-Royce, which had a drink cabinet in the back. I had a large whisky and soda and then went to sleep until we hit the customs check at the Brenner pass.

We stayed in Austria, because there was no other customs check, and at ten o'clock that night we turned off a side road along a private drive through pine forests.

It was too dark and I was too tired to have much curiosity about the place at that moment, though I could guess that it was some hunting lodge or mountain chalet that belonged to Malacod.

A fat old biddy with a cheerful face brought me a plate of smoked-salmon sandwiches and half a bottle of Chablis in my bedroom, and as I finished them Vérité came in.

She said, "You ought to let me look at that leg."

I said, "It'll keep until the morning. Where is this place?"

She said, "The nearest town, or village rather, is called Schwaz. We're not a long way from Innsbruck."

"And the house?"

"It's called Chalet Papagei and it belongs—"

"To Herr Malacod." I fished in my pocket and handed her the message which Baldy had written just before he died. "Translation, please."

She read it through and then gave it to me in English.

The note from Baldy – and I could imagine him, forcing it from himself, hanging on desperately to get it down – read:

> Zafersee again . . . heard them in hall . . . Zafersee, ten minutes away V. says . . . good place dump L.B. or K.S. which-ever. . . .

After she had read it Vérité stood looking at me. Somehow I was still not in the mood for explanations.

I said, "When is Herr Malacod coming?"

"Tomorrow."

"I'll give you the whole picture, so far as I know it, in the morning."

She said, "I don't care about that. You must have lost a lot of blood from that leg. Please let me."

"Don't fuss around. It's all right."

"It's not all right. You've got some dirty piece of rag around it. It could go septic."

I gave in, and I got the whole treatment right through, leg dressed, hands and face washed like a small boy, and finally tucked up in bed and given a goodnight kiss.

While she was doing it I said, "Would the Zafersee be what I think it is? A lake?"

"Yes." She gave me a look but said nothing, though she must have known what was on my mind. L.B. and K.S. meant to her what they meant to me.

When she was gone I reached for the telephone and called London.

I said, "Ringmaster. I'm at the Chalet Papagei, Schwaz near Innsbruck."

The voice at the other end said, "*Papagei*, that means parrot."

I said, "Thanks."

I lay back and tried to sleep, but it was a long time coming. I could finish Baldy's message for him. Whichever girl was to be eliminated, L.B. or K.S., would finish up in a lake not ten minutes from. . . . Well, that wasn't difficult to work out. And, wherever it was, the big lead case had gone there last night.

She brought me coffee and rolls in the morning and sat on the side of the bed sharing the tray with me.

I said, "I'm sorry I was a bit edgy yesterday."

She said, "I understood."

"You did?"

"When you asked me to translate that message, you already knew what was in it, didn't you?"

"Yes, I did."

"Because if it had suited you, you weren't going to pass it on."

"Could be. I took a chance and got the desk clerk at the Danieli to translate it for me."

"Because you'd seen the initials L.B. and K.S.? Oh, it's all right. I know how you feel about her. And all yesterday you were thinking about her. I didn't exist."

I started to make some protest, but she shook her head and smiled, saying, "Even if there were no K.S. you'd have done the same thing. It's the one thing which is wrong with you. You want something, something far more than you've got, and you're always taking stupid chances in the hope of getting it. True?"

"True. Don't we all want something more than we've got?"

"Yes, I suppose we do. But most of us, after a time, learn to be content with the way things are. Why don't you try to be that way?"

"I do. All the time, but somehow it doesn't work. At least, only for short stretches. I'm sorry about it."

She stood up and walked to the window, tall and lovely, her dark hair tied loosely back on the nape of her neck, and I knew what she wanted and I knew that I could never give it to her. There was no use kidding myself. I couldn't. And there wasn't any point in hiding it. So far as she was concerned I was a short-stretch man, and being honest about it.

"Find me a cigarette," I said, "and I'll tell you all that happened."

She came back to the bed, taking cigarettes and a lighter from her dressing-gown pocket. She sat down close to me and then, suddenly, her head came down to my neck and I put my arms around her and held her.

After a time I began to explain what had happened and she lit a cigarette for me, and things levelled out between us. We both knew that there was no bonus to be had from kicking out at the truth. The only man she'd ever loved was dead, and the only woman who was really under my skin stood a chance of finishing up in a lake. She'd known with him that she was taking on big trouble, and I knew that Katerina probably meant big trouble for me, too. Vérité had gone ahead until the thing had blown up in her face, and I was going ahead and hoping to be luckier.

Herr Malacod, Herr Stebelson and another man arrived together in the Rolls which had gone to fetch them from Innsbruck. They turned up just after lunch.

We met in a sun room looking out over the garden. Five of us. Malacod, Stebelson, the other man, Vérité and myself. Malacod was in an old-fashioned tweed coat and knickerbockers and there were dark shadows under his eyes, giving his dead white face a pathetic, clownish look. Stebelson had his usual brightly polished plastic look, and Vérité had become a shadow in the background, notebook and pencil in hand. The other man – to whom I was not introduced – never said a word during the whole interview. But he was restless. He kept moving up and down by the window, leaning heavily on a thick stick. He was well over sixty, white haired and with one of those sad, leonine faces that have forgotten how to smile. It looked to me, from the way he walked, as though he had an artificial right leg from the knee down.

I gave Malacod the whole story, including everything about Severus, except that I said he was a man I had known before in Venice whom I had enlisted to help me.

Malacod heard me through in silence, nodding now and then over a fat cigar, and when I had finished, he said—

"And your conclusion from all this, Mr Carver?"

I walked over to the window and looked out at the garden. My shoulder was itching from Frau Spiegel's bite and I rubbed it. The old boy with the gammy leg moved away from me, shaking his head a little as though all he'd heard so far distressed him.

I said, "It's obvious to me that I'm not going to be let in on the truth or whatever it is behind all this. Okay – why should I grumble? I'm just a hired hand. But, working in the dark, I suppose it goes something like this. The lead case has been lifted from the Adriatic. It left the Villa Sabbioni, but it never arrived at Munich. It was dropped off somewhere. That somewhere is presumably within ten minutes of this Zafersee – into which, at some time, either Lottie Bemans or Katerina Saxmann is going to be dumped." I turned and looked at Stebelson. He gave me a bland, unmoving full-moon stare.

I went on, "You know all the angles behind this, though it isn't hard to guess that they must be mostly political since London, Moscow and possibly Bonn and Washington are interested. I'm not over interested in the political angles. I just don't like the idea of any girl being dumped into a lake. So where do we go from there? We can trace this Zafersee place and then I can find, with luck, this place where Siegfried is almost certainly holed up with a lead case and two blonde German girls, one of whom, I think, he means to marry and the other – to keep his records clear – he means to murder. Is that the way it is?"

I looked at Malacod now and he met my eyes squarely through a little veil of cigar smoke.

He said, "Correct. But there is one assumption which you are wrong about."

"And that?"

"You are no longer, as you put it, a hired hand." If he had said it with that warm smile of his I should have expected promotion. But there was no smile.

I said, "What do you mean?"

He said, "I have always been prepared, up to a point, to accept some of the terms you have imposed upon your contract, Mr Carver – whether you knew I was aware of them or not. But I can no longer do this – for my own good reasons. You are specifically working for a certain Mr Sutcliffe. . . . Oh, I know quite a lot about him. And, also, you have withheld information from me. Information which you have collected while in my employment. I'm referring to the colour slide. I say none of this in anger. I have known and I have accepted. But now a moment has been reached where I must have complete confidence in those working for me. And undivided loyalty. Would you say that you can give that?"

I hesitated for a moment, looking across at Vérité. I knew that she qualified when it came to undivided loyalty. She had told Malacod about the slide.

"Well, Mr Carver?"

"I'm only interested in one thing. I don't want any girl dumped in a lake. I rate that higher than undivided loyalty."

He shook his head, and said, "I thank you for all your help. If your secretary sends me your account you shall have my cheque."

"If that's the way you want it."

"That," he said, "is the way I want it. And may I say that, whatever amount you charge, I shall add a bonus to it."

"Do that," I said, moving towards the door. "And perhaps you'll tell your chauffeur to drive me into Innsbruck. I'll be ready in half an hour."

I went up to my room and kicked the mat across the floor. I had to kick something. All right, so they were going to take over and work on their own. They had every right. I had been hired and now I was fired. But I couldn't be fired from the way I felt about Katerina.

There was a knock on the door and Vérité came in.

I said, "If you've come to help me pack, I can manage. But I'd like about fifty quid in Austrian money. You can knock it off my account when it comes in."

She came over, lifted my case on to the bed, and began to pack. She said, "I understand how you feel."

I said, "Do you?"

She nodded. "Of course. If I could help you, I would. I want only good things for you. Even her – if that is what you want."

I went to her and put my hands on her shoulders, looking into her large dark eyes, and then I leaned forward and kissed her gently on the lips.

"There's nothing you can do. The wheel started spinning some time ago. I've just got to wait and see where the ball finishes."

"I know. And when it comes to that moment you can always find me if you want to."

"If I'm still walking after the big bang, I might hold you to that." I didn't know the hidden truth in those words then. I went on, "Who is the old boy with the tin leg?"

"A business associate of Herr Malacod's."

"Jew?"

"Yes."

"How come the leg?"

"It was amputated in a concentration camp."

At that moment the telephone bell rang. I picked it up and a voice said, "Ringmaster?"

"Yes?"

The voice went on, plummy, as though, whoever it was, was finishing off a soft-centred chocolate. "Innsbruck Railway Station. 21.00 hours today."

"Okay," I said, and rang off.

Vérité looked at me and I said, "My bookmaker. He's tracked me down at last. You won't forget about the money, will you?"

I could see her fighting not to say anything. Then she turned and went from the room.

My packing finished, I went down to the hallway. Stebelson was there by himself and he walked out on to the front steps with me, where we waited for the Rolls to come round.

Because I was feeling that way, I said, "Care to listen to a little theory I've got?"

He said, "No."

I said, "Good. That makes me even happier to lay it out for you. You got Katerina into this racket, whatever it is. Not because you wanted to do anything for Malacod. But because you hoped somewhere along the line to do something for yourself. Maybe, like me, you don't like being a hired hand. But it isn't going to work. You picked the wrong girl, and you know it. Like you, at the start, I thought there might be a big picking somewhere, but this thing is out of our class. Take my advice – if you can see it, settle for a small, quick profit now and get out."

To my surprise, he smiled and said affably, "Perhaps I shall take your advice. Katerina is definitely unreliable. I had thought she would not be. But I had a letter from her which makes it very clear."

"You had a letter?"

"From Venice. It is the first time I have heard from her since she left Paris."

"I could go and tell Malacod this."

"I should deny it and say it was just a ruse for you to stay in the job. And, anyway, I don't think you want to stay now. You have other plans. If you remember, I once advised you against falling in love with Katerina. Here is the car."

The Rolls drew up smoothly below and the chauffeur got out to open the door for me.

I went down, watched by Herr Stebelson, who lifted a plump

hand in farewell. Behind him in the doorway of the hall I saw Vérité standing. She half raised a hand to me and then turned away.

I was matey and sat up with the chauffeur. We made Innsbruck in well under the hour.

It was just after six, so I went and had a drink and an early dinner.

Over dinner I read a note which the chauffeur had handed to me from Vérité when he had dropped me.

"Madame Latour-Mesmin," he had said, "asked me to give this to you."

The note read:

Darling,

I know that you are going to be foolish. Nothing I can say or do can stop that. I know this better than most people could. Please try and look after yourself. All the love I have is waiting for you whenever you want it.

To save you the trouble of looking it up, which I know you would soon, the Zafersee is not far from the Achen Pass, on the German side of the border. Love. V.

She was quite right. She had saved me the trouble of looking it up.

I was picked up at nine o'clock by a young man in a sports jacket and tightly-cut twill trousers. He had a sandy moustache, wore a Tyrolean hat with a feather in it, and he was driving an old Mercedes which, as we moved off, showed quite clearly that no matter how shabby the coachwork was the engine had had constant and loving care.

He was English and chatted away quite affably about nothing at all. I let him ramble on.

We went over the frontier into Germany at Scharnitz and

headed north along the Munich road. After five or six miles he turned right handed off the main road along a side road. Now and again through the trees I caught a glimpse of lake water.

After about four miles we pulled sharp left into a narrow driveway and the headlights picked up the façade of a low, grey stone house with the shutters drawn across all its windows. The car lights were flicked off before I could get a good look at it.

I was taken around to a side entrance and ushered by my friend into an old-fashioned kitchen at the end of a long corridor.

I found myself facing Sutcliffe. He was sitting at the kitchen table with a plate of cold beef and salad in front of him.

He looked up and beyond me, to the young man, and said, "All right, Nick. I'll ring when I want you."

I heard the kitchen door shut behind me. Sutcliffe waved me to a seat at the end of the table, facing him. There was a bottle of whisky, a siphon, and a glass waiting there. I sat down and helped myself. Sutcliffe pushed salad into his mouth, chewed, and studied me. I didn't like the way he looked at me. But then I never did.

He cleared his salad and said, "Start from the beginning – and go right through, omitting nothing. Nothing."

I lit a cigarette, sipped my whisky, and began, giving him everything from the moment I had arrived in Venice until the moment I had been picked up in Innsbruck, everything, that was, which was of professional interest. I didn't go into any details of my private affairs concerning Vérité, or of my feelings about Katerina, but he got everything else, and he listened like a sphinx, just chewing gently to himself at cold meat and salad, and occasionally taking a sip at his wine. I knew that when I had finished, the questions would come, and I was not even tempted to make any guesses at them. Guesses never worked with Sutcliffe. And all the time I grew more and more uncomfortable because I suddenly realized that, although he was using me now, had used me in the past, and might use me again, he didn't really like me. And as long as I didn't carry the establishment stamp he never would. Plonk that on me for keeps and he would loyally make an effort to tolerate me.

He said, "This white-haired man at the Chalet Papagei – are you sure he had an artificial leg?"

"Vérité Latour-Mesmin confirmed it."

"Which one are you in love with? Her – or the Katerina girl?"

I didn't answer right away. I gave him a dirty look and myself another shot of whisky.

"Which?"

I knew the tone. This was Sutcliffe on the job. There was no question of this being an affable after dinner chat. He was all cut and kill to get the thing he wanted and God help whoever got in his way.

"Katerina," I said. "And I don't want to see her finish up in a lake."

"Naturally. But – if the timing works that way – she may do just that."

"First things first, eh?"

It didn't rile him.

He said, "Unfortunately, yes. So let's come straight to the point. From a professional point of view you've got one flaw. It puts a practical limit to your usefulness. You involve yourself personally. That means under emotional stress you cease to obey the reins. If our moment for taking action has to be timed later than the elimination of one of these girls, you'd never accept it."

"You mean that I've got a warm little heart throbbing under my rumpled shirt? That I shouldn't care – so long as some dirty political tangle is smoothed out – that some girl finishes up with minnows chewing her eyeballs?"

"Precisely."

Old Spiegel could have made the same sound with his Toledo blade.

I stood up. "You're dead right. That's the way I am. I don't like those things."

He looked up at me and took a cigar case from his pocket. His eyes were like dry pebbles. He pulled out a cigar and inspected it. It was certainly Havana, and probably a Ramon Allones. He ran the cigar under his nose to get the bouquet.

"Quite," he said. "And that's why you're fired."

"Well, well," I said, "soft-hearted old unreliable me. And no union to take up my case." I let soda hiss gently into my glass. "So perhaps you'll ask old Nicky boy to drive me to the nearest hotel."

He struck a match and lit his cigar, and he took a lot of care doing it.

When it was going, he said, "It's not as simple as that. You've served your purpose. I'm grateful. But you know a great deal. You're a security risk, whether you like it or not. Nick and I are going to drive you to Munich. Casalis is there. He and Nick will take you to London. When you reach London your passport will be taken from you for a month – things should have cleared up by then. I'm sure you won't mind. That, in fact, you'll see the good sense of it all. Also you will hand over the little pill case you got from Frau Spiegel. Now sit down and finish your whisky."

He reached out a hand and pressed a bell push somewhere under the table for Nick. He was smiling in a positively fatherly way now, because he had it all sewn up. Carver had done a good job, within his limits. Carver would now be isolated, sealed off . . . and somewhere not fifty miles away in the hills was a lake into which, for all he cared, Lottie or Katerina might be pitched if it proved expedient. I saw her then in my mind as I had first seen her on Brighton pier, misty blue eyes and the wind in her golden hair; I saw her face below mine in the back of the car up

on the downs, saw the loose drift of sand on her legs at Melita
. . . and there was a swift, sudden ache in me for her. No matter
what she was, we'd never had a chance to prove what we could
be, and I wanted that chance. For God's sake, a man had to be
given some chances, or had to make them, and he didn't have to
be a knight in shining armour. He could be a grammar-school
boy from Honiton, a simple little snooping inquiry agent from
London with an overdraft. He could be anything, so long as he
had a warm little human heart and the courage to spit in the eye
of authority.

I heard Nick's footsteps coming along the corridor.

Sutcliffe blew a cloud of cigar smoke. As it cleared, I saw that
his hand had come from his jacket pocket and he was holding a
gun on me.

"No nonsense, Carver," he said gently. "Believe me, in many
ways I sympathize with your feelings. But that is as far as it goes."

Nick opened the door behind me. I turned to look at him. As
he came forward, I picked up the soda siphon and I let Sutcliffe
have it. The liquid streaming out, I swung behind Nick, so that
there could be no gunplay, and I whirled the hissing jet round
catching him in the side of the face. Then I was through the door
and racing down the corridor.

I don't often pray, but I offered up a simple, direct number which
I didn't think called for a lot of deliberation above. Just, O Lord, I
said, let Nick have been innocent enough in his profession to have
left the car key in the Mercedes.

He had. And my case was on the back seat, too. Sutcliffe would
murder him for it. The engine fired and I shot around in a wide
dark circle on the gravel, kept the lights off and headed her down
the drive. I took a large chunk off the nearside wing as I scraped
one of the gate posts – and then I was away, lights flicking up and
the narrow side road all mine. Okay, so I was mad. But where do

you get in life if you just fill up all the forms, hand over your passport when told, queue here and queue there, and never do anything that gives the old adrenalin pump a chance to work into top gear? I'll tell you. You just get to be old and pensioned with nothing but a lot of dusty memories that no one wants to hear about.

CHAPTER SIXTEEN

SNAKES AND LADDERS

I drove for about two hours and then I pulled off the road, about a hundred yards down a grassy ride, into a pine forest. I slept soundly in the back of the car until the dawn began to creep up and the birds inconsiderately started their chorus.

I started the car and jockeyed it off the ride and into the wood as far as I could get it. With luck it would be a day, maybe a couple of days, before anyone found it. Then, case in hand, I started walking, heading roughly north-east.

By ten o'clock I was in a small place called Lengries, where I bought myself a torch, a map, and a rucksack, and dumped my case. From Lengries I took a bus to a place called Bad Tölz. Here, I changed the Austrian money I had and then found a chemist. I handed over one of Frau Spiegel's pills to him and asked him if he could analyse it for me. He looked a bit old-fashioned about this, but in the end told me to come back in an hour.

I went away and settled down to an early lunch and studied the map. Bad Tölz was about thirty kilometres north of the Achen Pass which marked the border between Austria and Germany. I worked out a route for myself back southwards to the Zafersee, which was a tiny pinpoint of blue on the map some way north of the pass and, so far as the map was concerned, had no road leading to it.

After lunch I bought a large pair of sunglasses and a flat cloth cap, and then went along to a garage and hired a small motor scooter for a week. That gave me trouble at first, but, by offering to double the usual deposit, I persuaded the garage man to overlook the fiddling details of credentials and guarantees. I drove along to the chemist shop and the old boy there was looking even more old-fashioned. He told me that, as far as he could make out, the pill was some compound of nembutal and veronal. One pill was enough to put a man flat on his back for a few hours. Three or four pills and a man would go on his back and never get up again. He started then on some spiel about how dangerous the pills were and that ordinary citizens should not have them in their possession, and it really was his duty to . . . I backed out of the place at this point.

I went out of Bad Tölz fast, not wanting to give the chemist a chance to put the police after me. By late afternoon I had found the Zafersee, and also lodgings for myself.

The lake was two miles off the road running up to the pass. A small cart track led to it. It was in a little bowl in the hills, hemmed in with steep-sided, pine-thick slopes. The water was still and clear and deep. I guessed that the bottom was a tangle of long-submerged, waterlogged tree trunks where a body dropped in, properly weighted, would sink and be trapped for ages in the maze of dead timber. It was the kind of place where an expert frogman would think twice before going too deep.

The lodgings were a mile beyond the Zafersee, at the head of a small col over which the rough track rose and then dropped, through more forest, to a river with a large road running alongside it. It was a small wooden farmhouse, perched against the slope of a small alp, and it was run by a German of about fifty-odd and his wife. They gave me a room at the top of the house with a wonderful view down the near side of the pass to the Zafersee.

For the next three days I left early with sandwiches packed by Frau Mander and returned late for supper. I worked a ten-minute scooter range all round the place. This I'd marked on the map as a circle, centred on the lake, of about ten or twelve miles in diameter – and that covered a fair bit of ground. I never once saw anything that resembled the place I was looking for. I checked the local telephone directories for Hesseltod and Vadarci and drew a blank. I did everything I could and still drew a blank. Whenever I reached a hilltop or a view point I took out my field-glasses and went over the country below me. If any house or feature looked interesting I would go and check it. I asked postmen, publicans, and any local looking people that I met on the forest and hill tracks. To help with the language difficulty I flourished a drawing I had made from memory of the details of the slide. I got nowhere.

Every evening before I returned to the farmhouse I would stop half a mile from it and give it a good going over with my glasses before homing. I knew that Sutcliffe would have someone looking for me, and he knew roughly where to look.

The third evening my caution paid a dividend. Through the glasses I saw Nick talking in front of the farm to Herr Mander. I got back on the scooter and freewheeled away down the track. I had all I needed in my rucksack, the torch, the glasses, the *Le Chasseur*, my battery razor, a shirt and a pair of socks.

That night I slept rough in a hay barn a good twenty-five miles from the Zafersee. I woke hungry, and headed for the nearest village to get some food.

I was coming down a steepish hill towards a wide easy corner on a mainish sort of road when a car came down behind me, blared its horn, and went by, missing me by about an inch. The blare of the horn and the near swish of the car's passing made me wobble, and I went into a skid that took me off the road. I finished up on the grass, cursing the bastard to hell. The scooter lay on its side against a heap of road stones.

I got up, dusted myself down, and eased off the cursing. I'd taken a patch of skin off my left hand and the wound was full of grit. On the other side of the road was a small cottage with a neatly kept garden. To one side of the cottage an iron pipe came out of the bank and a spout of water fell into a stone trough.

I went up to the cottage. An old man was sitting on a bench in the sun. I showed him my hand and pointed to the stone trough. He nodded. As I went to the trough I heard him call something in German into the house. I washed my hand clean and was about to wrap my handkerchief round it when a woman came out of the house. She was much younger than the man and could have been his daughter. She carried a towel in one hand and a tray in the other. On the tray was a length of bandage and a glass of wine. She gave me the wine, said, "*Bitte . . .*" took my left hand, and began to wipe and then bandage it. She was about forty and smelt good, like fresh hay and baking bread. When she had finished I pulled my drawing from my pocket and began to go through my ritual, "*Kennen Sie . . .*" and so on.

She took the drawing, shook her head over it, and then went to the old man and handed it to him. He looked at it in silence for a while, and then started a long conversation with her. I got the impression that they seemed to be arguing about something. In the end the old boy got up wearily from his seat and started down the garden path. The woman, with a big smile, motioned me to follow him.

Outside the gate the old boy paused, pointed to the scooter, and said something. I didn't have to know German to realize that the old man preferred riding to walking.

I started it up. He climbed on to the tiny pillion seat and motioned me away down the road. He sat behind me for two miles, chuckling to himself, gripping tight to my waist, and now and then breaking out into bursts of German which meant nothing to me.

Then on a long curve of new road, he tapped me hard on the shoulder. On our left was a run of tall stone wall. We got off and we walked along the wall in the grass for a couple of hundred yards until, to accommodate the new road, the wall turned almost at right angles. Round the corner he stopped and smacked the wall as though it were the flank of a favourite horse. This next section of wall was much newer than the one we had been following. He said something in German and shook his head at my obvious stupidity. Then he made the obvious motions of opening big gates. He then stepped to one side, sank unsteadily on one knee and crossed himself. This done he turned to me and began to count on his fingers aloud, "*Ein, Zwei . . .*" and so on. I could count fairly well in German. He stopped at "*Zehn*".

I got it then. I walked across to the other side of the road and took a look at the wall. From the turn of the angle, to where it ran away into the rise of a wood, the stonework was years newer than the first part we had walked along. From where I stood I was looking at the view I had seen in the background of the slide . . . the same mountains, the same grouping of trees. But there were no gates, and no wayside altar. I could have searched for months and never found it. Ten years ago clearly, the road had been widened and straightened and the gates had gone. More than likely the slide had been a colour transparency taken for sentimental reasons before this work was done. Something else became obvious, too. I'd been working on the basis of a ten-minute road drive from the Zafersee – that at a generous estimate gave a radius of five miles from the lake. This place was at the limit of a twenty-mile radius. I couldn't see Siegfried doing the body-dumping trip, almost certainly at night, at a speed of over a hundred miles an hour – except by using a helicopter!

I took the old man back to the cottage by way of the nearest inn, bought him a couple of brandies, and finally left him at the cottage gate with a handsome tip.

It took me until late afternoon to beat the bounds of the place. The stone wall was its frontage only to the two-mile strip of main road.

The rest of the estate was bounded by a tall wooden fence which carried three strands of barbed wire, angled outwards to stop anyone climbing in. I guessed there might have been a couple of hundred acres of ground inside, roughly in the shape of a natural bowl, surrounded by wooded mountain slopes that ran up to bare crests. The new entrance was a mile up a side turning, a twisting, tree-hung road; a tall pair of barbed-wire topped wooden gates with heavy iron drop-ring handles that didn't move an inch when I tried them.

I climbed the hill on the far side of the gates until I came out in a small clearing where I could get a good view of the bowl. There it was, an enormous *Schloss* with a centre block and two side wings. From my view point I had the whole of the side of one wing facing me. The roof was cut into small towers of blue slate. To one side there was a small lake surrounded by parkland. A narrow stream ran out of the lake and disappeared down-valley in the direction of the main road. I went over the whole place with my glasses, and the thought of what it must cost to heat it in winter made me shudder. The only sign of life was Herr Hesseltod.

I held him in the glasses for an hour and the sight of what he was doing cheered me up. He was repairing a patch of bad slatework on the roof of one of the higher towers on the wing facing me. He'd got three ladders; a long one from the ground up to a wide terrace on the fourth floor, another ladder up to a flat roof about twenty feet above this, and then a longer ladder up to the slope of the tower. To one side of the tower I could see part of a rounded dome, that looked like glass. It was clearly a great warren of a place where you could get lost in a maze of rooms. I had to get Katerina and Lottie out of the place as fast as possible, and I had to do it myself. If I went to the German police with my cock-and-bull story, I knew exactly where I would finish – in Sutcliffe's hands. He would already have taken care of that one.

I waited until Hesseltod had finished for the day, and then I went back down the road on my scooter and found the stream which ran out of the lake.

It came out through a culvert in a bank, with the wall two yards above it on a slope. It was a simple brick tunnel, about four feet high, and there was about six inches of water flowing down it. Ten feet up the tunnel was a wooden framework, latticed with barbed wire.

I drove five miles down the valley, bought myself a pair of pliers at a garage, and then went and had dinner at a *Gasthof.* Before I left I bought myself half a bottle of brandy, and a great length of sausage which I tucked away into my rucksack.

It was eleven o'clock when I went into the culvert. The barbed wire gave me no trouble. Beyond the wire the culvert ran for about twenty yards, and then I was out and into a small plantation of young spruce. I kept their cover up towards the *Schloss.* It was a night bright with stars and I could see the ladders still in position. I had now, too, a better view of the front of the place. There was a big gravelled forecourt held between the two wing arms. One or two lights showed in the far wing, and there was a light over the main door in the face of the centre block.

I sat in cover for a couple of hours across the lake until there was only one light burning in an upper window of the far wing. Then I made my way cautiously round the top end of the lake. When I was a hundred yards from the foot of the first ladder, I took off my shoes and hung them by the laces round my neck.

I'm not good at heights and I went up without looking down. Two-thirds of the way up the last ladder I stepped sideways from it on to a parapet top that protected the edge of the leaded roof flats from which the towers rose. I went exploring cautiously around the acres of leaded roof. There were four towers or pinnacles on my wing and one had a small door at roof level. On the inner side of the wing there was a thirty-foot drop to the roof run of the centre block. I found a piece of rusted iron rod lying on the leads and decided to tackle the tower door. I prised open the door and slid inside to pitch darkness. I then sat down with my back to the door and decided to wait until first light.

I was wakened by the sound of pigeons love-making on the roof outside. It was a quarter-past four. I was not prepared for the comfort which was awaiting me.

A little run of stone steps went down from the roof door to a narrow corridor. Dust was thick on the floor and bat and mouse droppings crunched under my feet. At the end of the corridor a door led into a small kitchen. It had a stone sink with a cold-water tap, rows of tarnished copper pans, and a small electric grill festooned with cobwebs. Beyond the kitchen was a hallway with a moth-eaten carpet, an antique armchair, a dower chest, and an oil-painting of some white-haired old boy in court dress.

Off the hall I found a bedroom with a fourposter, stripped of everything except the mattress and uncovered bolster. There was a sitting-room with an alcove at one end which was lined with shelves that held rows of leather-bound books. Around a small marble-fronted fireplace were a couple of settees and a chair. The walls, which were lined with leather and studded with copper-headed nails, were covered with oil-paintings, most of them dark and dirty. At the end of the hall were two doors. One led into a tiny bathroom and lavatory, and the other, which was locked from the outside, led out, I guessed, into the main body of the wing. I tried to look through the keyhole but it was blocked by the key on the other side. It wasn't hard to figure what kind of person had lived up here – some embarrassing old relative shoved out of the way and conveniently forgotten. As it stood at the moment, except for the dust, cobwebs and bat and mice deposits, it was all ready for occupation; water ran from the kitchen cold tap, the electric grill and lights worked, and there was water in the bathroom.

I cut myself a slice of sausage, drew a glass of water, and sat just back from the sitting-room window, looking down on to the front courtyard of the *Schloss*. At eight o'clock I heard Hesseltod overhead working on the roof and whistling contentedly.

I sat for four hours at the window, and a very interesting four hours they were.

The first person to appear in the courtyard was the old man who, I was pretty sure, was Professor Vadarci. He walked over to a wide, stone-rimmed bowl which was full of water. Through the glasses I could see goldfish and water-lilies. He spent some time fiddling with three or four big arc lamps set up around the pool. He was there for about ten minutes and then Madame Vadarci appeared. She was wearing a long white summer dress, one of her big floppy hats, and carrying a lace-bordered parasol.

She joined the Professor and they strolled over to the lakeside and sat down on a seat under a large weeping willow. The old man smoked and Madame Vadarci read a newspaper; a pair of simple, innocent people, enjoying the morning sun.

An hour later Siegfried appeared. He was wearing bathing trunks and white sandals and he joined them by the willow and did a few press-ups and back-flips. As he finished I saw Katerina come into the forecourt and walk towards the lakeside group. With her was another girl.

I put the glasses on them. Katerina was wearing a towelling tabard, and her head was bare, the blonde hair drawn tightly back from her forehead and caught at the nape of the neck with a ribbon. I got her face in profile and saw that she was laughing as she talked to the other girl. Katerina's blonde hair, the blue eyes, the firm suntanned skin, the way she walked and smiled, all made enchantment for me. I gave her half a minute's silent worship, didn't care if I was a damned fool about her, and then slid the glasses to the other girl. She was a shade taller than Katerina, blonde and she carried her bathing wrap instead of wearing it. She went across the gravel in a white bikini. It had to be Lottie Bemans.

When they joined the group, Siegfried came up to them and put an arm around each one's shoulders. I didn't care for that. He looked altogether too matey with both of them.

He talked to them both and pointed down the lake, explaining something. The girls tossed their wraps aside, kicked off their sandals and lined up on the bank. I saw him drop his hand and both girls went in with long, racing dives and they headed away down the lake like a couple of torpedoes. The edge of the window cut off part of my view of the lake. When they passed out of sight I saw that there was nothing to choose between them. They appeared, heading back, in about thirty seconds and now one of them had about a yard lead. I could not tell which one it was until she came into the lakeside and Siegfried reached down and gave her a hand ashore. It was Lottie, and I had her face full on, panting and laughing.

Katerina came out of the water unaided, and for a few moments was ignored. I didn't know how the elimination process was going to be worked – but she already had big competition from Lottie.

I turned away from the window, trying not to think of the Zafersee not many miles away. I took an angry swipe at a cushion that lay on the carpet. It exploded into a cloud of dust that got into my throat and sent me into the kitchen for water. When I came back the lakeside was deserted.

I beat some of the dust off the settee and stretched out on it.

After a while I realized that there was no tapping noise from the roof.

I went up, opened the door carefully, and slid out. Two or three pigeons went up indignantly from the leads. I walked over to the tower, and I realized at once that I had committed the cardinal sin of any military commander. I had failed to ensure my lines of communication with the rear. I was sitting on top of the *Schloss* with no way of getting down, except through the house. That snake Hesseltod had finished his job on the tower and the long ladder that had reached up to it was now lying on the lower roof twenty-five feet below me.

CHAPTER SEVENTEEN

THE KATERINA PHILOSOPHY

I couldn't tell how long I was going to be marooned in the suite and on the roof top, but, like a good castaway, the first thing I did was to carry out a much more thorough survey of my little double-decked island.

On the roof I found a plentiful supply of food. On a Pacific island it would have been seagulls and their eggs. Here, it was pigeons and their eggs. At least, I wouldn't starve.

I found drink, too, in the cupboard in the sitting-room. There were a couple of bottles of brandy and two unopened bottles of Rhine wine. Behind a silk screen to one side of some bookshelves in the sitting-room there was a glass door about four feet high with rows of drawers below it. It was a wall case and in it were a couple of hunting rifles and a twelve-bore shotgun. The drawers below held boxes of ammunition. At that moment my eye was caught by the title of one of the books on the shelf at my right hand.

The title of the book was *Les Crimes de l'Amour* by the Marquis de Sade. With it were *Justine* and *Philosophic dans le Boudoir.* And beyond these the whole row was taken by other authors . . . about thirty volumes of *erotica.*

I kept watch from the window but there was no more movement outside. As the sun went down I moved up on to the roof.

I didn't care a damn about all the political malarky involved around the girls. The people pushing it and the people trying to put a spoke in it wouldn't move an inch from their plans to accommodate a simple little human need like saving a beautiful girl from being dropped into a lake. That's how life was with the Sutcliffe, Malacod and Spiegel types. First things first. All I could think of was a helicopter flying low in the dark over the Zafersee and the weighted cargo being jettisoned.

I had to get in touch with Katerina, and that meant bursting out of the suite and taking my chance in the house. I had to get the girls out, and I might have to do it by force. For myself, I had the *Le Chasseur* – but it would be handy to have the girls armed. Katerina, I knew, could handle a gun.

As the darkness gathered over the bowl in the hills that held the place, I went down to the suite. There were thick velvet curtains in the sitting-room. I drew them and turned on the light.

I opened the gun-case and took out the shotgun. It was a twelve-bore, hammerless ejector gun by Cogswell and Harrison, a nice job, fitted with ornamental strengthening plates, and there was ammunition for it in one of the drawers below the case. The other two were German Walther rifles, one a ·404 that would stop an elephant, and the other a ·22 repeater. This last seemed a handier model to me. A ·22 slug can make a man think twice about coming on and, if that's all you need, there's no point in blowing his head off.

I put the two I had chosen on a table with their ammunition.

I shut the glass front of the case. It had a round brass knob as a handle. Maybe because it hadn't been opened for years, the door of the case stuck a little. To get it closed I pushed the handle hard, turning to the left as I did so, in order that the small lock tongue should not catch the lock casing until I had the door shut. The door went home into its frame with a jerk and I nearly fell over. The brass knob in my hand, held to the left, took another half turn and the whole gun-case moved away from me, hinging on its left like a door. I was staring into an aperture about four feet high and three feet wide. From the light behind me, I could see a narrow run of stone steps going steeply down for two or three yards and then the outline of another opening which looked about six feet tall and just wide enough to take a man who didn't carry too big a girth.

I stood there in the darkness, listening. A faint draught from the entrance funnelled up into my face. After a few moments I realized that on the draught there was coming to me the smell of frying onions.

I got my torch, and kept the beam well down to the ground. There was a thick layer of dust and mortar powder on the floor of the passageway. When I moved my arms just brushed the sides. After about twenty yards there was another drop down of six steps. Then the passage turned sharply and some yards ahead I saw a small patch of light striking across the passageway from left to right at about eye level. Switching off my torch I went quietly down to it.

I found myself looking through a small double-sided ventilator grille into a long, barely furnished room. The smell of onions and bacon was strong in my face.

It was probably originally the family schoolroom – there was a chalk-whitened blackboard fixed to the wall facing me. There were two iron beds, a deal trestle table, and a couple of whitewood cupboards. Near the door was a sink with a long draining board to one side and on this was a small electric ring. Standing at the ring, a frying-pan in hand, was a young man of about twenty-odd, his back to me, singing quietly to himself as he turned the onions and bacon in the pan. The table was set with a place for one. From a schoolroom it had now been turned into a barrack room. Hung on the wall between the beds was a sub-machine gun and a couple of pin-up photographs.

The young man turned away from the electric ring, came over to the table, and scooped his fry out on to a plate. He had very close-cropped sandy hair, wore a white singlet and black, tightly fitting breeches. He had his boots off with a right toe sticking through the grey wool of heavy socks. He had a pleasant enough face but was clearly tough, brawny, and a handy companion in a fight. He sat down and began to eat. Once he looked straight up at the ventilator grille, chewing reflectively, a far-away look in his eyes. Maybe he had a girl in some distant village and was wondering why she hadn't written.

I moved on. But now, I kept the torch beam dead in front of my feet. If this passageway did the round of the upper rooms in the *Schloss*, I didn't want any of my torchlight shining through the ventilator of an unlighted room. That could have caused trouble if anyone were inside lying awake and counting sheep.

This secret passageway had clearly been put in when the *Schloss* was built. One way and another I had a fair picture of the kind of fun that had appealed to the past owners of the *Schloss*.

The next patch of light was round a corner and about thirty yards farther on. It was the same arrangement, a ventilator grille, double-sided, and through it I had my first really good look at Lottie Bemans.

It was a pleasant little boudoir type bedroom, all hanging drapes and frills around the dressing-table, and bows of ribbon worked into the lace curtains that hung from a *baldacchino* affair over a small four-poster bed.

Lottie Bemans was lying in bed, reading by the light of a small bedside lamp. She had her blonde hair piled up in a sort of Grecian fashion on top of her head and her shoulders and arms were bare except for the thin straps of a silk nightdress. She was a good looker, but her face was longer and, in repose, more serious and intelligent than Katerina's. She was reading a magazine and smiling now and then to herself. It was a nice smile.

I moved on, hoping that I could find Katerina's room. I tried to keep in mind the twists and turns of the passageway. As far as I could judge, I had dropped down from the higher level of my wing and was now moving along the inner side of the centre block, with the bedrooms which faced the front courtyard on my left. Both ventilator grilles had been on my left.

I moved forward slowly so as to make the least noise possible.

After another thirty odd paces, the passage turned, dropped four steps, and turned again. Ahead, there was a much bigger, hazier patch of light coming through low down and on my right hand.

It was an inset of ornamental grille work, about three feet long and two feet deep and I had to drop on one knee to look through it.

I was high up, right under the large glass dome which I had seen bulging up in the roof of the centre block. The glass was hung inside with an elaborate arrangement of purple lengths of silk. From hidden lights, a soft haze of blue light flooded down from the dome into a wide circular hallway whose floor was about a hundred feet below me.

The floor of the hall was covered with large black and white tiles. Most of the way around the sides of the hall ran a roofed-in cloistered walk, supported by marble pillars. From my view point I couldn't see any windows lighting it and there was only one main door, a tall, elaborately carved wooden affair with great iron hinges and ornamental work. Standing with his back to the door, facing the centre of the hall, was a young man who seemed the exact counterpart of the one I had seen frying onions, except that he was dressed for duty. He was hat-less, blond, wore a black silk shirt buttoned tightly up at one side of the neck, the sleeves ballooning a little, black breeches, black, heavy, Army-type boots, and cradled across his arms was a sub-machine gun. He was standing with his legs slightly apart, in an attitude of complete alertness and there was no movement from him.

In the centre of the hallway, raised up on a three-stepped marble platform, was a sort of catafalque affair about ten feet long, three feet wide and about two feet high. The whole thing was draped in a great black velvet covering that fell from splendid golden, pineapple shaped knobs at each corner. Three figures stood facing the catafalque on my side of the hall.

They were Professor Vadarci, Siegfried and Madame Vadarci. The two men were in dinner jackets. Madame Vadarci wore a long black dress, that left her great arms bare, and a double rope of pearls cascaded from her neck over the generous curve of her bosom almost to her knees. In one hand she held a great black plumed fan, wide open, and on top of her red hair was a little coronet affair made of pearls. The three of them just stood there, their heads bowed a little, and as still as statues. They said nothing, they did nothing but just stand there, and they stood there for a good five minutes.

Then suddenly a little silver-toned bell rang gently somewhere and they moved to the great door. The guard came to life, stepped aside, and swung half of the door open. They went out and the guard followed them. The door closed and I had the place to myself. My eyes popped again as below me the great catafalque began slowly to sink into the ground. It went down as though on a lift. When it was below the level of the marble dais, a sheet of black marble slid noiselessly across the hole, and no one would have suspected that there was anything below it. Coinciding with the movement of the marble slab back into place, all the lights went out. Somewhere there was a good stage manager who knew his stuff.

I found Katerina early the next morning. Her room was on the left, just before the turn and steps down to the length of passageway which held the ornamental grille above the hall.

On the way to it I passed five or six ventilators that gave on to empty rooms. It was much easier going with the daylight let into the passageway from them.

I picked out Katerina's room – which was much like Lottie's

– because I could hear her singing to herself. The sound was coming through a half-open door on the far side of the bedroom, from the noise of running water clearly a bathroom.

She came out after a few seconds, wearing a loose green silk dressing-gown. She sat down on the edge of the bed and began to roll on a pair of stockings. Watching her in those few seconds, I knew that there was nothing I wanted from the world except her. . . .

I swallowed the lump in my throat and rapped gently on the ventilator grille. She looked up. I rapped again and called quietly, "Katerina. . . ."

She looked towards the bedroom door and then back at the grille. I had to admire the coolness and the quick thinking. There wasn't a loose or sloppy reaction in her. She'd recognized my voice just from the one word.

I said gently, "Katerina. . . . Over here."

She got up from the bed and went to the door and locked it. You'd have thought that voices coming from ventilators were part of her daily routine.

She came back and stood where I could see her. As she looked up she was smiling, violet eyes wide, a delicious wrinkle line below the soft curve of her blonde hair.

"Darling. . . . Are you a ghost?"

I said, "If I could get in there you'd know I wasn't."

She shook her head. "You are mad to be in this place."

"Okay, but I'm here."

She put her finger tips to her lips and blew me a kiss. "Darling, I love you. You do such crazy things for me. Why?"

"I'll show you later. Listen to me now and—"

"Oh!" She put her hand to her mouth suddenly. "You watch me for long? You have seen me go to the bathroom without clothes?"

"Unfortunately, no. Now listen. I've got to get you out of here."

"But why? I like it here."

"That's because you don't know what's lined up for you or Lottie Bemans. One of you is going to be murdered."

"Murdered!"

I had her serious and listening then. Keeping my voice down I explained about the apartment and the key that was on the outside of the door. She had to get up there so that we could make our plans for a get-away.

"Don't say anything to Lottie yet. Do you think you can find the apartment?"

"I think so. I'll try." Her voice was shaky.

"Tonight. The moment it's dark."

She nodded, and then said, "You are sure about this? About this bad thing?"

"Absolutely and—"

I broke off as there came a couple of knocks on her door.

"Katerina!" It was a girl's voice.

Katerina looked up and motioned me to go. She blew another kiss.

The voice outside the door called, "Katerina. . . . *Schläfst du?*"

Katerina moved towards the door. As I drew back, I heard her call, "*Nein, ich schlafe nicht, Lottie. Ich komme.*"

I had enough German to cover that lot, and Lottie calling again, "*Das Frühstück ist fertig.*"

I went back to my own *Frühstück*: pigeons' eggs, and the last slice of my sausage. Katerina would make it. Between us we would work something out.

That day passed like water wearing away a stone, so slowly that the tension built up in me until I felt like some caged animal. I walked round and round the place, unable to settle for more than a few minutes at a time.

And then, at three o'clock that afternoon, I saw Howard Johnson and Herr Stebelson. I was on the roof with my field-glasses, taking a cautious look around the property. I swung the glasses across the far hillside in the direction of the main gate. There was a movement across an open space high up on the mountain.

Two men had just come out of a line of trees and were climbing, their backs to me. I held them in the glasses. They paused in the middle of the open space and turned, looking back at the *Schloss*. There was no mistaking Herr Stebelson, and then Howard Johnson turned full face into my field of vision. I slipped behind the edge of the tower wall and watched them through a gap in the parapet. It was a good thing I went into hiding for they both took out field-glasses and sat down, watching the *Schloss*. They stayed there for about half an hour and then they moved down and back into the trees and I lost sight of them.

Keeping in cover I went to the tower door and below. It was an interesting combination – Stebelson and Howard Johnson. It seemed likely that Stebelson, knowing now that he was not going to get any co-operation from Katerina, was selling out his Zafersee information to Frau Spiegel's group. It looked, too, as though he'd tumbled to the helicopter radius from the lake ... and the Lord knew what other information he had ... probably plenty. I hoped that he had had the good sense to insist on payment before he had handed over his goods.

Time, after that, dribbled away. Darkness came and I had some food. I smoked, had a drink, and I kept away from the erotic books. I sat with the door open into the little hallway so that I should hear her at the door.

She came at half-past ten. I heard the key turning in the lock and I was in the hallway as the door opened and she slipped in. She turned to me, held up a warning hand in silence, and put the key into the lock and carefully twisted it home. Then she turned right round and held out her arms.

It was like the burst of a great rocket filling the darkness of the sky with a sudden chrysanthemum blaze of light. Blonde hair, misty violet eyes, a simple little yellow frock and gold slippers, and her brown, bare arms reaching for me. I took her into my arms, kissed her, and held her. Then we were sitting together on the settee in the main room. I had her hands in mine and she was rubbing her cheek against the side of my neck, saying silly little things in German to me which I didn't need to have translated. Her lips moved to mine and it took me ages before I could force myself to come to the most important item on the agenda.

I got up and went and fixed a couple of brandies. I handed her one.

"Now listen," I said. "We're all in big trouble here and we've got to get out. You, Lottie and me."

"But why?"

"Never mind the whys for a moment. How is the only thing. So I want straight answers – and quickly. Just how closely are you watched or guarded?"

She sipped her drink, gave a little frown and said, "Too closely. Some parts of the house we cannot go. At night we sleep on the third floor and are locked in until morning."

"How did you get up here?"

"We can go up, to the higher floors. But not down. I have a terrible time finding this place."

"Why can't you go down?"

"There's a door at the top of the main stairway. The man Hesseltod has the key. He sleeps in a room by the door and unlocks it in the morning."

"Are you friendly with him?"

"We chat sometimes at night when we come up. Sometimes he asks Lottie and me to have a drink. He's nice. But why do you ask all this?"

"Never mind for the moment. I'll come to that. Could you slip something into his drink if I gave it to you? So that we could get his key?"

"Yes . . . yes, I think so. But not tonight. He sleeps already. Tomorrow night, yes."

I didn't like that. It meant passing another day in the place. But I had no choice.

"Darling, why you frown?"

"Because I don't want to have to wait until tomorrow night. However. . . ." I went over and sat down by her.

She put a hand on mine and said, "I don't understand all this. Why is it so dangerous for me and Lottie? We are not allowed to do some things – but we have been told that it will all be explained. That it is a good thing for us in the end."

As she spoke I was thinking, another day, a whole day, for things to go wrong. But there was no other way. We couldn't go down now, wake Lottie, explain things to her, and risk getting the key from Hesseltod as he slept. . . .

I said, "Okay. Then it's got to be tomorrow."

Katerina said, "You don't answer my questions. Why do we have to go?"

I said, "There are a lot of questions and a lot of answers to come. It looks as though we've got time on our hands so why don't we start at the beginning."

"That's what I want. How can Lottie or I be in danger?"

I said, "Let's leave that for a moment. And get this—" I put my hands on her shoulders and looked straight at her. "I want the truth from you. And don't pretend I've always had it in the past, because I haven't. Promise?"

She leaned forward and kissed me gently on the lips, and then said, "I promise."

"First of all. What was the exact set-up between you and

Stebelson? He's admitted that there was one, but that you've now gone back on it."

She was silent for a moment studying me. Then she said, "All right, I'll tell you. Stebelson works for Herr Malacod. You know this. Well, Malacod is interested in Madame Vadarci. Madame Vadarci is looking for girls, my age, blonde like me, strong, healthy, good at sports and intelligent. Also, they must be absolutely purest German blood, back for many generations. You know this is not so easy to find. Particularly, too, when the girls must be beautiful. I am beautiful, yes?"

"Yes. But get on with it."

She did. Malacod and Stebelson knew what Madame Vadarci was after. Stebelson had suggested to Malacod that he find a girl, that he fake her antecedents, birth, parentage and so on, and then bring her to the notice of Madame Vadarci without her knowing anything about him or Malacod.

"There is a man in Cologne, a friend of Stebelson, who worked on genealogical research for Madame Vadarci. Stebelson paid him money, he fixed papers for me, and then gave my name to Madame Vadarci – she came to England to find me in Brighton."

"You were a decoy?"

"Yes."

"And then they roped me in on the same tag – because they wanted someone to follow you and find out what Madame Vadarci was up to and where she was going?"

"Yes."

"And Lottie Bemans?"

"The same thing – only she is chosen before me without any faking."

"Aren't you German?"

"Of course – but my parents are dead. Nobody knows about them. So Stebelson and this man make up a whole family history for me."

"So you and Stebelson had an arrangement that if during all this something came up that might offer a quick profit – then you'd double-cross Malacod."

"In a way."

"But you've gone back on that. Why?"

"Because perhaps he wants to marry me."

"He?"

"That way I get better things than ever Stebelson can arrange."

"He," I said firmly. "Who is he?"

"Alois . . . the one here, the one you saw in Venice."

"What's his other name?"

"Vadarci – he was adopted by them."

"But you must know why Lottie's here. He's going to choose between the two of you. He might choose Lottie."

"Perhaps – but perhaps it will be me. So, I finish with Stebelson."

"And what's behind all this? Bringing you and Lottie here secretly? And this big case, the lead affair – I saw it go into the helicopter at the Villa Sabbioni and you went with it. You must know about that."

"No. Truly. They promise we shall know soon. But they swear us to secrecy, Lottie and me. Both of us will get many good things."

"One of you might. Whichever is chosen. The other, no matter what she's sworn or what she expects, is going to be killed, dropped in a lake and never seen again. That's why I'm here. That's why I've got to get both of you away fast!"

"Oh, no!" She was really shaken.

"Oh, yes. You've both got to get out of this place. There's no profit here for anyone, you, me, Stebelson, or anyone. There's something, too big for you or me to handle, cooking here. What about all these guards?"

"All this we are promised to have explained."

"And you've accepted all this?"

"Why not? They are good to us. Maybe something nice comes from it."

I looked at her hard then. She had promised me the truth. I seemed to be getting it. But how could I know with a girl who was so sure of herself, so much herself, her own mistress, that you could never tell what was going on inside her beautiful blonde head?

I said, "What does Lottie think about all this?"

"Sometimes she says she is frightened."

"But you aren't?"

"No."

"I wonder. You chucked Stebelson. You did that from Venice. But you kept me coming along. Why – if you thought you might end up marrying this Alois?"

She took her time over answering, smiling at me.

"Because I love you – truly, I do. I want you near."

"But if you married this type? What then?"

"I have plenty of money. I travel. And we could see each other. You and me. Have little good times together."

"You think I'd stand for that?"

"Maybe you would. Why not? For me, nothing is black and white. I don't say *Yes*, I don't say *No*, until the last moment. How can I tell what I will do tomorrow until it comes? You are not like that?"

She sat there as pretty as a pin-up and said it, laying out the whole Katerina philosophy and expecting me to go along with it.

"For God's sake," I said, "don't you ever think about anyone else? If you marry Alois, then Lottie gets dropped into a lake! You'd know about that. You couldn't keep that secret as the price of marrying him. Could you?"

For a moment she hesitated, and then she shook her head.

"No. But I did not know all this. You sound so angry."

"Well, you know now. And I'm getting both of you out of here.

There's big and dangerous trouble behind it all. Get that into your head! It's big enough to have people like Malacod spending money to ferret it out, and others spending government money. If it suited the book, both you and Lottie could finish up in the lake." I stood up, and I was angry, angry because I was afraid for her and Lottie, and also because of what she had said about me, that I would have accepted the "little good times together" if she had married this Alois.

"Darling, I like you when you get angry."

I pulled her up to me, holding her tightly by the shoulders.

"From the moment I saw you on that pier I knew exactly what I wanted. From now – if it takes the rest of my life – I'm going to knock some sense into you. Do you understand?"

I shook her shoulders a little. She nodded her head slowly, and my arms went round her, holding her, and it was at this moment that I heard the sound of the helicopter.

It roared overhead as though all the girders were falling out of heaven, and the window-panes rattled until I thought they were going to crack.

I let Katerina go, ran across the room and switched off the small table-lamp that was burning, and then went to the window. I jerked the curtain partly aside.

In the courtyard below, the lights around the ornamental water basin were turned on and pointed upwards. I was just in time to see the great clumsy dragonfly affair swing in from the lake, hang poised, racketing and whirring, and then drop gently to the gravel. The moment it touched the ground the lights went out. The motors died and there was the quick movement of people passing, shadowy and vague, across the gravel.

Close behind me, Katerina said, "That is the way I come here. Lottie also. Inside the helicopter you see nothing because the windows are covered. We do not know where we are; though we guess Austria or Germany. Also, tonight we are told there is a special conference and not to mind the noise of the helicopter."

"Special conference?"

I saw the great hall with its velvet catafalque and the dim blue lighting. Because I had a memory stuffed like a jackdaw's nest with odds and ends, I remembered a book I had read, and knew then that one's mind never knocks off working, clicking away quietly in the subconscious. Alois. Had it been Alois? Yes, I was sure it had.

I turned and looked at Katerina, and I was thinking that the whole thing was just too fantastic for words.

CHAPTER EIGHTEEN

THE ASHES OF ATONEMENT

We went to the conference. I took Katerina with me along the ventilator passage to the large grille that looked down into the main hallway. She looked through and then turned back to say something to me. I put my hand gently over her mouth. Acoustics could be tricky right up under a dome. Crouched behind the grille Katerina and I could hear every word that was said without any difficulty.

The great door to the hall was shut and both guards were on duty, standing one each side of it, sub-machine guns cuddled across their arms, their black silk shirts fresh pressed and their boots shining . . . stirring memories from old newsreels and documentaries.

Since I had last seen the place two rows of gilt chairs had been placed between the door and the marble platform. There was no sign of the catafalque. Under the cold blue light that drifted down from the heavy hanging silks of the dome a cold, unearthly atmosphere of fantasy seemed to possess the place.

Standing at the foot of the marble platform were Professor Vadarci and Alois Vadarci. The professor was dressed in an ordinary lounge suit, but Alois was in the same rig as the guards. Instead of a sub-machine gun for a weapon, I noticed, he had a dagger with an ornamental handle tucked into the top of his breeches. In his hand was the whip I had seen in Madame Vadarci's room.

Sitting on the chairs were about ten men; with them was Madame Vadarci, swathed in black silk, gently pluming her fan in front of her face. They were mostly middle-aged, and a couple were well over sixty. The youngest one there, I guessed, was Manston. He sat at the end of a row, monocle screwed into one eye, one hand toying with its black silk cord, and wearing a well-cut suit of soft tweed. He was listening to what Alois was saying and nodding gently to himself in approval. I knew then that under the cover of being Sir Alfred Coddon, K.B.E., C.V.O. – who had certainly been put away for the time being in ice-cold iron-bound storage – he had worked his way into the centre of the web by a direct route. His only trouble would be that, although he sat now in the centre, he would not know its location on the map. The Vadarcis and their helicopter made that security tight. Next to Manston sat the white-haired old boy with the tin leg whom I had seen at the Chalet Papagei. He had his thick walking-stick between his legs and was leaning forward, resting his chin on it, his eyes never leaving Alois. Malacod had had the same idea as Sutcliffe – a personal representative straight to the unknown centre.

As for the rest of the bunch, they all looked prosperous, hard-bitten types who had long ago worked things out and knew just how to handle the delicate and complicated business of getting the most out of life for themselves. You could tell it from their good clothes, the silk shirts, the polish on their hand-welted shoes . . . from the way they sat, almost from the way they breathed. They understood about men and employing them, about deals and swinging them, about compromises, and profits . . . about nice, clean commercial murders, and the way to push them out of mind and conscience when they went back to the bosom of their families. I didn't have a moment's thought that they might be here simply because they enjoyed playing at secret societies or being members of archaic guilds with elaborate rituals. They were here on business. They were the kind of men who often employed me.

I put out my hand and held Katerina's. It was good to have her beside me. It was going to be good to take her out of this fantasy and keep her by me for good . . . or, at least, for as long as I could.

Alois was speaking in English but after each few sentences he would stop and then translate his words into German, pause, and then give it all again in French.

Alois was saying—

"Until now, all of you – and scores of others who are not here tonight – have been approached individually. All of you are trusted and influential members of our party. Not from Germany alone – but from other countries where, when the moment of trial comes, your support will be invaluable. You are men, too, who, in the past, when you have seen change coming, have known how to accommodate yourselves and your interests to the change. . . ." He paused, went into his translation act, and then went on: "At some stages of a party's development it is wiser to talk obliquely, leaving wise men to read between the lines. But tonight a direct statement is going to be made."

He had a good strong voice, spoke well, and standing there, blond hair shining, a blue sheen running like liquid metal over his black shirt, he was a commanding figure.

"The *Sühne Partei* at the moment – and I admit it frankly – is nothing. It is a wishy-washy organization for doing good. The world is crammed with similar organizations. But ours has one difference. The day is coming when it will be given its true birth, its true strength, which will make it a power in Europe, and in the rest of the world. No great party can run on logic alone. It must have a great dream behind it, a splendid promise ahead of it, and a soul, and a legend to defend."

He was a great talker, and he had them hanging on every word.

"You are all men of different countries, men of influence in commerce, industry, the law. Let us be frank, you are men who control politicians, men whose activities are only nominally subject to government because you are the government. When you go from here you will take with you a secret knowledge, the certainty of an inevitable development. You have pledged yourselves, and I have pledged myself, to one end – a new Europe. In a very few days we shall have our rally – from that moment forward there will be no turning back. I have only one dream – the reunification of my country; complete, unshackled national reunification. Soon this hand will put the match to the powder, and thenceforth every hour of my life will be dedicated to one end."

He paused, one hand held aloft.

Beside me Katerina whispered, "What is it all about?"

I put my lips to her ear, kissed it, and then whispered back, "Maybe he wants to knock down the Berlin wall."

"So. . . ."

I smiled to myself. It was a good comment.

As Alois's hand dropped, Manston spoke.

He said, "None of us here, I am sure, have any argument with what you have said. We all, too, can see the difficulties involved – unless these facts you promise are entirely beyond question. Even then, there will be attempts to discredit them."

Alois said sharply, "The facts are incontrovertible. When they are presented at the rally – then no one in Germany will doubt them."

Manston said, "Could we have the facts?"

I don't think Alois liked being rushed. After all, this was his big scene. He frowned. Then without a word he went up one step of the marble platform. Somewhere the stage manager must have picked up his cue. The black marble slab at the top slid aside and slowly the draped catafalque rose from the ground. Beside me I heard Katerina's breath sigh in surprise.

Alois said flatly, without emphasis, "I have to tell you that I am the son of Adolf Hitler."

It knocked Katerina. I felt her grab my arm, the fingers biting home.

Nobody in the hall batted an eyelid. I would have given a lot to know Manston's thoughts. The only reaction from him was to take his monocle out and slowly polish it on a silk handkerchief.

"By whom?" It was said in German and I didn't need the translation, and the voice of the old boy who spoke was as unemotional as though he were making an office query. They were a tough lot and they had to be. Each of them ran a full stable of political and industrial horses and they knew all about nobbling and fixing and ringing.

"My mother was Eva Braun. Before you leave here, you will each be given a statement, drawn up by Professor Vadarci, setting out all the facts and dates, and also photostatic copies of all the relevant documents and certificates, including a statement made in writing by my father, signed by Eva Braun in the presence of two witnesses, both of whom are still alive, and whose affidavits are also attached. After our rally these facts will be made public."

A bald-headed man wearing a black stock with a large pearl-headed pin in it said, "*Votre jour et lieu de naissance?*"

Alois said, "The Bergof, Obersalzberg, the 16th June, 1942. The birth was kept secret. I was named after my grandfather, Alois Hitler. I am the only child and was, of course, legitimized by the marriage of my father to Eva Braun in 1945. For reasons of state at the time of the birth, and ultimately for dynastic and political reasons at the time of the collapse of the Third Reich, clearly foreseen by my father, the birth and my existence were never made public. I was placed in the care of Professor Vadarci, and was brought up under his name."

He went on, "All the evidence is set out incontrovertibly in the statement. If this is contested, the people involved, who are still living, are prepared to come forward. Let it not be forgotten that in our people there was and there still is a loyalty to the Third Reich and to my father which he alone commanded and which, at his death, became mine to command."

Manston crossed one leg over the other, and said in a mild voice, "He is incontestably dead?"

"Yes."

"And Martin Bormann?"

"I am not at liberty to answer that question." He began to speak very deliberately now, translating after each few sentences. "There are only two pertinent facts – I am my father's son, and my father is dead. As for my father's death you will also be given the full facts before you leave here. I do not propose to go into them now, or to discuss the validity of the evidence of people like Guensche, Linge, Rattenhuber, Baur or Mengerhausen, names which will be familiar to you if you have taken any interest in those last days in the Chancellery Bunker. The facts are set down for you to examine and test. Much more pertinent is the importance that was placed on the identification and whereabouts of my father's body. The Russians were the only people who were in a position, during the months of May and June 1945, to establish these. Let me remind you that, in early June, they first said that the body had been recovered and identified with fair certainty. A few days later Marshal Zhukov, in a public statement to the Press, described the last days in the Chancellery – but on the vital question of the death and the whereabouts of the body he said, 'The circumstances are very mysterious. We have not identified the body of Hitler. I can say nothing definite about his fate'. Later, in September, they were openly accusing the British of harbouring my father and my mother somewhere in their zone of Germany. And Stalin himself assured people like the American Secretary of State at the Potsdam Conference that he believed Hitler to be alive and probably in Spain or the Argentine. From those days to these, governments and private individuals have talked, written about, and investigated this mystery. And the purpose behind it is very clear. No government ever found the body. But every government which had fought the Third Reich wished to know him dead. They wanted nothing left on which myth or legend could be built, no relics, no pilgrimages, no proof even that he died a soldier's death, at his own hand, with a soldier's weapon, rather than surrender. It is for this reason that it has been said that he poisoned himself, a coward's refuge. My father shot himself."

He paused, breathing hard. And he had reason. It was some performance.

Suddenly he raised the whip aloft, and went on, "Let it be frankly understood – my father died a soldier's death, but he was a tyrant! It is not the Third Reich we wish to bring back – but a new Germany, a new Europe. My father's death ended a tyranny. But when tyranny is done, there comes atonement. The atonement of a whole people, the demand of a people to be whole again, to seek their true destiny, their true greatness against odds no matter how great. And it is then that they demand the myth, the holy relic, the reminder of greatness, the shrine on which can be focused the memory of a black past and from which they can draw the strength for a glorious future. Be assured then that I, the returning son, shall give to the people of Germany the shrine they need, the tyrant soldier dead, the fires of oppression now turned to the ashes of atonement. This I promise to do. This I can do – for that shrine is here. Here is the body of my father!"

He stepped a little aside and turned to the catafalque. I felt Katerina shiver beside me, but whether it was from cold, excitement or fear I did not know.

The stage manager took over again and the velvet drapes slid away from the catafalque, revealing a large glass case. As the curtains fell away, lights came on inside the case.

He was lying there, raised on a small gold bed, dressed in full uniform.

I crouched there with Katerina and we watched them. Each man got up, one at a time with no rush, slowly, almost as though each were bowed with some great, unseen burden which they knew they would have to carry for a long time. Each man went up to the catafalque, looked, walked around it, and then went back to his gilt chair. And while it all went on the guards stood at the door, staring over the heads of the men, over the top of the catafalque, soldiers on duty, remote, but alert, crystallized by their last orders, waiting until the next should set them in motion.

I remembered Malacod saying to me about politicians, "Expediency is the only god they acknowledge." The rally at Munich in a few days' time would put a bomb under the table of every cabinet room in the world. Vadarci knew what he was talking about in *Stigmata*. "Atonement could be as good a rallying cry as 'Death to all infidels!' I knew then, too, why Manston and my friend with the tin leg had worked their passage into this company, understood why Howard Johnson and Frau Spiegel had been set on this trail. The news had leaked, but there wasn't one security service that trusted another. They all wanted the same thing – to stop any shrine being set up. But they each worked separately for fear that, at the last moment, if one were successful in laying hands on the catafalque, then a moment of expediency might intervene, destruction of the body be delayed, maybe, even the shrine set up, for some suddenly burgeoning political advantage. And Malacod – he was a Jew. German Fascism, Atonement Party, Neo-Nazism . . . the whole list of names only echoed other names right back through the ages, and he had seen the danger to his people, and now worked on his own account, bent on destruction of the shrine, just as the others were, but trusting none of them.

Down below Alois was talking again. Now, he was interrupted

by question after question, as he set out the details of the way the body of Hitler had been taken from the Chancellery Bunker, the trail confused, the body embalmed and hidden. . . . The sound of the voices washed into my ears. I listened, fascinated, and knew – as though I hadn't before – that the witness men give can never be truly checked.

But two things I knew without needing cast-iron proof; the body in that case was not Hitler's, and Alois was no son of Hitler. Some things in life you know by instinct. The mind computes and rejects and then closes firm against the alien touch of a too bizarre probability, like a sea anemone prodded with a stick. If the whole thing was not a fake, then grass was really blue and the sky green and no one had noticed it so far.

Not that any of this mattered a damn. Professor Vadarci – it had to be him – had spared no expense to make the fake seem genuine, all the authentic proofs laid out in a row, and the body of some unknown, maybe one of Hitler's old doubles, stretched out in uniform, and the whole package deal sold to Alois years and years ago when his voice began to break and the first hairs appeared on his chest. Alois believed. Watching him, listening to him made that clear. It really was a work of art – and Manston, by God, had said just that.

Put this masterpiece on exhibition at the Munich rally and trouble would spread from it. People would believe what they wanted to believe – so long as you could give them an inflammatory rallying cry, sell them a phoney relic . . . anything that would sanctify the course that in their hearts they wanted to follow. It was the biggest fake of all time, and Vadarci was going to get away with it if he could last out until he got his travelling circus to Munich.

I took Katerina's arm.

"Come on," I said. It was like getting a tight cork from a bottle. I had to tug to get her to move.

And all the way back to the apartment, I was asking myself – if this thing had leaked, as it had to Sutcliffe, to Spiegel's lot, and to the Jew Malacod, why hadn't it got to Bonn? It wasn't like them to miss the smell of drains in their own backyard.

CHAPTER NINETEEN

LOVE IS THE STRANGEST THING

In the apartment, Katerina kept walking restlessly up and down, and there was a faint hysterical note in her voice, as she kept asking, "What does this mean?" and then not listening as I tried to explain. In the end I grabbed her by the arm and made her sit on the settee alongside of me.

"Just stay here," I said, "and listen. I told you this thing was too big for either of us to look for a profit in it. And so it is. Just let's get the hell out of this."

"You think this thing will happen at Munich?"

"Yes. All the men down there know it. They know what's coming now, and they'll begin to make their dispositions, to work out new alignments."

"I don't understand."

"A lot of people have suspected what was in the wind. All they want really is to suppress it. That's what they've been after. To find this place and then grab Alois and the body and destroy both – and never a word of it ever leaking out. At least two of the men in that crowd, I know, are there for just that purpose. Now they've got some sort of a fix on this place, we've got to get out before the real action begins!"

She looked at me intently for a moment, her violet eyes wide, excited.

"You know this?"

"Yes. And maybe Alois does. I'm sure he won't take any chances. He's too clever for that. The moment these men go, he'll clear everything out of here to some new hiding-place. Anyway, we've got to go – and quickly. Lottie, you and me."

"But we can't before tomorrow night."

"Let's hope that's soon enough. Here—" I pulled out Frau Spiegel's little silver case and handed it to Katerina.

"What is this?"

"There are some pills inside. Tomorrow evening you make sure that Hesseltod offers you a drink. Can do?"

She nodded, smiling, her eyes shining.

"These knock him off?"

"Out. Not off. One will fix him for an hour – and that's all we need. Wait for him to keel over, take his key, and then come up here for me. And don't explain anything to Lottie until Hesseltod goes under. Clear?"

She nodded. "I think so. But my head, it goes round and round with all this." Then she leaned forward and kissed me lightly on the lips. "You are a clever one. Always so clever. You saved me from marrying this Alois, from getting mixed up in this big business."

"It's big. And I saved you."

"And now there's nothing we can do until tomorrow night?"

I stood up, and pulled her up to me. "I wouldn't say that."

She smiled, then kissed me, and her arms went tightly around me. When she let go of me I nearly fell over.

I said, "We've had a hard evening. Time for a nightcap and then bed."

"There is a bed here?"

"In the other room. No sheets or blankets."

"What for we want those?"

She walked across the room to the bedroom door and opened it and looked in. I went to the cupboard and fixed us both a brandy.

She came back to me. I stood there with a glass in each hand and she came close up to me and touched my lips with hers. Then she laughed and took the drinks from me and said, "You go first."

I went into the bedroom, flopped on to the bed, and kept my

eyes on the open doorway which was lighted from the small lamp in the room beyond.

I heard her kick off her shoes, and I imagined I could hear the fall of her dress. After a few seconds, she came to the doorway. Her loose hair fell, glistening and smooth, about her neck, and she was naked, the light behind her touching the silhouette of her hips and arms and the long run of her firm legs with a faint silvery outline, and my throat was suddenly dry and parched.

She came over to the bed, holding the two glasses in her hand, and I said, "For God's sake, give me a drink."

She laughed, keeping her distance from me, and handed me a glass, and she said, "I am beautiful. You see me in the doorway?"

"I see you in the doorway. I'll see you like that all my life. Pack up the sun, the moon and the stars and put them in cold storage. I don't need them. You're all I want now and for ever." I raised the glass and drank deeply to her, and she raised her glass and drank to me.

She said, "It is nice, the thing you say. You always say such things to me?"

"Always."

This was no moment for a man to waste valuable time in drinking. I drained the glass hurriedly. "Come here."

She put her glass down on the bedside table. I don't know what I did with mine. It went overboard somewhere. I put out my hands and she came down to me, smooth and cool, like a dream coming true. She lay, naked and eager, in my arms, and her lips were suddenly hard and hungry against my own, and my hands on the freedom of her body were burning and impatient so that she broke from me after a moment and said softly, "We don't rush, no? There is so much of the night left. So many hours. . . . Darling. . . ."

She raised herself on one elbow and bent and kissed me with a warm, soft passion. I felt her fingers slip the buttons of my shirt

and then her hand moving across my breast. All I could see was
the outline of her blonde hair haloed against the far door light –
and then the halo broke and shimmered, became blurred, and
danced in a crazy way before my eyes. I put one hand up to caress
the proud, firm curve of her breasts. Suddenly, my hand floated
away from me, a million miles away, and my senses began to rock
and swim, darting in and out of consciousness like a trout in a
mountain stream, out of light into shadow. . . .

She slipped off the bed and stood at its side looking down at
me, and I was powerless to move. But as my mind slid across a
sunlit stretch of shallow water, I was calling myself all the names
under the sun. Knocked out by my own pills. . . . No, by Spiegel
pills. . . . Spiegel pills. . . . Why hadn't I worked it out properly?
This was her whole philosophy. Wait and see where the profit
lies. Maybe she had meant to go away with me, but an hour's
teutonic peep-show had changed her. She was German . . .
German, blonde, beautiful, chosen to be the bride of Alois Hitler
. . . . The myth had taken her, possessed her, her eyes were dazzled
with the golden future . . . and it would be the same for thousands
of others.

I struggled to get off the bed, but nothing would work. I went
in and out of consciousness, each time going deeper and taking
longer to come back. Once she was in the room, then gone, and
then back again; and this time she held her dress in her hand and
began to slip it on and she was speaking from far away. . . .

"I am sorry, darling. . . . Sorry for you. You are so nice and
exciting . . . but not enough for Katerina. . . ."

I tried to speak, just to call her a bastard, but all I managed was
a grunt. She leaned over me and kissed me on the forehead and
then was gone . . . and I went too, but some hazy, crazy dream
carried on, mixing me up and playing ducks and drakes with reality.
I was back again, watching through the dome grille, listening to

Alois talking away, explaining those last days in the Bunker . . .
telling how the body was taken away . . . names, names, that meant
little to me but would to others . . . of Johannmeier, Lorenz,
Zander, and Hummerich, and others, making their way to the
Havel lake . . . of a Junkers 52 seaplane that didn't pick them up,
and then of another . . . of the body being shipped aboard, of men
being abandoned, killed . . . the trail obscured, and the long flight
over a disorganized Europe to the Adriatic, to some Vadarci retreat,
long established . . . of embalming, secrecy, men being killed to
iron-clad the secrecy . . . and the questions, hard, probing, coming
from the men assembled under the unearthly blue light of the dome
. . . lies and deceit and even then, so many years back, the planning
beginning for this moment. . . . Then, the whole dream did a
sickening whirl-about. I heard myself gasping and choking as I
began to take the long back slide down into unconsciousness,
fighting against the slippery slope. My eyes opened for a moment,
and the last craziness came upon me – for I could have sworn that
Howard Johnson stood at the bedside and said, "Bad luck, lover-
boy – you really bought it. King-sized and gift-wrapped. . . ."

There were four of them in the room. It was a little study affair,
book-lined, cosy, deep leather armchairs, and on a marble mantelshelf an elegant French ormolu clock that said half-past two. That
had to be in the morning because the curtains were drawn and the
lights were on. I'd been out about two hours. I was sitting in a swivel
chair behind a low, walnut-veneered desk. There was a big bowl of
gladioli on the desk. My head was pulsating like a chrysalis about
to let out the biggest butterfly ever seen by man.

Madame Vadarci was there, fan waving, and – always something new from that source – smoking a cigar, probably to steady
her nerves. Katerina was there in her yellow dress and gold shoes.
I glared at her. Professor Vadarci was there, his face screwed up,

as though he was sucking on a sour sweet, and he had a gun in his hand which I recognized as my *Le Chasseur*. And Alois was there black shirted and breeched, dagger still stuck in the top of his belt. He had a whip in his hand, and I'd seen the whip before, in Paris, a fancy affair with an ivory-banded gold grip. Greek key pattern on the leather stock and a long, four foot thong.

I was sitting, unbound, free as air, behind the desk, and for the third time I said, "There must be *some* aspirin in this place *somewhere*."

And for the third time Alois pulled his fancy trick. The whip flicked in his hand and the long thong curled out and took a bloom from a gladioli spike four inches from my nose. He was no flower lover.

He said, "Answer the question."

I said, "I can't remember what it was. Headache, you know."

Alois looked at Professor Vadarci and the old boy scratched his chin, and then said, "All right. We will come to an understanding with you. All the visitors are still here. You just name the two you know. After that you stay here for a few days and then we let you go. You and Fräulein Lottie Bemans. We give our word for this."

"I want aspirin, not promises."

Alois was angry then. I saw his mouth tighten and this time the whip snaked and the tip of the thong took me across the side of the neck. There was a heavy silver cigarette lighter on the desk. I picked it up and slung it at him, hard. He was some number, reflexes and eyesight A1 at Lloyd's. He must have moved, because I was dead on target. His hand came up – left, too – and caught the lighter at baseball speed. It came back, not at me, but at the vase which shattered like a bomb going off. Cold water surged across the desk and swamped my knees, and my arms held a couple of flower spikes so that I must have looked like some pantomime sprite arising from a pond. Alois smiled then.

He said, "All right, we do it the hard way."

I said, "You can do it any way you like. But don't expect me to take anything on promise. You don't mean to let anyone go, me, Lottie, or anyone else."

"I'm sure he would."

It was Katerina.

I gave her a hard look. It didn't ruffle her, so I decided to try something that might.

I said, "Katerina, here, sees herself as Frau Katerina Hitler. You know, of course, that her whole pedigree has been faked? You're not getting yourself a pure Aryan bride. Take my advice, drop Katerina in the lake and hitch up with Lottie."

It was all right saying it, but the ache for her was still there, an ache that no aspirin would ever touch. You can't escape it. You can try and kill it with words, but you hate yourself for it, and your stupid little heart and mind always long for a second chance.

Alois said, "She has proved herself tonight. That is all the pedigree I need."

If I couldn't make a dent in Katerina, maybe, I thought, I could in him. A little family trouble might take some attention away from me.

I said, "Pedigrees in this establishment are cheap enough. Professor Vadarci sold you a phoney one years ago after he'd picked you from some orphanage or refugee camp. You're no more the son of Hitler than I'm the son of Tarzan."

Alois didn't even look towards Vadarci. His whip hand went back and I got the full blast across the side of my neck, followed by the single word, "Swine!"

I bit my lip, and then I gave him the second barrel. "You're nobody's son. Strictly nobody's from nowhere. And that poor old mummy out in the hall, pumped full of embalming juice, never came within a hundred miles of being your ever-loving daddy. Why don't you grow up fast, give up the amateur theatricals, and get yourself a job as a P.T. instructor? A good honest job."

He heard me through, every word, and I could see Professor Vadarci smiling faintly, confident, because he knew that he had only to show the boy a hoop for him to jump through it like one of Pavlov's dogs, and Madame Vadarci looking bored, and then I got the whip again in the same place, but this time he said nothing.

As I jerked back in my chair from the blow, Madame Vadarci took her cigar from her mouth and flicked ash on to the floor.

She said, "I am bored with these playactings, and this foolish talk. It will be light soon and our guests must go, or be kept for another day. That would be unwise. Also, Alois, after this, we must move quickly. So . . ."

She put the cigar back and gave it a hearty suck, puffed smoke, and fanned it away with her ostrich plumes.

I said, "Fat Mamma's got a point there."

The whip flashed out and I took it on the other side of the neck.

"Be respectful, please," said Alois.

I noticed then that Katerina's eyes were shining. Not the way I had ever seen them shine before for me. Usually, for me, they were misted, and soft. Now they glittered, hard, bright amethysts; and she was breathing a little quickly so that I could see the press of her breasts against her dress. She was enjoying the whip work, enjoying the whole situation. All this was for her, this excitement, this precipice walking, the promise of a rich future . . . and it was really bringing her alive, every sensation double-edged.

Alois said, "All right. We make him speak." He looked at me. "Move!"

The whip thong half curled itself around my shoulders, biting through the thinness of my shirt. I moved, not too fast, but I moved. It was common sense.

As I went out of the door after Alois, Katerina stood aside for me to pass. For a moment we were very close together. I could have slapped at her, found some words to try and wound her, but I didn't. She looked at me, through me, and I knew that already I had ceased to exist for her. The shine was still in her eyes and she was deep in the trance that had come upon her at some moment as we had crouched together behind the grille.

They were all in the great domed hallway still. They all turned as I was led in and it was obvious that they had already been alerted that something had gone wrong. Not a word was said by anyone as the two guards took me by the arms and led me to one of the pillars that supported the low sort of cloistered walk that ran right around the hall. I was pushed against the outer side of the pillar. My wrists and ankles were tied, and the ropes taken round the column and fastened. I stood there, my head free and to one side, so that I looked into the centre of the hall where the catafalque was still on its dais, lights blazing. All I could see of its occupant were the soles of a pair of brand new military boots, yellow, unsoiled.

In a ragged half circle to one side of the gilt chairs stood the guests. Manston and the man with the tin leg were at one end, and Manston was watching me with a little frown on his forehead and I knew that already he must have made up his mind. Nothing would come from him. I might crack and name him, but he would do nothing first to save me. That I might name him he must already have accepted as a possibility. He would be concerned now with his own moves. I had no quarrel with that. He had a job to do – and I had been dismissed, told to keep out of the way, and I had broken the rules. I always broke them somewhere, and then paid. But this time I was setting up a record.

Alois and his group stood a few yards from me, and Alois, when I was bound, turned to the men and said in a calm flat voice—

"This man was discovered in the house. He has worked, or is still working, for the British Secret Service. On his own admission he has stated that there are two men amongst you who work for the same or comparable organizations of other governments. These men – unlike the rest of you – are here in bad faith, planning to destroy me and all I work for. I do not intend either of these men to leave here alive. This man is going to be whipped until he names them." He smiled for a moment. "I don't expect any chivalry, but since, in the end, he will speak, and no one leaves here until he does, it would save time and unpleasantness if the two men revealed themselves." He paused, looking at them, and then when there was nothing but silence, he said, "No? Well, then we must do it the hard way."

The whip in his hand, thong gathered neatly into the right palm against the butt, was held out towards Katerina.

"You. Give him the first dozen."

I saw Katerina hesitate for the merest fraction of a second, so slight that it was like the flick of a swallow passing. Then she took the whip. Whatever she thought, she was still under trial with him. She knew it, too.

She came round behind me and I lost sight of her, but I heard her speak to one of the guards.

"*Das Hemd!*"

A hand went to the back of my neck and my shirt was ripped away from my back in two pieces. I was bitter and bloody-minded. If I ever walked out of this place, I told myself, and she was around, I'd get her. No matter how much I loved her, I would get her. . . . All I wanted for her was some great humiliation. I longed for it so much that I scarcely felt the bite of the first lash across my back.

But I felt the second and the third. I couldn't stop my body jerking, and had to bite at my lower lip to keep back sound. She didn't hurry, and, by God, she could handle a whip. Alois couldn't fault her on that.

I yelled at the seventh stroke. There was now a sweaty haze across my eyes, through which I could see Manston watching me, monocle still in place, face untouched by any emotion. Beside him the man with the tin leg sat in a chair, his eyes on me.

After the eighth stroke, Alois said:

"Enough." He came up to me, put out a hand and jerked my face up by the chin. "You wish to speak?"

I took a deep breath and nodded.

"Good. Speak."

I said, "I thought you'd like to know, I shan't need the aspirin. My headache has gone."

He stepped back, ignored me, and nodded to Katerina. The lash bit into me. She was a strong girl. I didn't yell. I twisted my head back as far as I could get it and she was just in my sights. I could see the flush on her face, the shine in her eyes, and the rise and fall of her shoulders as she breathed hard, and I shouted, "Go on, you beautiful blonde bastard! Go on – enjoy yourself!"

Her arm swung back and the lash caught me across the neck and the side of my face. She gave me the round dozen and the marrow had gone from my legs. I was slumped down the pillar, most of my weight on my wrists, and I could feel my head lolling like a puppet's on half slack strings.

Katerina came round past me and handed the whip to Alois. He gave her a little pat on the arm. They were going to make a fine pair. Both of them would enjoy setting a match to the Munich powder keg. But I didn't have much time to worry about them. My mind wasn't functioning too smoothly from the remains of dope and this treatment, and I had difficulty in focusing. I could see old tin leg standing up now, supporting himself on his stick. In his free hand, he was holding his artificial leg which he must have unstrapped while the beating was going on. No one seemed to be taking any notice of him. I thought that damned odd, because his boot was still fixed to the end of the leg, and it looked so ludicrous that I wanted them all to see him. After all, if ever there was a moment for a good giggle it was now.

Alois came up alongside me, flicked the thong to loosen up his muscles, and then started to go by me to get into position for his first strike. Katerina's efforts would seem like love caresses compared with his, and I knew that two or three smacks from him would have me talking.

Fortunately it never came to it. As he was level with me, a voice said, "I don't think it will be necessary to torture this man any longer."

It was tin leg. He had moved behind the group of men and was standing on the first step of the dais, leaning heavily on his stick, the length of an empty trouser leg swinging grotesquely against the glass case.

"Come down from there!"

It was Madame Vadarci and there was anger in her voice, anger, I supposed, for the sacrilege he was committing of leaning against the Führer's show case. But that was nothing. On top of the case he had carefully placed his tin leg.

From somewhere close behind me, Alois said, "Why?"

"Because I am one of the men you want." He said it as calmly as though he were announcing himself as the local gas man come to read the meter.

Alois came by me then. I pulled myself up a little and tried some real weight on my legs. I could feel the whole of my back wet and burning like hell.

Alois said, "Please come down from there and remove that object from the top of the case."

Tin leg shook his head. "No. It stays there. And I advise you all to vacate this hallway immediately. This very useful artificial leg of mine is filled with high explosive which I have now timed to explode within about sixty seconds." He looked straight at Alois, the sad, leonine face lined now with a dignity and nobility I wondered I'd never noticed before. Then he said, "You can order your guards to shoot me, of course. But it won't help. The timing mechanism in the leg is such that any attempt now to pick it up will cause it to detonate." He smiled then, a thin, wasted, bitter smile. "We are not going to allow a myth and a legend to be re-created. We suffered enough while this monster lived. Too many people suffered. Now the myth and the legend are to be destroyed. Without this," he put a hand on the glass case, "you are nothing. Here is the power and here is the true evil. I advise you to move quickly. Your time is running out."

Alois moved. It was like lightning. One moment he was standing watching the man, the next a hand flashed and the large dagger was whipped from his belt, and it seared through the air. He'd certainly been well trained in all the arts. The knife point took the man in the throat. He went down without a sound, except the clatter of his stick as it rolled across the steps of the dais.

Alois turned round and shouted, "Back, everyone! Back to the door."

They moved, like a panic-struck flock of sheep, crashing and pushing through the chairs, heading for the doorway and the cover of the cloistered walk. I couldn't move. I had a stall seat again, and was tied to it, and no one cared a damn for me. Not even Manston, cold-blooded, professional, cerebrating right up to the last moment, knowing that if he came to release me it would mark him as the other man and, who knew . . .? that could still be dangerous if success should come out of the mad risk that was being taken now by Alois. It was clear what he intended to do. He was moving towards the glass case quickly. I heard the big hall doors open away to my right and the rush of feet, but I kept my eyes on Alois, waiting for the moment when I would jerk my head back behind the pillar and pray.

Alois moved quickly through the scattered chairs. But when he was free of them, and the catafalque only a couple of yards away from him – there was a shot.

I saw his body jerk and his left arm fly upwards. He spun half round, swayed, recovered himself and then kept moving on. Far up under the blue dome the shot echoes rolled and wickered like thunder. There was another shot and it must mave taken Alois in the side. He spun round like a top and dropped full length on the marble steps. Blood ran out through his fingers as he clutched at his side. The shots were coming from the grille high up in the dome. I remembered Howard Johnson leaning over me, his face wavering like running water in my doped dreams, and saying, "Bad luck, lover-boy – you really bought it. King-sized and gift-wrapped." He was up there now, Hesseltod's ladder hoisted from the lower roof for the final climb, to give him, first, a ringside seat at my doping, then to leave him free, when I had been carried away, to take the ·404; his orders as clear as Manston's, and the other's – trust no one, but destroy the myth for ever.

Alois crawled forward, reached blindly for the sides of the case and began to haul himself up.

Another shot came from the grille and this time Alois's body jumped, spun and fell sideways down across the marble steps. For a moment I had a glimpse of a smashed face, of blond hair red with blood, and then I saw no more because the time was up.

The sixtieth second dropped from now into the past, and there was a roar like the heavens opening. The blue-lit cavern was sheeted with orange flame, and the shock wave beat at me and slammed me away and then back against the pillar and I went out, listening to the whistling, crackling, exploding fall of glass from the dome.

CHAPTER TWENTY

AND ALL THAT'S LEFT FOR ME

What did I learn from it? What did I lose? What did I gain? It's not a long list.

A broken arm, right. The shock wave did that when it slammed me away from the pillar and then back again.

Some scars on my back which will always be partly there. Some other scars, too; around the heart, I suppose you could say, if you cared for whimsy. I don't know what happened to Katerina. She went through the hall door and disappeared. All the people I've questioned since know nothing about her. The Vadarci pair went into the blue, too, with Katerina. But it could be that Manston and Sutcliffe have tabs on them and aren't saying. A girl like Katerina will pop up again somewhere. My guess is that they know where she is and what she's doing, but they're giving nothing away – just as nothing was given away, to Press or public, about the whole affair in the *Schloss*. So, that leaves you free to call me a liar.

Of course, I got some money. A handsome cheque from Malacod and – after a struggle – my full fee from Sutcliffe. He handed it over with the biggest dressing down I've ever had and I had to listen just to get the fee. That was all right by me. I just went into a trance until he had finished.

I got hell from Wilkins, of course, but I expected that. After all she had to have some way of showing her relief that I was safely back.

Oh, and a whip. I got that about a month afterwards. I keep it on my desk now just in case Wilkins gets difficult.

Manston brought it in. He was very pleasant.

"I picked it up after the big bang. I thought you'd like it. You should keep it handy for dealing with girls like Katerina. Stebelson had more sense than you. He knew when to write her off – the moment she saw Alois. That's why he sold out fast to Howard Johnson. Big money, too. Everything he knew. But he never collected. Frau Spiegel drove him to Lake Zafersee for a picnic and he was fished out some weeks later."

"And Howard Johnson?'

"Posted to Moscow. Staff training job."

I put my hand round the whip.

"And the white-haired number with the artificial leg. He's going to be missed in some synagogue."

"Not only there. Didn't you know you were working for Bonn? They really want a new Germany, you know. Not the Alois kind. There's no racial discrimination these days. Just co-operation. Malacod was their man, and so was our friend with the white hair. Well, see you some time."

He went, leaving me with the whip. No question of any apology for not raising a finger to help me in the *Schloss*. We both knew the rules. But he had been helpful for the month's convalescence I had taken to get over the scars and a broken arm.

He lent me a little cottage he had on Lake Annecy, near Talloires. It was a good spot and, because I was in funds, I could afford to eat now and then at Père Bise. But mostly Vérité and I did our own cooking and ate on the little terrace overlooking the lake. It was a perfect month, even with a broken arm and having to sleep mostly on my side.

And what did I learn? That you get used to anything, even to the fact that perfection is only a month long, and then there's the office waiting, clients being clever with you, and two roads running away north and south, and that you've got to be honest and take your own road because somewhere at the end of it – with luck – there might be the thing you really want. Or am I just kidding myself? Probably.